the beautiful ASHES

A Broken Destiny Novel

JEANIENE FROST

the
beautiful
ASHES

A Broken Destiny Novel

ISBN-13: 978-0-373-78501-8

The Beautiful Ashes

the beautiful ASHES

To JBA, now more than ever.

chapter one

I'm twenty, and already, I've got nothing left to lose. That's why I didn't care that Bennington, Vermont, looked like a postcard for autumn in the country. The two-story bed-and-breakfast I pulled up to was no different. It even had a white picket fence and a steady swirl of sunset-colored leaves drifting down from the many trees in the yard.

My picturesque surroundings were in stark contrast to how *I* looked. If I hadn't been exhausted from grief and stress, I might've cared that my brown hair now resembled greasy mud. Or that my breath was in desperate need of a Mentos, and don't get me started on the coffee stains decorating my WMU shirt. Since I had more important things to worry about, I didn't even bother to cover my head against the downpour as I left my car and ran into the bed-and-breakfast.

"One moment!" a cheery voice called out from farther inside. Then a heavyset older woman with graying red hair came down the hallway.

"Hello, dear. I'm Mrs. Paulson. Are you—oh, my, you're soaked!"

"It's nothing," I said, but she bustled out of sight, returning moments later with a towel.

"You sit down and dry yourself off," she ordered in the same *tsk*ing tone my mother had used a million times before. A surge of grief had me dropping into the chair she waved at. The things you didn't realize you'd miss until they were gone…

"Thanks," I said, determined not to cry in front of a total stranger. Then I pulled out the Ziploc bag I'd carried around most of the day. "I'm looking for two people who might've stayed here the weekend before last."

As I spoke, I pulled out a picture of my sister, Jasmine, and her boyfriend, Tommy.

Mrs. Paulson got a pair of glasses from her apron pocket. Then she sat behind a large antique desk and accepted the picture.

"Oh, what a pretty girl," she said, adding kindly, "just like you. But I've never seen either of them before, sorry."

"Thanks," I said, although I wanted to scream.

I'd spent the day showing Jasmine's picture to every hotel, motel and inn in Bennington, yet no one had recognized my sister. She'd been here, though. The last texts she'd sent came from Bennington, but the police already hinted that they thought she'd sent them while driving through. To them, Jasmine was an impulsive eighteen-year-old who'd gone on a road trip with her boyfriend. My sister might be impulsive, but she wouldn't have disappeared for over a week unless she was in real trouble.

I stuffed her picture back into the plastic bag and rose, so upset that I barely registered what Mrs. Paulson was saying.

"…can't let you go back out in that, dear. Wait here until the rain stops."

I blinked in surprise at her unexpected kindness. Every other proprietor had been anxious for me to leave once they knew why I was there, as if losing a family member could somehow be contagious. My eyes stung with a sudden rush of tears. Maybe it was. My parents' funeral was the day after tomorrow.

"Thank you, but I can't," I said, voice husky from emotions I couldn't let myself feel yet. The shock helped with that. Ten days ago, my biggest concern had been making a bad impression on my Comparative Revolutions professor after my text message alerts kept going off in his class. Then I read Jasmine's texts, and everything had changed.

Mrs. Paulson gave me another sympathetic smile. "At least let me make you a hot cup of tea—"

A dark, hazy double image suddenly appeared over the reception lounge, making it look as though it had aged over a hundred years in an instant. I stifled a groan. Not *this* again.

The pricey antiques vanished, replaced by broken-down furniture or nothing at all. The temperature also plummeted, making me shiver before movement in the hallway caught my eye.

A blonde girl walked past the decrepit-looking reception lounge. Her face was smudged with dirt and she was bundled up in a tattered blanket, but I didn't need a second glance to recognize her.

"Jasmine," I whispered.

Mrs. Paulson came around the desk and grabbed me, coiling shadows suddenly darting across her face as if she had snakes trapped beneath her flesh. Jasmine continued to walk by as if she wasn't aware that we were there. If not for the innkeeper's surprisingly strong grip, I could have reached out and touched my sister.

"Wait!" I cried out.

The house blinked back into elegant furnishings and warm, cozy temperatures. Just as quickly, Jasmine disappeared. Mrs. Paulson still held me in a tight grip, although the shadows on her face had vanished. I finally managed to shove her away, heading down the hallway where I'd glimpsed my sister.

Before I made it three steps, pain exploded in the back of my head. It must've briefly knocked me out, because the next thing I knew, I was on my knees and Mrs. Paulson was about to hit me with a heavy picture frame again.

Get out! The single, emphatic thought was all my mind was capable of producing. My body must've agreed. I don't know how, but I was suddenly outside and slamming the door shut on my Cherokee. Then I sped away, wondering what had made Mrs. Paulson turn from a kindly old lady into a skull-smashing maniac.

I drove back to my hotel as though on autopilot. After I parked, I sat in the car with the engine off, trying to fight back nausea while I figured out my next move. I could call 911, but I didn't want to admit that I'd had another weird hallucination right before Mrs. Paulson attacked me. If I told anyone *that,* I'd be signing up for a stay in a padded room. Again. Second, the cops in Bennington already didn't like me. As soon as I'd arrived this morning, I'd bitched them out for not doing enough to find Jasmine. They'd probably take Mrs. Paulson's side and assume I'd done something to provoke her.

I paused. Had I? I didn't remember getting away from Mrs. Paulson. What if I'd done something else I didn't remember? Maybe something that had scared her so much, she'd hit me in self-defense? The idea that I might be having blackouts in addition to hallucinations soured my already bleak mood. I got out of the car and went to my hotel room. Once inside, I dropped my purse as though it were a fifty-pound anchor, then flicked on the light.

Everything in me stiffened. The couch should've been empty, but a guy with hair the color of dark honey sat there, his large frame taking up most of the space. Strong brows, a straight nose, high cheekbones and a sensual mouth made up a face that was striking enough to adorn billboards. He didn't look startled by my appearance, either. In fact, if I didn't know better, I'd swear he'd been expecting me.

Gorgeous guys do not spend their evenings waiting around for me. That's why I thought he was another hallucination until he spoke. My hallucinations had never spoken to me before.

"Hi," the stranger said, his deep voice tinged with an accent I couldn't place. "Sorry to tell you, but you're about to have a really bad night."

I knew I should turn around, open the door and run, preferably while screaming. That was the only logical response, but I stood there, somehow unafraid of my intruder. Great. My survival instincts must've secretly made a suicide pact.

"If you knew the week I'd had, you'd realize that whatever you had planned could only make it better," I heard myself reply, proving my vocal cords were in on the death wish.

Then again, I wasn't wrong. My sister? Missing without a trace after texting me "help" and "trapped!" last Monday. Parents? Died in a car accident two days after they arrived in Bennington trying to retrace Jasmine's steps. Me? In addition to losing my whole family, I'd nearly gotten my head bashed in. By comparison, being robbed sounded like a vacation.

A grin cocked the side of my intruder's mouth. Whatever response he'd been expecting, it hadn't been that.

"If I win? Probably. If I lose, things are about to get much, much worse," he assured me.

"What's the contest?" I asked, wondering why I was having a conversation with my intruder. Brain damage from the head wound?

He rose. Despite my baffling lack of fear, I flinched as he came nearer. He had to be a foot taller than my five-six height, with shoulders that would fill a door frame and muscles no bulky overcoat could hide. The only thing more striking was his eyes: a deep blue rimmed with gray so light, it almost gleamed.

"The contest is to see who walks out of here with you," he replied, that silver-and-sapphire gaze sliding over me.

"What if I don't want to go anywhere?" I countered.

"It's too late for that," he said softly, reaching out and drawing my attention to the fact that he wore leather gloves.

I darted away. For some reason, I still wasn't consumed with terror—wake up, survival instincts!—but I wasn't about to let him grab me. He didn't try to stop me as I ran past him into the bedroom. Then again, I realized with an inner groan, why would he? Now he stood between me and the room's only door.

He came toward me, and my heart started to hammer. Why hadn't I left when I had the chance? And *why* wasn't I screaming for help right now?

Three hard raps on the door startled me. Then I couldn't believe it when I recognized the voice.

"Miss Jenkins, could you let me in? It's Detective Kroger. We met this morning at the police station."

A cop when I needed one? Miracles *did* happen!

To my shock, my intruder turned around and opened the door. The two men stared at each other, and though the intruder had his back to me, I saw Detective Kroger size him up.

"He broke into my room," I said, making a "do something" gesture.

Kroger's brow went up. "Is that so, mister?"

"Guess you'd better take me in," my intruder drawled.

I expected Kroger to reach for his handcuffs. Instead, he came inside, shut the door, and turned off the lights.

"What are you doing?" I gasped.

"Move over to the couch," Kroger said, and I didn't know if he was talking to me or my enigmatic intruder.

I wasn't going to remain in the dark to find out. I felt around the bedroom until I reached the nightstand, then turned on the lamp. Light flooded the room, showing that my intruder was still in the mini lounge area with Kroger. In fact, it didn't look like either man had moved an inch. What was going on?

"Why aren't you arresting me, Detective?" the intruder asked in his silky, accented voice.

"Good question," I added.

"Shut up, bitch," Kroger said harshly.

My jaw dropped. Before I could respond, Kroger's fist shot out, punching the bigger man in the shoulder. Then he frowned, as if surprised that it had no effect. The intruder caught Kroger's fist when he swung at him again.

Kroger stared, disbelief creasing his features as he tried to yank free and couldn't. Then, understanding seemed to dawn.

"You must be Adrian," Kroger spat.

"In the flesh," my intruder responded lightly.

I was about to ask what the hell was going on when shots rang out. I dropped down right as one of the men hurtled toward me, too fast to see who. I managed to leap away without getting flattened, though I took out the nightstand in my wild lunge.

The room went dark as the lamp broke. My heart pounded at the instant blindness. I hadn't been afraid before, but I was now, trapped in a room with two men who clearly wanted to kill each other. I began to feel my way around the bed again, and this time, stumbled on something big. That something grabbed me, and I freaked out, kicking, punching and clawing to get free.

Then I was yanked away and shoved viciously into the wall.

Pain exploded over me, and when I swallowed, I tasted blood. I started to fall, dazed, when a rough grip hauled me up.

A beam of moonlight landed on my attacker's face, and I recoiled. Shadows flickered like snake tongues across Kroger's skin, turning his features into a sickening mask of evil. Worse, I knew I wasn't hallucinating. The pain I felt was too real.

"You want to know what happened to your sister?" Kroger's voice was harsh. Guttural. "You're about to find out."

Without thinking, I punched him as hard as I could. He looked surprised, but the blow didn't even make him flinch.

Suddenly, he was snatched backward and then flung straight up. As Kroger fell back down, Adrian kicked him hard enough to send him crashing through the bedroom window. Before I could even scream, Adrian leaped after him. Then all I heard were thumping noises and groans before a distinct snapping sound made something primal tense inside me.

One of them had just died, I knew it. But which one?

A dark form rose in the gaping hole where the window had been. I began to back away, every movement painful, when I saw something silvery gleam in the moonlight.

Adrian's eyes.

"Looks like you're coming with me after all," he said while vaulting through the window.

I wasn't bothered by his casual tone or the fact that he'd just killed someone. I was too busy trying to absorb what I'd seen on Detective Kroger's face, let alone what he'd said.

You want to know what happened to your sister? You're about to find out.

Hope clawed through my reeling emotions. If the snake-like shadows on Kroger's face were real, then maybe so was my vision of Jasmine at the bed-and-breakfast!

"We need to…get Jasmine," I managed to gasp, feeling something wet where I clutched my abdomen.

Adrian pried my hands away and sighed.

"You're hurt. Sorry, he was one of Demetrius's dogs, so he was harder to kill."

He picked me up. Despite Adrian's touch being far gentler than Kroger's, I couldn't stop my pained moan.

"Don't worry, you'll be better soon," he said, carrying me toward the door.

We need to get Jasmine! I wanted to insist, but my tongue seemed to have gone on strike. The tingling in my limbs and buzzing in my ears probably wasn't a good sign, either.

"What's your name, anyway?" I heard Adrian ask, his voice now sounding very far away.

I managed one word before everything went dark.

"Ivy."

chapter two

A familiar song was playing, but I couldn't remember the name. That bugged me enough to open my eyes. A wall of black met my gaze, slick and smooth like glass. I reached up to see what it was, and that's when I realized my hands were tied.

"Silent Lucidity" by Queensryche, my mind supplied, followed immediately by, *I'm in the backseat of a car.* One that was well taken care of, going by that flawless, shiny roof. With those details filled in, I also remembered what had happened right before I'd passed out. And who I was with.

"Why are my hands tied?" I said, heaving myself into an upright position.

For some reason Adrian didn't have a rearview mirror, which was why he had to glance over his shoulder to look at me.

"Does anything make you panic?" he asked, sounding amused. "You're tied up in the backseat of a cop-killer's car, but I've seen people get more upset when Starbucks runs out of Pumpkin Spice flavor."

Anyone normal would panic, not that it would do any good. Besides, I ran out of "normal" a long time ago, when I realized I saw things no one else did.

Speaking of which, why wasn't I in pain? The lump where Mrs. Paulson had whacked me was gone, and my shirt was red from blood, but aside from a mild kink in my neck, I felt fine. When I pushed my shirt up, somehow I wasn't surprised to see smooth, unbroken skin on my abdomen. Well, that and a bunch of crumbs, like I'd eaten a dessert too messily.

"Why does it look like I have angel food cake on my stomach?" I wondered aloud.

Adrian snorted. "Close. It's medicine. You were injured."

"You can tell me how I'm not anymore," I said, holding out my bound hands, "after you untie me."

Another backward glance, this one challenging.

"You may be the calmest person I've ever been sent to retrieve, but if I tell you now what you want to know, that will change. So pick—the truth, or being untied?"

"Truth," I said instantly.

He let out a laugh. "Another first. You're full of surprises."

So was he. He'd just admitted that he regularly kidnapped people—which was how I translated "retrieve"—so I should be trying my damnedest to get free. But more than anything, I needed answers. Besides, I still wasn't afraid of him, and somehow, that had nothing to do with him magically healing me.

"Truth, Adrian," I repeated.

He turned once again and his gaze locked with mine, those odd blue eyes startling me with their intensity. For a moment, I could only stare, all thought frozen in my mind. I don't know why I reached out, awkwardly touching his arm to feel the hard muscles beneath that bulky jacket. If I'd thought about it, I wouldn't have done it. Yet I couldn't make myself pull away.

Then I gasped when his hand covered mine. At some point, he'd taken off his gloves, and the feel of his warm, bare skin sent a shock wave through me. The touch seemed to affect Adrian, too. His lips parted and he edged over the back of the seats—

He yanked on the steering wheel, narrowly avoiding another car. A horn blared, and when the driver passed us, an extended middle finger shook angrily in our direction. I leaned back, my heart pounding from the near collision. At least, that's what I told myself it was from.

"*Dyate*," Adrian muttered.

I didn't recognize the word, and I was at a loss to place his accent. It had a musical cadence like Italian, but beneath that was a harsher, darker edge.

"What's that language?" I asked, trying to mask the sudden shakiness in my voice.

This time, he didn't take his eyes off the road. "Nothing you've heard of."

"I picked truth, remember?" I said, holding up my bound hands for emphasis.

That earned me a quick glance. "That is the truth, but you don't get more until you meet Zach. Then we can skip all the 'this isn't possible' arguments."

I let out a short laugh. "After what I saw on Detective Kroger's face, my definition of 'impossible' has changed."

Adrian swerved again, but this time, no other car was near. "What did you see?"

I tensed. How did I explain without sounding insane? No way to, so I chose to go on the attack instead.

"Why were you in my hotel room? And how did you heal me? There isn't even a mark—"

"What did you see on his *face,* Ivy?"

Despite his hard tone, when my name crossed his lips, something thrummed inside me, like he'd yanked on a tie I hadn't known was there. Feeling it was as disturbing as my inexplicable reaction to his clasping my hands.

"Shadows," I said quickly, to distract from that. "He had snakelike shadows all over his face."

I expected Adrian to tell me I'd imagined it, a response I was used to hearing. Instead, he pulled over, putting the car in park but keeping the engine running. Then he turned to stare at me.

"Was that the only strange thing you saw?"

I swallowed. I knew better than to talk about these things. Still, I'd demanded the truth from Adrian. It didn't seem fair to lie in return.

"I saw two versions of the same B and B earlier. One was pretty, but the other was old and rotted, and my sister was trapped inside it."

Adrian said nothing, though he continued to pin me with that hard stare. When he finally spoke, his question was so bizarre I thought I'd misheard him.

"What do I look like to you?"

"Huh?"

"My appearance." He drew out the words like I was slow. "Describe me."

All of a sudden, he wanted compliments? I might have finally met someone crazier than me.

"This is ridiculous," I muttered, but started with the obvious. "Six-six, early twenties, built like Thor, golden brown hair with blond highlights, silvery blue eyes…you want me to go on?"

He began to laugh, a deep, rich baritone that would've been sensual except for how angry it made me.

"Now I know why they came after you," he said, still chuckling. "They must've realized you were different, but if they'd known what you could see, you never would've made it out of that B and B."

"You can stop laughing," I said sharply. "I get that it's crazy to see the things I do."

Lots of kids had imaginary friends growing up. I had imaginary places, though at first, I hadn't known I was the only one who could see them. Once my parents had realized that what I kept describing went far beyond childhood fancy, the endless doctor visits and tests began. One by one, diseases and psychoses had been crossed off until I was diagnosed with a non-monoamine-cholinergic imbalance in my temporal cortex.

In other words, I saw shit that wasn't there for reasons no one could figure out. The pills I took helped a little, though I lied and said they got rid of all my hallucinations. I was sick of doctors poking at me. So whenever I saw something that no one else did, I forced myself to ignore it—until Mrs. Paulson and Detective Kroger had tried to kill me, of course.

Adrian did stop laughing, and that unblinking intensity was back in his gaze.

"Well, Ivy, I've got good news and bad news. The good news is, you're not crazy. The bad news is, everything you've seen is real, and now, it'll be coming for you."

chapter three

Even on a good day, I hated when guys were cryptic. Those of the Testosterone Persuasion already came with a mountain of senseless tendencies—did they really think they needed to add purposefully vague statements on top of that?

The fact that Adrian refused to elaborate on his enigmatic warning *while I was tied up in his backseat* made it unbearable. As the time ticked on, I consoled myself by imagining hitting him in the head with something heavy. Or leaning over the seat and choking him with the band of duct tape around my wrists. If the back of this vehicle had had a cigarette lighter, I might've gotten creative with fantasies about that, too.

Guess being kidnapped turned me into a violent person.

"Are you a sex slaver?" I asked abruptly.

"Someone's watched *Taken* too many times," Adrian said, and the amusement in his tone grated on my last nerve.

"Why wouldn't I think that?" I shot back. "You saved my

life, but you're taking me somewhere against my will, and you refuse to untie me."

"You picked truth, remember?" was his infuriating response.

I swear, the first heavy object I got a hold of...! "You didn't give me *that*, either."

"Yes, I did." He said it with a heavy-lidded, backward glance that would've made me straighten up and smile if he'd done it while we were sitting at a bar. "Just not all of it, but don't worry. We're here."

With that statement, Adrian turned down a long road that led to a set of soaring, elaborately carved gates.

"Wait a sec while I open the gates," he said, turning the car off and taking the keys with him.

I waited...until he was far enough away for me to make my move. Then I leaped over the seats. When I yanked on the driver's side door, however, a large hand on the window prevented it from opening.

"Why am I not surprised?" Adrian said with irony dripping from his tone.

I stared at his hand, as if that could explain how the rest of him was attached to it. A second ago, he'd been in front of those barbarically ornate gates, doing something that caused them to swing open with a mechanical moan.

No one could move that fast. Or, more accurately, no one *should* be able to move that fast.

"What are you?" I breathed.

His teeth flashed in a smile that was predatory and sexy at the same time.

"A couple hours ago, I wondered the same thing about you."

Me? Before I could ask what he meant, he opened the door and let me out. Ice raced through my veins when I saw the knife in his other hand. That was also the moment when I noticed the sign on the gates: Green-Wood Cemetery.

"Don't," I gasped.

He raised a brow, cutting through the duct tape around my wrists. "You're the one who wanted to be untied."

My arms fell to my sides while relief roared over me, replacing the surge of fear-fueled adrenaline. Just as quickly, something snapped inside me. All the grief, anger, fear and frustration of the past ten days hurtled through my defenses, turning me into someone I didn't recognize.

A rage monster.

My hand cracked across Adrian's face with enough force to make it tingle and burn, and still, it wasn't enough. I began beating on his chest, part of me horrified by my actions, but the rest urging me to hit him harder.

"What is the matter with you?" I yelled. "You pull out a knife with no explanation? I thought you were going to *kill* me!"

Adrian grabbed my hands. Any sane person would have recognized how overmatched I was and calmed the hell down, but I was way past sanity. With my hands out of commission, I kicked his shin hard enough to send pain shooting up my leg. He grunted, backing me up until I was pressed against the car hood. Now I had a wall of steel behind me and a wall of muscled flesh on top of me.

"Stop it," Adrian ordered, his strange accent thicker with his vehemence. "I *promise,* I'm not going to hurt you!"

My breath came in pants. Adrian countered my attempt to drop down and wiggle free by pressing his thigh between my legs. I stopped *that* course of action at once, which was the same as admitting defeat. I couldn't use my arms to push him away. He felt more solid and heavy than a stone gargoyle.

"Get off me," I said between ragged breaths.

"Not until you calm down," he replied sternly. Then the barest grin tugged at his mouth. "Feel free to take your time."

I glanced down, only now registering that my breasts were pressed against his chest just as tightly as his thigh was wedged between my legs. Any movement on my part caused an embarrassingly personal friction, as if inhaling each other's breaths while we panted wasn't intimate enough.

I tried to slow my breathing, not to mention my galloping heartbeat. If not for his grin, I wouldn't have known he thought anything of the compromising position he had me in.

If nothing else, he didn't seem angry that I'd slapped, kicked and pummeled him. Now that my reckless rage had passed, I realized how stupid I'd been. One punch from his massive fist would've meant lights out, but he hadn't hit back. Instead, he'd promised that he wouldn't hurt me. Despite his kidnapping me and his refusal to give me answers about what was going on, I decided to believe him.

"Sorry I attacked you," I said, my voice no longer shrill.

He shrugged like he was used to it. "Don't worry. You were overdue for a breakdown, anyway."

Just how many people have *you kidnapped?* I almost asked. Since I didn't really want to know, all I said was, "Can you get off me? You're heavy."

He slowly uncurled his body from mine, but that silvery blue gaze stayed glued to me. I shivered, suddenly aware of how cold it was, now that I wasn't covered by over two hundred pounds of warm-blooded male.

Adrian shrugged out of his coat, revealing a crew-neck black shirt that hugged his physique like it was paying homage. Of course he'd noticed the shiver. I wondered if anything escaped those piercing eyes.

I put it on. The hem had been midcalf on him; it pooled on the ground with me. I'd never felt dainty around a guy before. I was comfortable at a size eight because I didn't have to starve to maintain it, and my five-six height meant I could usually wear heels without being taller than my dates. Next to Adrian, however, I seemed to drop twenty pounds while also shrinking a few inches. Of course, his bulk was all muscle. Feeling him on top of me had made that clear....

I nixed that line of thought before it led to other, more dangerous musings, and tightened his coat around me.

"If we're not here so you can kill me and bury my body in an empty plot, what else is there to do at a cemetery?" I asked with admirable calm.

He laughed, the deep, masculine rumble teasing something inside me that was too stupid to realize kidnappers were off-limits. That's why I refused to notice the chin dimple it revealed, or how his lower lip was fuller than the top one.

"Lots of things, but we'll get to that later."

"Sure there's going to be a later?" I challenged him.

"Of course." Another tantalizing smile. "Since you and I are from the same line, you'll be seeing a lot more of me."

Line? "You think we're *related?*"

His gaze brushed me like a physical caress. "Not like that, thankfully. That would make our first date awkward."

I stared at him in disbelief. "You're *hitting* on me?" I finally managed. "Do you have any idea how twisted that is?"

He shrugged. "I don't do subtle, it wastes time. Besides—" the silvery part of his eyes gleamed like liquid moonlight "—if you say you don't find me attractive, I'll know you're lying."

Under other circumstances, I might have blushed at being busted ogling someone I'd just met, but my *kidnapper* was hitting on me! Should that make me more afraid, or less? He'd already saved my life once and had had plenty of chances to harm me since, yet he hadn't.

Plus, I wouldn't be much fun as a date if I was dead.

"How about we hold the date talk until you give me the answers you promised?" I said, part of me wondering if tonight could get any stranger. The other part felt happy for the first time in over a week. Stupid ovaries. *Down, girls, down!*

Adrian's expression turned serious. "I'm taking you to the person who can give you those answers."

"Zach?" I asked, remembering Adrian mentioning the name.

"That's him. This cemetery is almost five hundred acres, so if you don't want to spend hours walking around in the cold—" he went over to the passenger side of the vintage-looking muscle car and opened the door "—get in."

He was giving me a choice. Or at least, the illusion of one. If I ran, we both knew he could catch me.

The car's interior light showed a hint of stubble trying to break through the smooth skin along his jaw, shadowing it in a way that was far too attractive. His exotic accent wasn't helping, either. If I was ever kidnapped again, it had better be by an old, ugly guy. That would be less confusing to my emotions.

And less embarrassing. What idiot got caught lusting over her kidnapper? No wonder he'd asked me out. He must have thought I gave "easy" a whole new definition.

I walked over, thinking that even if I could run away from him, I wouldn't. My sister was trapped in a place that shouldn't be real, yet somehow was, and Adrian was my only ally because he could see the same crazy things that I did. More importantly, Adrian had proven that he was able to kill those things.

If he was able to help me save my sister, I'd not only take him up on his date offer. I'd pay for everything and seriously consider putting out.

I got in the passenger side, hearing the door lock as soon as he shut it. I tried to open it. Nothing. My sense of unease returned. What kind of person saved people just to kidnap them, and had a vehicle you could only exit from the driver's side?

Then again, as Adrian slid into the seat next to me with an almost spooky fluidity, I realized what kind of person he was might be less important than *what* he was.

chapter four

Whoever had designed Green-Wood cemetery must have done so while puking drunk since it lacked a single straight road. I felt like we were driving through a child's maze game with all the twists and turns. Then again, maybe lots of cemeteries were laid out like this. I wouldn't know. I'd never been in one before. My parents' funeral wasn't until the day after tomorrow, both sets of my grandparents had died before my birth, and neither of my parents had siblings or cousins. Until ten days ago, I hadn't lost anyone close to me.

Now, I'd lost everyone, and while I buried my grief with the same determination I'd used to ignore seeing impossible things, it wasn't enough. When Adrian drove by a large tomb engraved "Beloved Parents," the ache that had burned in my throat since their deaths grew into an impassable boulder.

Adrian stopped the car at the same time that I suddenly found it difficult to breathe.

"What's wrong?" he asked urgently. "You see something?"

I shook my head, managing to draw in a breath despite that awful squeezing in my throat.

"Ivy." A large hand cupped my face, forcing me to look at him instead of the headstone. "What is it?"

Right then, I was glad that Adrian was so hot. Thank God for the deep hollows under his cheekbones, those sapphire eyes, and the blondish-brown hair that looked like it had been tousled from too much sex. If I hadn't had his looks to distract me, I might've had to focus on how bad it hurt to lose two people who'd never let me down, even when I'd been a stranger to them.

"It's just…my parents died five days ago."

My voice was husky from the emotions I kept trying to shove back, but the strangling tightness had eased. Another few deep breaths, and all that was left was a familiar burn.

"I'm sorry," Adrian said, taking my hand and squeezing it.

I'd heard those words from friends and fellow students a lot in the past week, often with an added cliché about all things happening for a reason. Adrian didn't say any of that crap. He just kept holding my hand while looking at me with an understanding that transcended compassion, as if he knew what it was like to lose everything within a brutally short amount of time.

"Thanks." I drew in another breath, blinking away the tears. Crying felt like giving up, and I wasn't doing that because I needed to find a way to bring my sister back home. "That's why I need answers, because I'm not about to lose my sister forever, too."

He let go of my hand and looked away, his jaw tightening. "Answers don't mean miracles. I heard what that cop said to you. If they have your sister, I'm sorry, but she's as good as dead."

"Bullshit," I snapped, instantly angry. "I know where she is. I just need a...way in."

Adrian sighed. "You see things no one else does, yet you're still in denial, aren't you? The creatures that have your sister are too strong, Ivy. Even if you got in, you'd never get out."

Creatures? Before I could respond, something flashed ahead, as if a spotlight had briefly turned on. Adrian began driving toward it. A few minutes later, we pulled up to what looked like a tiny castle, with circular turrets on the four corners and a tall, windowed dome blooming out of the center.

Adrian parked, going around to my side to let me out. "Welcome to Green-Wood chapel."

The door was ajar, soft light emanating from within. Adrian entered and I followed, hugging his coat around me as though it were a protective shield. I was so disturbed by what he said that the equally ornate interior was lost on me. He must've meant "creatures" in a metaphorical way, my logic argued.

A young African-American man stood at the end of the pews, his face partially concealed by the blue hoodie hanging over his bent head. I would've thought he was praying except that he faced us, not the altar, and his hands were at his sides instead of folded in the universal gesture for piety.

"Ivy, this is Zach," Adrian said. "Zach, meet Ivy, the girl you sent me to rescue."

Zach looked up, his hoodie fell back, and—

Light exploded around him like thousands of camera flashes. My eyes burned, unable to adjust to the blinding intensity, and yet I couldn't close them. I stared, stunned, as the glow around him became even brighter, until I saw nothing except Zach. A multitude of voices roared through my mind, deafening me to everything except their beauteous, painful crescendo. My body vibrated, caught in the thunderous echo, until it felt like my flesh would be shaken right off my bones—

"Don't be afraid."

The church morphed back around me, Adrian standing a few feet away like he'd been before. Zach hadn't moved, either. I had, though. Somehow, I was on my knees, hands raised, my face wet from tears I didn't remember shedding.

"Don't be afraid," Zach repeated, coming toward me.

I staggered to my feet. The lights around him were gone, as was the terrible noise that had made my whole body ache. Right now, Zach looked like half the guys around my campus, but I knew, with every fiber of my being, that he wasn't human. He was something else.

A creature, like Adrian had said.

I kept backing away, but then strong hands settled around my shoulders, gripping me with protective gentleness.

"Don't worry. He's not one of the bad ones," Adrian said softly. "Zach plays for the other team."

"The creatures have teams?" I choked out.

"Yes, they do," Adrian said, a note of grimness coloring his tone. "And both sides play for keeps."

I stared into Zach's walnut-colored eyes, seeing the *otherness* beneath the facade of a twentysomething man with closely cropped hair, thick brows, and smooth, dark skin. I didn't need Adrian to tell me he could rip me limb from limb if he wanted to. An instinctual, animalistic part of me knew that. In fact, I was painfully aware of how easily my bones could shatter, how little my skin protected the vulnerable parts beneath, and how useless my average strength was to defend myself. Fear made me want to edge farther into Adrian's embrace, but I forced myself to stay where I was.

Zach might terrify me, but Adrian said he fought against the things that had Jasmine. That made him my new best friend.

"I think freaky shadow people kidnapped my sister," I said, proud that my voice wasn't shaking. "So I need to know how to get her back."

"Did I mention she could see beneath demon glamour?" Adrian asked in a wry tone.

My stomach clenched at the word *demon,* but I didn't do anything embarrassing, like puke. Okay, so demons had my sister. Not much different than saying that freaky shadow people had her, right?

I might puke after all.

"Of course she can see through it," Zach replied, as casual as if he were noting that I liked chocolate more than vanilla. "It's in her bloodline."

I was standing so close to Adrian, I felt it when his whole body stiffened. "You knew what she was?"

A faint smile touched Zach's mouth. "I've always known."

"What do you mean, what I am?" I wondered.

Adrian ignored that and strode over to Zach, his height forcing the shorter man to look up in order to meet his eyes.

"You lied to me," Adrian bit out, his finger stabbing Zach in the chest with each word. "You said that I was the last of my line, yet you knew all along about Ivy?"

I couldn't believe Adrian kept jabbing Zach like he was a roast that needed tenderizing. Didn't he sense the blasting power beneath Zach's average-guy disguise?

"She's not a descendent of your line," Zach said, his hand closing over Adrian's with enough strength to hold it immobile. "You *are* the last of that, but she sees past the disguises of this world because she is the last descendant of David's."

"Last of whose?" I began, then stopped, stunned into silence as Adrian turned toward me.

Horror didn't begin to describe the look on his face. Adrian stared at me like I'd crushed his world, ground it up and then forced it down his throat until he died choking on its remains. If my skin had suddenly been replaced by scales oozing poison, I still wouldn't have thought I deserved such a look.

"Last of a line of rulers dating back to ancient times, when King David sat on the throne of Jerusalem," Zach replied.

History was my major in college, but I'd also been a fan of the arts since I was a little girl.

"King David as in the guy from Michelangelo's famous marble statue?" *The naked one?* I mentally added.

"The same," Zach agreed, a slight arch of his brow making me wonder if he'd guessed what I hadn't said out loud.

"Nice story," I said flippantly, "but all anyone knows about my biological parents is that my mother was an illegal immigrant who left me on the side of the road after the tractor trailer she was hiding in jackknifed."

In some ways, I couldn't blame her. All the illegals who'd survived the accident had run, and disappearing in a new country would have been harder with a newborn. The Jenkinses, who'd also been caught in the multicar pileup, had found me, and after a series of court battles, officially adopted me.

Zach shrugged. "Your disbelief doesn't change the truth."

Adrian was suddenly at the back of the church, his silhouette a dark outline against the stained glass panels.

"If you knew she was the last Davidian, how could you send me to get her?" His voice lashed the air like a whip. "How could you let me anywhere *near her,* Zacchaeus?"

Now I knew what *Zach* was short for, but that wasn't why my mouth dropped. "What is your problem?" I sputtered.

Adrian turned away as if he couldn't stand the sight of me. Amidst my disbelief, I felt a sliver of hurt. Why was he acting like I was viler than the cop he'd killed with his bare hands?

"You have to be near her," Zach replied in an implacable voice. "You cannot escape your fate."

At that, Adrian whirled, fists clenched, shoulders rigid and anger roiling from him in palpable waves.

"Fuck my fate," he snarled.

I didn't see him pass me. He moved too fast again. I only knew that he'd left when the chapel door slammed behind me.

chapter five

The sun was up by the time Zach returned. He'd gone after Adrian, but since he came back without him, that must not have gone well. My mood was pretty foul, too. I'd only waited in the church because I still didn't have the answers I needed. All I knew was that Adrian now hated me, demons existed, and Zach was...well, with the light show he'd given off, I could guess what sort of creature Zach was, but it was too unbelievable to say out loud.

"We're also known as Archons," Zach said, throwing me a sardonic look. "Is that word easier for you to handle?"

Once again, he'd guessed my thoughts, and I was starting to believe it was more than luck. No, I was in the presence of a creature with untold supernatural abilities, and unless I wanted to spend more time crying on my knees, I had to deal with that.

I'd start with the challenge he'd just thrown down.

"It's not my fault that you don't match up with the brochure," I replied flippantly. "You could've paired that hoodie with a harp and a halo, at least."

He smiled, reminding me that every species except humans showed their teeth to convey a threat.

"This mortal shell conceals my true nature. Because you and Adrian are the last of your lines, you see beneath it, but the rest of humanity does not."

I shrugged as though my already-careening world hadn't been turned upside down within the past several hours.

"Or I'm hallucinating again. I missed taking a couple doses of my meds—"

"Makes no difference, they're placebos," Zach informed me.

I stared at him, my lips parted, but my brain processing too many thoughts to speak.

"That's why your adoptive parents always filled your prescriptions for you," Zach went on, as if each word wasn't blasting apart what was left of my life. "Your psychologist provided the placebos as part of your therapy, but there is nothing medically wrong with you. Your adoptive parents were going to tell you the truth when you turned twenty-one—"

"Liar," I whispered.

A thick brow arched. "Demons lie. My kind does not. If you require proof, take one of your pills to a pharmacist for analysis."

My knees wobbled, but I didn't sit down. If I did, I might not be able to get back up. Zach might be a mind reader, but he couldn't have known that my parents always filled my prescriptions because I hadn't been thinking of that. He also couldn't know something that I didn't—if the pills were really placebos instead of actual meds.

Adrian was right. Despite everything I'd seen, I still hadn't accepted that it could actually be *real*. Now Zach was destroying my denial one revelation at a time.

"Your real mother didn't leave you because she was running from the police," Zach went on pitilessly. "She did it to save you, just as your dream revealed—"

"Stop!" I shouted, my breath now coming in pants. No one knew about that dream. I hadn't told my parents, Jasmine or the countless therapists I'd been to. How could Zach know, unless he was exactly who—*what*—he claimed to be?

"Enough."

Adrian's voice cracked through the chapel, startling me. I hadn't seen him come back in. I turned toward him, glad for anything that kept me from hearing revelations that were too incredible to be real.

"Don't mind Zach," Adrian said, an edge coloring his tone. "Archons have no tact when it comes to delivering big news."

Zach shrugged. "She asked for the truth. I gave it to her."

Adrian came nearer, his gaze glittering with anger. "Yeah, well, you want me to play this fate thing through? Then from now on, *I* tell Ivy what's what, not you."

My mind still felt like it had been thrown into a blender, but at that, I stiffened.

"Don't talk about me like I'm not even here."

Adrian turned that darkly jeweled gaze my way. "Believe me, Ivy, I know you're here."

The flat way he spoke somehow gave his words more weight, but this time, Adrian no longer looked at me with horror. Instead, he stared at me like I was the most dangerous person he'd ever met, which, all things considered, was ridiculous.

"You want to save your sister?" he asked evenly. "You'll need something strong enough to kill demons."

This was too much, too fast. "Like holy water? Or crosses?" I asked numbly.

His look became pointed. "Those are for vampires, and

they don't exist. To take down demons, you need one of three weapons, and the second and third ones will probably kill you."

"Okay, so we skip those," I muttered, part of me wondering if I was really having a conversation about how to kill demons. Placebos or not, right now, I missed my meds.

"Right," Adrian said, a glint appearing in his eyes. "Problem is, the first weapon is lost somewhere in one of the demon realms."

"Of course it is. Shopping for it on eBay would be too easy."

His lips curled, as if he knew my glibness masked a rising sense of disbelief. "You've already seen one demon realm. They appear as creepy, dark duplicates of the same place, just like that bed-and-breakfast you described."

If that was true, I'd seen others over the years, but they all had the same problem.

"How do we enter one long enough to save Jasmine? After a few seconds, they seem to disappear."

At that, Adrian shot Zach a frustrated look. "If her abilities are so weak that she only sees the other realms for a few seconds, she's nowhere near ready to do this."

I'd be offended if I didn't agree. My athletic skills were limited to occasionally dancing all night, as if *that* was any advantage in a demon fight. Still, ready or not, I didn't have a choice. Jasmine had no one else to come for her.

"I'll do whatever it takes," I said firmly.

The hardness in Adrian's stare made me wonder if I'd regret those words. Then he smiled, wolfish and challenging.

"All right, Ivy. To answer your question, you get into a demon realm the same way you get in anywhere. Through a door."

I wanted to start looking for the demon-killing weapon at once, but Zach insisted that we sleep. Due to my exhaustion,

I didn't argue until Adrian showed me my "bed." Being in an underground mausoleum was bad enough, but sleeping in one of the tiny rooms that contained a body?

"Hell no," I said.

Adrian rolled his eyes. "What's dead can't hurt you. Living demons can, and they can go anywhere except hallowed ground."

"Then I'll sleep in the church" was my instant response.

"Tourists visit the church," he replied inexorably. "They don't visit the catacombs, so we're sleeping here."

As he spoke, he gestured to another crypt that also had a sleeping bag in it. I looked back at my crypt. A small spider descended from the ceiling and landed right on my sleeping bag.

"I'll just sit in the hallway," I said grimly.

Adrian sighed. "Zach?"

I felt a tap on my shoulder. When I turned around, Zach was behind me. Before I could say anything, he touched my forehead, and like a switch had been flipped, everything went dark.

When I opened my eyes, I was in Adrian's car, my head resting against the cool glass of the passenger window. Lights blurred by, and with mild shock, I saw that it was evening.

"W-what happened?" I mumbled, sitting up.

Adrian didn't look away from the road, but his mouth twitched. "Zach compelled you to sleep."

Memory returned with a vengeance. "In a spider-infested crypt?" I began slapping at my clothes. If I saw anything with eight legs, I was launching myself out of this car.

A stronger twitch of his mouth. "Nothing beats an Archon sedative."

"You think this is funny?" I unlocked my seat belt, took off his coat, and threw it into the backseat. With luck, now I wouldn't have things crawling all over me.

That earned me a slanted look. "You want to fight demons, and you're freaking out over spiders. That's *damn* funny."

Put like that, he had a point. "Speaking of, uh, them—" would I ever say *demons* without feeling like I should be in a straitjacket? "—why do we need this special weapon to save my sister? You killed Detective Kroger just fine without it."

"Kroger wasn't a demon, he was a minion. Demons can't tolerate our realm for long, so they take willing humans, mark them, and send them out to do their dirty work. They have their own signature marks, too. The shadows you saw on Kroger meant he belonged to Demetrius. Marks make minions a lot tougher than humans, but compared to their masters, they're easy to kill."

I hardly knew where to begin with my questions. "Our realm? You mean...this?" I asked, waving at the scenery we drove past.

"Yeah, this," he said, the words heavy with emotion. Regret? Resolve? I didn't know him well enough to be sure.

"And we can see demon marks and demon realms because we're the last of King David's line," I said, trying to piece the impossible facts together.

Adrian stiffened, his mouth tightening until white edged his lips. "You are. I'm not."

That's right, Zach had said he was the last of another line. "What are you, then?" I asked softly.

The look Adrian pinned me with seemed to compress me, until every breath I drew felt like a hard-fought victory.

"I'm something else," he bit out.

I was glad when he glanced back at the road. My heart was thumping as if I'd been jogging. Whatever Adrian was, he didn't like it, and if a man who wasn't afraid of demons didn't like what he was, then I should be scared shitless of him.

So why did I have a strong urge to smooth away the hardness in his expression? I swear, my reactions to him made *no* sense. I never went for the tortured bad boy because I had enough issues of my own. On top of that, Adrian had made it clear that, given his choice, he'd be nowhere near me. Whatever strange pull I felt toward him, I had to get rid of it. Fast.

"Where are we headed?" I asked in a neutral tone.

"Gold Hill, Oregon," he replied, his voice equally emotionless.

All the way across the country? "What's in Oregon that makes it so special?"

His grunt sounded grimly amused. "A door to multiple demon realms."

chapter six

I learned a few things over the next twenty hours. Not about demons or the mysterious weapon—Adrian refused to talk about those—but about him. Like, for example, his pathological hatred of mirrors.

Every time we stopped to refuel, Adrian would smash the mirror in the ladies' room before he let me inside to pee. I was convinced he'd be arrested, but I soon found out another fact: no one but me could see what Adrian really looked like.

"He's five-eight, skinny, with black hair," the gas station attendant snapped into his phone, his Spanish accent thickening as he yelled, *"Pendajo!"* at Adrian for destroying his bathroom mirror. "And he's driving...*a mi Dios!*"

That last part was screamed when Adrian moved with his incredible speed, yanking away the shotgun the attendant had pulled out. Then he broke it over his knee and handed the two pieces back with a growled, "Have a nice day."

"Diablo," the attendant moaned, sinking behind his counter.

I didn't think Adrian was a devil, but I still didn't know

what he was. The fastest way to get the silent treatment from him was to ask again what "line" he was from. He did explain that Archon glamour masked his appearance, so he wouldn't be recognized by minions. Now I knew why Detective Kroger's first punch had hit Adrian in the shoulder. He thought he'd been striking a much shorter opponent. That was also why Adrian had demanded that I describe him soon after we met.

"You could see through demon glamour," he'd explained, throwing me one of those hooded looks. "Minions can do that, too, but only humans from one of our lines can see through Archon glamour, so I needed to find out what you were."

"What if I'd failed to describe you accurately?" I'd asked.

A shrug. "Then you'd have been a minion, and I'd have killed you."

Between that admission, the compulsive mirror smashing and his impenetrable secretiveness, I was well on my way to getting over my attraction. Adrian wasn't just damaged goods, he was *deranged* goods, and coming from someone with a history of psychosis, that was saying something. By the time we pulled into a motel at the halfway point of Kearney, Nebraska, I would've been happy never to see him again.

I called shotgun on the bathroom as soon as we entered the hotel room. Adrian obliged after smashing the mirror—he had to have ten thousand years of bad luck by now—then finally, I was able to take a shower. Thank God the motel had complimentary bottles of shampoo and conditioner because I wasn't about to ask Adrian for any. For all I knew, the bulky duffel bag he'd brought in was filled with severed minion heads.

After I showered, I washed my clothes, making a mental note to insist that we shop before hitting the road tomorrow. With everything I owned now hanging to dry, I donned Adrian's coat over my towel before leaving the bathroom.

He stood in front of the motel door, flicking something

from a glass vial onto it. He did the same with the window, all while muttering in that strange, harshly lyrical language.

He probably wouldn't tell me, but I asked anyway. "What are you doing?"

"Setting supernatural locks," he replied, with a jaded glance at me. "This motel isn't on hallowed ground, so we have to demon-proof this room. I don't think we were followed, but I'd rather you weren't murdered in your sleep."

I swallowed. I'd rather that not happen, too. "So, that stuff you're sprinkling around is like demon-mace?"

His mouth twitched, making me wonder if he fought back a smile. "Close. Know how a priest blesses water and then it's considered holy? This is the Archon version of blessed oil, which briefly renders any place it touches as hallowed."

"How brief is 'briefly'?" I wondered.

A shrug. "Long enough for us to sleep."

"If it hallows out any place, then *why* did we spend last night in a spider-infested crypt?" I asked at once.

Now I was sure he was fighting back a smile. "You looked like you slept there just fine to me." At my instant glower, he added, "I can only get this stuff from Zach, and he's stingy with handing it out. This is the last I've got, so after tonight, we'll need to sleep on real hallowed ground until he decides to show up and give me more."

A stingy angel. Now I'd heard of everything. Guess I'd better enjoy the real bed tonight. Who knew what I'd be cuddling up next to tomorrow. Speaking of that, I needed to handle some things before I went off the grid any longer.

"You have a phone I can use? I need to call my roommate, Delia. Tell her I'll be gone for…a while."

Adrian's expression changed from suppressed amusement to stern refusal. "Not a chance. No calls, texts or emails."

Who did he think he was, my new father? "Let me rephrase—

I'm *calling* my roommate, either with your phone or with someone else's."

I couldn't just disappear on Delia. I, of all people, knew
how awful it was to wonder if someone you cared about was
alive or dead, and she wasn't just my roommate. After Jasmine,
Delia was my best friend.

"You call her or anyone else you know, you're making them
a target," Adrian replied coolly. "Not many people escape a
demonic kidnapping attempt. The ones that do are usually
helped by me, so that makes the demons extra mad. By now,
minions have combed through every aspect of your life, and
they're waiting for you to connect to someone so they can use
that person against you."

Nothing changed in the room, but it suddenly felt smaller,
as if the walls were edging toward each other.

"What's the point? They already have my sister," I said,
anger and despair sharpening my tone.

Adrian leveled that gemstone stare at me. "Right, so don't
give them anyone else."

I sat down on what I guessed was my bed, since Adrian's
duffel bag was on the other. The zipper was open, revealing
nothing more sinister than clothes and toiletries. And here I'd
been so sure about the severed minion heads. I did give the
toothbrush a longing look. This motel didn't have those as
freebies, and my breath could probably slay a dragon.

"Help yourself," Adrian stated, nodding at the bag. "Zach
packed supplies for both of us."

He didn't need to tell me twice. I went to his bed and began
to rummage through the bag. Thanks to his large build, it
wasn't hard to distinguish what was meant for Adrian and
what was intended for me. The only surprise was that Zach
had guessed my size, even on the intimate items.

"What kind of angel notices cup size?" I muttered under my breath as I added a bra to my pile.

Adrian's bark of laughter let me know that I'd said it too loud. "Zach is nothing if not detail-oriented."

"You sound like you've known him a long time," I observed.

His face closed off in a now familiar way. I could let it go, like I had most of the drive here, but I was getting tired of his frequent bouts of silent treatment.

"I get that you don't want to be here and you *really* don't want to talk about whatever it is that you are, but if we're going to be fighting demons together, I should at least know more about you."

Adrian walked toward me, a hard little smile twisting his features. Then he bent down until his face was level with mine. His eyes looked even more vivid in the overhead light, and he was so close, I could see that his lashes were dark brown instead of black.

"Here's the most important thing you need to know. I hate demons more than you do, so you can trust that I'll help you kill them. But, Ivy—" harsh laughter brushed my skin in its own caress "—whatever you do, don't trust me with anything else."

The last time we'd been this close, he'd had me pinned to his car. He wasn't touching me now, but somehow, his gaze made the moment equally intense. The scary part was, I liked it. Without thinking, I moistened my lips.

His gaze dropped there, and I sucked in a breath at the hunger that flashed across his face. So finding out about my supposed lineage *hadn't* killed his attraction to me! With that knowledge, things lower down began to tighten. Adrian was maddening, confusing, dangerous…and what would I do if he tried to kiss me?

Suddenly, I saw a blur of motion and then he was gone, the door vibrating from his exit.

I awoke to the wonderful smell of hot, greasy food, and the even more tantalizing aroma of coffee. When I opened my eyes, a bag of McDonald's was on my nightstand. I hadn't heard Adrian leave to get it, but then again, I hadn't heard him come back last night, either. He must have since his bed was mussed, and from the sounds of it, he was now in the shower.

I fell on the food like a starving animal. A candy bar and a small bag of peanuts had been all I'd eaten over the past two days. Getting yelled at by multiple gas station attendants after Adrian broke their mirrors hadn't made me want to browse for more substantial fare. After I finished, I quickly put on new clothes, not wanting Adrian to come out while I was half-naked. Things were strange enough between us already.

My necklace snagged on my sweater as I yanked it over my head, reminding me there was one mirror Adrian hadn't smashed yet. Since the shower was still running, I opened the locket, a pang hitting me when I saw my sister's picture on one side and a small mirror on the other.

This way, we'll always be together, Jasmine had said when she'd given it to me the night before I left for college. She'd cried a little then, and I never admitted it, but when I was alone in my room that night, I did, too. Sure, we fought like mad sometimes, but no one was closer to me than Jasmine. With everyone else, I had to keep faking so they'd believe everything was fine. For my parents, it was so they wouldn't worry about me. For my psychologist, it was to avoid more tests or inpatient stays. For my friends and the occasional boyfriend, it was so I wouldn't have to explain things they probably didn't want to understand. With Jaz, I could be myself because who-ever that was, she was okay with it.

"Nuts, normal, doesn't matter," she'd said years ago when I was upset after my psychologist told me I might never be cured. "You're my sister, Ives, so no matter what, we're stuck with each other."

As I stared at her picture next to my own reflection, her loss hit me all over again. It took everything I had to hold the tears back. After several hard blinks, her image became less blurry. As I looked at her, I silently made her a promise. *No matter what, I will find you.* She'd never given up on me. I sure as hell wouldn't give up on her.

Vow made, I could look at her picture without tearing up again. We didn't resemble each other, of course. Jasmine was a blue-eyed blonde like my adoptive parents, and I had hazel eyes and brown hair. My greenish-brown eyes, light skin tone and other markers had caused my pediatrician to speculate that one of my parents had been Caucasian. We guessed the other was Hispanic because that was the nationality of the immigrants who'd been unable to flee the tractor-trailer accident, but who knew?

Thinking about my biological parents made Zach's words steal through my mind, though I'd done my best to forget them. *Your real mother didn't leave you because she was running from the police…she did it to save you, just as your dreams revealed…*

"Good, you're up."

Adrian's curt voice made me jump. I snapped the locket shut, glad my back was to him so he couldn't see what I tucked under my sweater. He was *not* smashing the last gift my sister gave to me, mirror phobia or not. With the locket safely hidden, I turned around.

"Thanks for…breakfast."

I couldn't help my pause. Some things should come with a warning label, and seeing Adrian stalk through the room wearing only a towel was definitely one of them. I hadn't known ab definition like that existed without airbrushing, and the network of muscles on his arms, back and chest rippled as though dancing to a song that reverberated beneath his flesh.

Michelangelo had it wrong, I thought, tearing my gaze away. With that body, Adrian was the one who needed a marble statue made in his image. Good thing he was so fixated on shoving his things into his duffel bag, he didn't notice my admiration.

"We're leaving in ten minutes," he stated, still in that brusque tone.

After he'd stormed out last night, I told myself it didn't matter if Adrian was still attracted to me. I needed to rescue my sister, not start something with a guy who'd warned me he wasn't trustworthy, let alone all the other reasons why Adrian was off-limits. No matter the dazzling packaging, he was six feet six inches of undetermined supernatural bad news, so his coldness now suited my purposes.

His barked orders, however, didn't. We needed to get a few things straight before we went any further.

"Just because you're pissed about our little road trip doesn't mean you get to keep taking it out on me," I said. "For whatever reason, you chose to come, and we don't need to be friends, but you do need to quit acting like my boss. So we're not leaving in ten minutes, Adrian. We're leaving in twenty because I'm taking a shower, too."

He swung around, arms crossing over that muscled chest in obvious annoyance. I continued on as if I didn't notice.

"It's not my fault if you've never had a serious girlfriend, but believe me when I tell you that it's impossible for a girl to get ready in less than twenty minutes."

"Fine," he said, his tone only slightly less rude.

"You may want to wait until I'm in the bathroom to get

dressed, too," I said airily. "If you drop that towel now, I'll think it's your way of telling me you still want that date."

I didn't wait for his response before disappearing into the bathroom. All jokes aside, if he *did* drop that towel, I might forget all the many reasons why I should stay away from him.

chapter seven

Twenty minutes later—okay, twenty-five, but close enough—we climbed into his car. I wasn't much for old muscle cars, but I had to admit that his Challenger was in great shape. Still, I'd kill for a satellite radio. This only had AM and FM.

"You don't need to drive the whole way. We can take turns," I offered.

"No," he replied at once.

"So you're one of those," I muttered.

His brow went up. "One of what?"

"Guys who think a girl can't handle their precious metal babies," I said, rolling my eyes.

At that, he laughed. "I rebuilt this car from the axle up, so yeah, you can call it my baby. But no one, male *or* female, drives it except me."

"So you're an equal-opportunity control freak?" I replied without missing a beat.

"You have no idea," he said, voice lowering while his blue eyes slid over me in a phantom caress.

My breath caught. Until that moment, I hadn't realized he'd avoided looking at me since he stormed out last night. Now, his gaze moved over me as if he already knew which parts to touch first and which parts to leave until I was breathless and begging. My heart began to beat faster. How could he affect me so much when we barely knew each other?

Then, like a switch had been flipped, he looked away as though the sight of me had burned his eyes. His whole demeanor changed, too, as if he were angry for revealing something that was supposed to remain hidden.

"When should we arrive in Oregon?" I asked, needing something, anything, to break up the tense moment.

He revved up the car and glanced at the clock. "Three a.m., if we don't get caught in traffic."

Nineteen hours until I crossed into one of the places that countless doctors had sworn were merely figments of my imbalanced mind. Once again, I had so many questions, I hardly knew where to begin.

"Have you been to this particular 'realm door' before?"

"Yes."

One tightly spoken word that warned me to drop the subject, if I didn't want another round of the silent treatment. I stifled a frustrated sigh. I needed more information, and he was moodier than a tween girl with her first PMS attack.

"How did you know minions were trying to kidnap me the other night?" There. Total change of subject, and something I'd been wondering about, anyway.

Adrian didn't look at me as he pulled out onto the road. "Zach told me. He's the one who sent me to retrieve you."

I'd have to drag everything out of him, wouldn't I? "Okay, how did Zach know?"

He grunted. "Archons get information about future events. Every so often, they interfere to change the outcome."

"Every so often?" I repeated with angry disbelief, thinking of Jasmine's kidnapping and my parents' deaths. "Why not every time? Or do Archons have days where they're just not in the *mood* to save people from harm and death?"

Nothing changed in his expression, but his tone hardened with what I thought might be remembered pain. "That's the million-dollar question, isn't it? I don't have an answer, and when I asked Zach the same thing, all he said was something about 'orders.'"

"That's such bullshit," I muttered.

"I couldn't agree more," Adrian said dryly.

Neither of us spoke for a few minutes. Not strained silence like before, but silent, shared reflection while both of us thought of things that we wished had turned out different.

"So that's what you do?" I finally said. "Rescue people for Zach after he tells you that minions are after them?"

He shrugged. "Gives me a chance to piss off demons."

"Most people would *avoid* doing that," I pointed out, suppressing a shudder. If not for Jasmine, you wouldn't catch me near a demon, minion, realm or anything freakily supernatural. Why did Adrian run toward the danger instead?

"You and I aren't most people, Ivy," he said softly. "Because of what we see, we don't get to pretend the world is a beautiful place where monsters don't exist."

I was the one who looked away that time, unable to handle the truth of his statement or the intensity in his stare. Until a few days ago, I *had* been doing that. Even as a child, as soon as I'd realized no one else saw the things I did, I'd wanted it to stop. I hated feeling like something was wrong with me, so after I'd jumped through almost a decade of medical hoops looking for a cure, I started pretending that I'd found one.

I told my parents, the doctors and even eventually Jasmine that I no longer saw the strange, dark worlds hanging like nightmares over regular places. I certainly never told Delia or my other friends about them. I said the pills I took were for a hormonal imbalance, and all my doctor appointments were for that, too.

Lies, lies, lies, all because I wanted to pretend I was normal. According to the gorgeous stranger across from me, I wasn't then and never would be.

"What happened with you?" I asked, my voice low as if we were sharing secrets. "I hid from what I saw, but you started hunting down the things everyone told me couldn't exist. You must've had proof that they were real, so what was it?"

He closed off so fast I was surprised I didn't hear a sonic boom. I shut my eyes, letting out a sigh as I tried to settle myself more comfortably into my seat. Looked like the question-and-answer segment of our time was over.

Eventually, as afternoon slid into evening during the long drive, the late hour and boredom lulled me into drifting off.

A thunderous boom woke the black-haired woman. Her baby began to wail at the multiple crashing noises. She left the baby in the backseat, walking through the brush that hid her car.

On the nearby highway, a tractor-trailer was on its side, multiple cars piled up around it. Each passing second brought a new screech of tires and, more faintly, screams. Then the back of the trailer opened, and people stumbled out, some disappearing into the tall grass that lined the road, others limping a few feet before collapsing onto the road.

The black-haired woman hurried back to her car, but as she began to strap her baby in the car seat, she paused. Then she turned around and stared. Sunlight broke through the clouds, streaming down to the side of the road about fifty yards from the accident. The woman began to shake.

"No. No, I can't leave her," she whispered.

The light grew brighter, and another sunbeam appeared, illuminating the same spot. Tears streamed down her face, but after a minute, she picked up her child and walked toward it.

"Promise me she'll be safe," she choked out, setting the baby in the grass. Then she kissed the child, whispering, "Mommy loves you. Always," before running to her car and driving away—

"What is that?"

Adrian's voice startled me. For a second, I was disoriented, the dream clinging to me as it always did. Yes, I was in a car, but I wasn't the unknown woman driving away from her baby. That wasn't real. The glare Adrian leveled at my chest was, though.

"Is that a mirror?" He sounded horrified.

I looked down. My locket was open, the mirrored side facing me. At some point while I was sleeping, I must've opened it. Adrian's hand shot out, but this time, I was too fast for him.

"Don't you dare," I snapped, holding it out of his reach. "It's the only picture I have of my sister after you left everything I own back at that hotel in Bennington!"

He lunged again, actually letting go of the steering wheel to reach the side of the car where I held it. With a sharp yank, he wrested the locket from my hands. I tried to snatch it back, but he shoved me into my seat with one hand, finally grabbing the steering wheel with the other.

"Are you crazy?" I shrieked. "You could've gotten us killed!" If this hadn't been a lonely stretch of desert road, our careening into the next lane might've had permanent consequences.

"You're going to get *yourself* killed," was his chilling response. Then, still pinning me to my chair with that single hand, he held my locket up.

I gasped. Something dark poked out of the small mirror, like a snake made of blackest smoke. It disappeared when Adrian smashed the mirror against the steering wheel, but an eerie wind whistled through the car, ruffling my hair and stinging my nostrils with its acrid scent.

Adrian muttered a word in that unknown language, and I didn't need a translator to tell me it was a curse.

"What was that?" My voice was hoarse.

He threw me a pitying glance, which frightened me even more. If he wasn't angry, we must really be screwed.

His next words proved that. "Brace yourself, Ivy. You're about to meet a demon."

chapter eight

I didn't consider myself religious. My parents used to take Jasmine and me to church on Christmas, but it was more a social event than a pious one. Hearing we were about to be attacked by a demon, however, made me pray like I'd never done before. I just wished I knew if anyone was listening.

Adrian wasn't praying. He was cursing up a storm, if I correctly translated the spate of words coming from his mouth. He'd also lost that pitying expression, because the looks he shot me now were distinctly grim. It wasn't the right time, but I couldn't stop myself from asking the obvious.

"How did it find us?"

Adrian stomped on the accelerator, and the muscle car shot forward like it had rockets in the engine.

"Through the mirror," he said shortly. "For stronger demons, mirrors act as portals, and you've been number one on their Most Wanted list since you escaped them in Bennington."

I gaped at him. "Maybe you should have *told* me that?"

"You think I smash every mirror near you because I don't

want you to get conceited?" Then his tone softened. "You're barely holding it together with what you *do* know, Ivy. I'm not about to tell you what you can't handle yet."

Anger flared, which felt better than the fear that made my blood seem like it had been replaced by ice water.

"No, I wasn't ready to know that demons used mirrors as portals. I also wasn't ready to know demons existed, or had kidnapped my sister, or that my parents were dead, or any of the horrible things I've dealt with in the past two weeks. But that didn't stop them from happening, so quit protecting me from the truth, Adrian! It doesn't help a damn bit!"

Adrian glanced at me, a gauntlet of emotions flitting across his features.

"You're right. If we survive, I'll apologize."

My laughter was bleak. "You? Say you're sorry? Now I *really* want to live."

To my surprise, he laughed as well, though it was colored with dark expectancy.

"Hold that thought. You'll need it."

Before I could respond, something filled the road in front of us. I would've said it was storm clouds, except clouds don't sweep along the ground like a heavy fog rolling in.

"Shut your vents," Adrian said, flipping the tiny levers on his side. I did the same, more apprehension filling me as he turned the entire air-conditioning system off. No, those weren't low-hanging clouds. They were something far more ominous.

"Turn around," I said, my voice suddenly breathy.

"It wouldn't matter" was Adrian's chilling reply. "He'd only follow us. I need you to find hallowed ground, Ivy."

I couldn't take my eyes away from the billowing clouds in front of us. They were so dark, they seemed to devour the beams that came from Adrian's headlights.

"All right," I mumbled. "Give me your phone, I'll look up the nearest church or cemetery."

"It's too late for that," he said, stunning me. "You need to find it yourself."

"How?" I burst out. We were almost at the line of black clouds. The temperature in the car plummeted, making my skin feel like it had turned to ice.

"It's in your bloodline," Adrian said, swinging off the road so sharply that the back end began to fishtail. "You can sense hallowed ground, so find some, Ivy. Now."

"I don't know how!" I shouted.

The car shuddered over the uneven terrain, bouncing so much I almost hit my head on the roof, but I didn't tell Adrian to slow down. That wall of darkness filled up the rear window of the Challenger until I couldn't see the glow of our tail lights anymore.

"Yes, you do." A growl that sounded comforting compared to the horrible hissing noises coming from outside the car.

"I don't!" What was that flash of white on my side of the car? Or that new, ripping sound? Oh God, were those *teeth* scraping away at the metal on my door?

"It's getting in, it's getting in!"

"He can't get in the car."

Adrian's strong voice broke through my panic. I stared at him, my eyes starting to burn from the acrid stench that crept in through parts of the car we hadn't been able to seal.

"I warded it against demons a long time ago," he went on.

I felt better about that for three seconds, which was how long it took before the car lifted up on one side like a gargantuan hand had swatted it. For a paralyzing moment, I wasn't sure if we were going to flip completely over. Then we crashed down hard enough to make the windows shatter, and I tasted blood from my jaw snapping shut on my tongue.

"'Course, that doesn't mean he can't tear the car apart around us," Adrian said, stomping on the gas as soon as all four wheels were on the ground. "We're running out of time. Where's the hallowed ground?"

"I. Don't. Know," I screamed. My heart was pounding out of my chest from terror. If I knew a way out of this, I'd take it.

"Yes, you do," he insisted, those sapphire eyes searing me when he glanced over. "Tell me which direction you want to run. That's the right way, I promise."

Which way did I want to run? In whatever direction this living nightmare wasn't! The car lifted again, and everything in me braced for another impact. That awful hissing noise grew into a roar, and Adrian's gaze met mine. In those darkly beautiful depths, I realized these would be the last moments of our lives if I didn't use an ability I'd never heard of before.

In the seconds before the car came crashing down, I closed my eyes. Concentrated on which direction I wanted to flee to, and tried to ignore the pain as flying glass pelted me from all sides. My instincts were screaming at me to run from the horrible thing outside these crumbling metal walls, and I let those instincts consume me, filling me until I couldn't focus on anything else. I needed to get out of here. I needed to leave right now and go…*there*.

"That way," I said hoarsely, opening my eyes and pointing.

Adrian's hand closed over mine, his grip strong and sure. Then the car crashed down hard enough to make my vision go black and my whole body ache, but he didn't hesitate. As soon as the worst of the impact was over, he grabbed his coat, yanked me into his arms, and then flung us out of the car.

His body took the brunt of the impact, but it still felt like I hit the ground with almost the same force as the car crashing down. My yelp was swallowed up by a tremendous *boom!* as Adrian threw something at the fog that rushed us. White flashed, more bright and brilliant than a lightning bolt. Those hideous clouds recoiled with a scream as though they were in pain.

Adrian leaped up, still holding me in his arms. Then he began to run in the direction I'd pointed, leaving that ugly, writhing darkness behind us.

Even without the nightmarish clouds surrounding us, I could barely see. Nothing but desert stretched out in front of us, and the headlights from Adrian's car were now too far away to do any good. That strange flash of light was gone, too. Even the moon seemed to hide, but Adrian's incredible strides never wavered. It was as if his eyes had night-vision technology built into them.

His speed had startled me when I was only an observer of it. Now that I was locked in his arms, hurtling through the night like I'd been strapped to the front of a bullet train, it filled me with terrified awe. His heart pounded next to my cheek, but he *couldn't* be human. No mere mortal could move this way. Hell, some hybrid cars couldn't go this fast.

"Where is it, Ivy?" he yelled, the wind snatching away his words almost before I could hear them.

I wasn't sure anymore. All the darkness had disoriented me, and it wasn't like there was a neon sign that said Hallowed Ground This Way. I didn't say that, though. What I saw when I glanced over his shoulder froze the words in my throat.

That roiling mass of evil was right behind us. I shouldn't have been able to see it against the midnight-soaked desert, but I could. The shadows forming it were filled with such seeth-ing malevolence that their darkness gleamed. Then something like a huge mouth gaped open, teeth long and razor-sharp.

"Adrian!" I screamed, tightening my arms around him.

He didn't look back, though his grip on me turned bruis-ing. "Tell me where to go, Ivy!"

I forced myself to look away from the appalling sight, but I couldn't look ahead. Sand-filled wind stung my eyes from how fast Adrian ran. I couldn't see, but maybe I didn't have to.

I closed my eyes like I had back in the car. Concentrated on my need to be as far away from the formless death monster as I could. My concentration broke when something sharp lashed my legs before digging in as though trying to claw its way up my body. I screamed again, and Adrian snarled, somehow increasing his incredible speed. With a final slice, the claws left my body, but something hot and wet ran down my legs.

I choked back my next scream, my heart pounding as fast as the booming beneath my cheek. Then I concentrated again, pain and panic finding the switch in my mind that I hadn't realized was there.

"That way," I said, pointing without opening my eyes.

Adrian changed direction, the hard pumping of his legs shooting pain into me from the endless impacts, but I didn't care. Another roar sounded behind us, growing closer, until I could almost feel its icy breath on my cheek. My legs throbbed, anticipating more claws slicing through my skin, and though I knew I shouldn't, I opened my eyes.

It was *right there,* faceless except for those grotesquely large teeth that snapped mere inches from my head. I stared, too horrified to scream again. It stretched, growing even bigger, until I couldn't see anything except the wall of evil that was about to come crashing down on us—

It split through the middle, breaking around us like water parted by rocks. An unearthly howl shook me, blasting my ears and blowing my hair back. Just as abruptly, Adrian slowed down, coming to a complete stop a couple dozen feet away from the thing, which surged and recoiled as though trying to break past an invisible barrier.

I didn't understand for the first few breathless seconds. Then

I saw the faint shimmers coming up from the earth and heard the faraway echo of long-dead voices chanting prayers. We'd made it to the hallowed ground, and the demon might rage along its perimeter, but it couldn't cross it to get to us.

chapter nine

Now I knew why people who'd escaped certain death broke into laughter. It had always looked strange in the movies, but I hadn't realized how quickly adrenaline turned to relief, the change hitting your bloodstream like a dozen tequila shots. For a few seconds, I didn't even feel any pain as I laughed from the wild, wondrous exhilaration of still being alive. I wanted to hug Adrian. I wanted to spin in circles. I wanted to scream, "Take *that!*" at the swirls of dark clouds that stormed along the edge of our supernaturally impregnable walls.

Adrian didn't laugh, but his wide smile conveyed both victory and savage satisfaction. He stared at the living darkness a short distance from us and said something in that strange, harshly melodic language.

To my surprise, the clouds began to shrink, dissipating as quickly as a fog machine in reverse. Soon, nothing remained except an inky pool on the ground, like the shadows had been transformed into liquid.

"What did you say to make it disappear?" I asked, my brain adding numbly, *and why didn't you say it sooner?*

"He's not gone," Adrian said, his tone edged with an emotion I couldn't name. "He's just shedding his disguise."

Those fluid shadows suddenly began to rise, forming into a pillar. Then they changed, coiling and swirling until a slender girl with long blond hair broke through them as though she'd been expelled out.

Jasmine hunched in fear as she looked around. When she saw me, she collapsed on the ground in relief.

"Ivy," she said, her hands trembling as she reached out. "Please, help me!"

I didn't need Adrian to keep holding me to stop me from going to her. This wasn't my sister. It was a *thing* wearing her image like a coat, and it infuriated me.

"Fuck you," I replied, all my fear and hatred rolled into those two words.

Jasmine's form blurred, turning into slithering shadows again. Out of those, a man emerged. He was almost as tall as Adrian, though not as thickly muscled, and he moved with snakelike grace as he prowled along the edge of the barrier. Long black hair hid most of his face as the wind tossed it around, but I caught a glimpse of pale skin, burning black eyes and a dark pink mouth that opened as he said—

"I can see why you like her, my son."

I barely noticed Adrian stiffen. I was too busy being shocked by the thing's identical, exotic accent and how he'd addressed the man holding me. *My son.* Was this the secret Adrian refused to talk about? It would explain his superhuman speed—

"Don't call me that." Adrian's voice lashed the air with palpable hatred. "I was never your son."

The demon sighed in the way my father used to do when

I was a child and he was explaining why some things, like dental visits, were unavoidable.

"Not by blood, but you're mine nonetheless. Now, Adrian, your little rebellion, while amusing, has gone on long enough. Carry her out to me. It will save us all from a lengthy, boring fight before the inevitable occurs."

Adrian's smile reminded me of a tiger baring his teeth. "I live to fight you, Demetrius, so it's never boring for me."

Demetrius. Wasn't that the demon who'd sent Detective Kroger after me? I started to squirm, wanting out of Adrian's arms while I processed this, but his grip only tightened.

Demetrius noticed, and the look he flashed Adrian was both knowing and cruel.

"Every moment you spend with her will strengthen the bond between you. Break it now, before it destroys you when you fulfill your destiny."

A noise escaped Adrian, too visceral to be called a snarl. "My 'destiny' won't happen if you're dead. How much did the Archon grenade hurt? Not nearly as much as David's sling-shot will, I hope."

Demetrius laughed, sending shivers of revulsion over me. If evil came in audible form, it would sound like that.

"Now that I've seen the last of David's seed, I'm even more confident of my people's success. You must be, too. That's why she has no idea what we're talking about." Another mocking, repellent laugh, then the demon's face turned serious. "Come home, my son. I miss you. Obsidiana misses you. You don't belong with them. You never did."

Adrian's grip hardened until it felt like I was encased in steel. "I'd rather die where I don't belong than live another day with you," he gritted out.

Demetrius shook his head. "So slow to learn," he said sadly. Then he looked at me, a smile playing about his lips.

"I make your sister scream in pain every day," he said in an offhand way. "If you want to save her, say my name in a mirror. I'll trade her life for yours."

My reply contained every filthy word I knew, plus a few I made up. Demetrius only laughed again. Then, with a swirl of shadows, he disappeared. Or did he?

"Is he really gone?" I asked hoarsely.

"He's gone. I told you, demons can't tolerate our realm for long. Even strong ones like Demetrius would be dead after an hour here."

As he spoke, he let me down, which was good, since I didn't want him touching me. The words *my son* kept resounding in my mind. Biologically related or not, the demon imprisoning my sister had close ties to Adrian—a fact he'd deliberately kept from me. Worse, Demetrius seemed very confident that their ties would be restored soon.

"So Demetrius is your stepdad?"

He sighed at the acid in my tone. "The simplest explanation is that Demetrius was...my foster parent."

The slight hesitation before those words told me he was hiding large chunks of the truth. Again.

"And Daddy Dearest misses you. How sweet."

Adrian's expression darkened so much, I half expected to see shadows appear beneath his skin.

"I get that you're pissed, but don't ever call him my father again. I was a child when he took me. Not all of us were lucky enough to end up with kind, *human* foster parents."

His raw tone melted away some of my anger. He might still be hiding something, but I couldn't imagine the horrors of growing up at the mercy of a demon.

"Why did Demetrius take you?" I asked with less rancor. "Does it have to do with your mysterious bloodline?"

As I watched his lips tighten in that familiar way, I knew

I was right—and that he still wasn't going to tell me what he was. Not part-demon, evidently, and I doubted he was part-Archon. If he was, Demetrius would've killed him, not raised him as his "son."

"Your legs are injured," Adrian stated, changing the subject. "Sit. I've got medicine in my coat."

If they hadn't been throbbing with pain for the past several minutes, I would have refused until Adrian told me the rest of what he was hiding. Since our car was busted and we probably had a long walk ahead of us, I sat, wincing when he pulled at the tears in my jeans. The wounds had already started to stick to the fabric.

After a few moments, Adrian let out a soft hiss. "Lots of gouges, and deep. Take your pants off."

"Geez, buy a girl a drink first," I said to cover my dread over how much that would hurt.

His lips curled as he retrieved a flask from his coat. "Ask and you shall receive."

"You've had liquor on you this whole time?" I didn't know whether to laugh or cry. "I could've really used some, oh, *every day* for the last few days!"

I snatched the flask and took a gulp, welcoming the burn that made my eyes water, and forced a sputter after I swallowed.

"Not a bourbon girl?" Adrian asked dryly.

"That's bourbon?" I let out a choking cough. "I thought it might be prison brew!" Still, I took another throat-scorching gulp. Beggars can't be choosers.

His snort was soft. "No, but let's just say the recipe doesn't come from a normal brew company."

"I'll bet," I muttered, then coughed out a protest when he took it from me. "Wait, I'm not done!"

"That's much stronger than regular bourbon," he said, putting it back in his coat. "Trust me, you've had enough."

When he started tugging my jeans down, the pain shooting through me made me want to argue, but I didn't. I hadn't eaten in hours, and I didn't want to add puking to all the other reasons why this night had been awful. Once my jeans were off, I stayed silent for a different reason.

Savage swipes had ripped open my flesh in at least a dozen places. I saw white in some of the gaping spaces, making my fear of vomiting a real possibility. If I'd been thrown into an angry bear's den, I probably would've fared better. How had I managed to even *stand* with injuries like this?

I must've said that last part out loud, because Adrian answered me.

"Shock and adrenaline, plus your bloodline. You're stronger, faster and tougher than you realize. You just didn't know it before because you never needed to be."

With that, he pulled a sealed plastic bag out of his coat. No wonder he'd made sure to grab it when we fled the car; liquor and medicine were necessities in any survivalist's book, not to mention the Archon grenade that had made cloud-Demetrius scream.

If I'd known then what I knew now, I'd have savored that scream. His taunts about Jasmine tormented me, as he'd intended them to. If I had any confidence that a demon would keep his word, I'd be tempted to trade my life for hers. Finding the weapon and taking on Demetrius might get me killed anyway, and then my sister would *really* be doomed.

Adrian scooped out some of the bag's contents, interrupting that bleak line of thought. The medicine looked like mashed-up macaroon cookies, and I tensed as he held that sticky mixture over the deepest gouge on my thigh. His eyes met mine, their silvery perimeter gleaming.

"Take a deep breath, Ivy."

I did, and still almost screamed when he brought his hand

down. The medicine hurt more than when Demetrius had made the wounds, but I bit my lip and didn't cry out. Adrian was trying to help. The less I distracted him, the faster this would end.

I repeated that like a litany while he smeared the agony-inducing substance on all my deeper gashes. He worked with quiet efficiency, thankfully not commenting on the sweat that beaded my forehead or how my breath came in pants.

"Almost over," he murmured in sympathy.

Something strange began to happen. The pain changed, turning into a tingling that reminded me of what it felt like when my foot fell asleep. Adrian finished with the final gouge and leaned back, watching my legs with an expectant expression.

The wounds began to close, expelling the now red-smeared medicine as smooth flesh filled in what had been gaping tears. Within minutes, the only marks left were shallower grazes that I could've made while shaving. I could hardly believe it.

"What is that stuff?"

His mouth curled. "Manna."

Where had I heard that word…? "The mythical bread that fed the Israelites when they wandered in the desert?"

His half smile remained. "As you see, it has a lot of uses. Now, turn over so I can get the other gouges."

I did, thinking it was a good thing that Zach had done my recent shopping. I normally wore thongs, but now, my ass was more modestly covered by bikini briefs.

Once I was on my stomach, Adrian's large hand covered a wound high up on my hip. Though the initial pain was just as sharp, something else flared through me. Maybe it was because I knew the harsh sting would soon fade. Maybe the bellyful of superpotent liquor contributed to the urge I had to see his expression as he dragged his hand over my skin, or perhaps it was the way his touch seemed to linger longer than medicinally necessary.

I could've told him to stop. Insisted on dressing the wounds myself; I could reach them, after all. But I didn't. He didn't speak, either, and as his hands continued their path down my body, treating and then smoothing over newly healed skin, the pain was a price I willingly paid to keep feeling him touch me.

It was wrong, of course. I kept telling that to my rapidly beating heart and the shivers that followed every stroke of his hands. He was danger wrapped in secrets tied with a bow of bad intentions, and it was totally unfair that no one had made me feel this way before.

"Almost over?" I asked, hating how much he affected me.

"Yeah."

He sounded angry, which made me flip over before he'd finished smoothing manna over a shallower cut. My quick movement must've surprised him, because it took a second for his expression to close off into that familiar, jaded mask.

In that brief, unguarded moment, I learned I wasn't the only one who'd been affected by his touching me. Suddenly, it seemed like a very good idea to put my pants back on.

chapter ten

Adrian made a fire out of plants, scrub and other things I wouldn't have thought to use, starting it by rubbing twigs together fast enough to get a spark. I huddled as close as I could to the fire without catching myself ablaze. Even so, my breath made tiny white clouds with every exhalation. Who knew a desert could be so chilly at night?

"How long do we have to stay out here?"

Adrian glanced back at me. He didn't appear bothered by the cold temperatures, or his pacing was keeping him warm. He hadn't stopped since he quit treating my injuries.

"Until morning. We can't risk another demon ambushing us if we leave the hallowed ground before sunrise."

"They can't enter our realm in daylight?" Interesting.

"Didn't I tell you that?"

"No, you didn't," I replied, adding, "along with a lot of other things," in case my tone hadn't been pointed enough.

He snorted, the slight breath pluming in the frigid air, too. "I'm not keeping secrets to make things worse for you, Ivy.

I'm doing it to help you. One thing I can say is that Demetrius is full of shit about your sister."

"How?" I asked instantly.

He came closer, until the firelight revealed every nuance of his intensely beautiful face.

"Right now, she's the safest, most well-treated human in all the realms. Your sister is the only leverage the demons have over you, and they might be evil, but they're not stupid enough to kill, maim or emotionally break their only advantage."

My sigh whooshed out, as if the part of me that had been holding its breath for days finally relaxed enough to release it. Even as relief seemed to blend with the liquor in me, creating a lethargic sort of high, a new question arose.

"Thanks for telling me, but…why did you?" He'd made it clear that he'd rather not be here, and keeping me scared about my sister's treatment was motivation for me to find the weapon as quickly as possible.

Adrian looked away, his jaw tightening. "Demetrius said it to hurt you, and I don't like to see you hurt."

The simple statement made me wonder all the more about him. Who was the real Adrian? The oddly charming man who'd asked me for a date right after he kidnapped me? The heroic one who'd saved my life two times in four days? Or the surly one who acted like I was a venereal disease he couldn't wait to be cured of? I didn't think the night was long enough to find out, but it might be too long for other things.

"What if Demetrius sends his minions after us?" I shivered as I looked around. "It's so dark, we wouldn't even see them coming."

"I would."

Two quiet, steely words that reminded me how different Adrian was from a normal person. To prevent myself from wondering for the umpteenth time what he was, I kept talking.

"What kind of hallowed ground do you suppose this is?" The ethereal shimmers coming up from the sand marked an area roughly the size of a football field.

Adrian shrugged. "This part of the Oregon desert? Indian burial ground maybe."

"That would explain the chanting," I said, cocking my head and listening. "I don't hear it anymore. Do you?"

His features tightened, but his tone was light. "I never heard it, Ivy."

I stared at him, understanding slowly dawning. "You don't see the shimmers coming up from the ground, either, do you?"

"No. Only you can sense hallowed objects." The smile he flashed held an edge of darkness. "My talents lie elsewhere."

I let out a short laugh as more pieces fell into place. "That's why you came with me even though you didn't want to. The demon-killing weapon is hallowed, isn't it? So you can't sense it, but with my abilities, I can, if you get me near enough."

That hint of menace didn't leave his smile. "I've wanted to kill Demetrius for years, but I've never had the means to. With you and that weapon, I finally will. Like I said, Ivy, when it comes to my hatred of demons, you can trust me completely."

"But once you kill Demetrius, all bets are off?" I filled in, a touch of anger coloring my tone. Adrian wasn't just some guy I was way too attracted to. He was also the only person who knew what it was like to see things that made everyone else believe you were crazy, until you believed it yourself.

Adrian stared at me, his smile wiping away. "I said I don't want to hurt you, and I meant it. So if we live through this, Ivy, I'm getting away from you as fast as I can."

I tried not to show how much that stung. What had I done that he relished the thought of never seeing me again? I'd think it was my hiding a mirror that almost got us killed, but Adrian had acted that way since Zach told him I was the last descendant of King David's line. I'd never forget the look he gave me when he found that out.

I paused. Maybe it wasn't what I'd done, but what someone else had done. After all, I hadn't misread some of the *other* looks Adrian had given me. Not every part of him wanted to run away from me as fast as he could.

"Did my ancestor do something terrible to your ancestor?" I guessed.

He looked shocked. Then he let out a laugh that was so bitter, I thought I'd finally stumbled on the truth. That was why his reply stunned me.

"No, Ivy. It was the other way around."

Despite my many attempts to get him to elaborate, he refused to say anything else.

Once dawn broke, I found out that manna could heal more than human injuries. Adrian spread a thin layer over his busted-up Challenger, and the vintage vehicle knit itself back together like I was watching an episode of *Counting Cars* on fast-forward. After that, we just had to brush the shattered glass out of the interior, and we were on our way.

When we made our first pit stop, I insisted on going into the ladies' room alone. Adrian kept getting caught destroying mirrors because it drew attention when a man entered a women-only area. He made me swear not to even peek at the mirror until after I'd shattered it. Demetrius might not be able to enter our realm during the day, but we didn't want him spying on us so he could ambush us once night fell.

That was how I found myself looking fixedly at the dirty tile floor as I approached the mirror in the Gas-N-Go restroom. Adrian had also given me a rock and a pair of oversize work gloves, so I didn't worry about cutting myself when I hit the glass with a hard bang, glancing at it only after I saw shards hit the floor. *Take that, Demetrius,* I thought, seeing only splinters of my reflection in its remains.

A flush sounded, and then the nearest stall door opened, revealing a fiftyish woman who looked back and forth between the ruined mirror and the rock in my hand.

"Why'd you do a thing like that?" she demanded.

Nothing I said would make it appear less crazy, so I might as well live up to her expectations.

"Ever have one of those days when you just *hate* your hair?" I asked, widening my eyes for maximum disturbed effect.

She didn't even wash her hands before she left. I made sure to be quick about my business as well, not surprised to see her talking to the store clerk once I exited the bathroom.

"Hey, girlie," the bald clerk said sharply. "Did you—?"

"This is for the damage," Adrian interrupted, slapping a handful of blank papers in front of the clerk. My confusion increased when the man snatched them up, his scowl turning into a grin.

"No problem," the clerk said, actually giving me a cheery wave. "Take care, girlie!"

I waited until we were outside before I said, "What was that?"

Adrian's mouth curled into a sardonic smile. "Zach's here."

That's when I paid attention to the hoodie-clad guy next to Adrian's car. Zach turned around, thankfully not projecting a blinding array of light as he faced us.

"I understand you ran into some difficulty last night," he stated, as if we'd only gotten a flat tire.

I blamed my response on being frustrated, under-caffeinated and hungry. "Yeah, and I hope you were too busy to show up because you were saving a bus full of nuns!"

A shrug. "I wasn't sent to you until now."

"Are you serious?" Incredulity sharpened my tone. "Is your

boss in a bad mood, or does he suffer from time-delay up there?"

Zach's face turned stony, but it didn't escape me that Adrian's smile widened.

"You don't know how many times I've wondered that," he murmured, nudging me in a sympathetic way.

Zach had a different response. "Why do you expect someone else to solve problems you are capable of handling yourselves?"

Adrian grunted. "Get used to hearing that. It's his favorite line."

Then you must want to punch him a lot, I thought before Zach's pointedly arched brow reminded me that my musings weren't private. That might not be all bad, though. I seized my chance.

Tell me what Adrian is, and why he's so determined to get away from me once this is over, I thought, staring at Zach.

"No," he said out loud. "I gave Adrian my word, and as I told you, Archons do not lie."

"What am I missing?" Adrian said, casting a suspicious look between both of us.

Don't you dare! I thought, but Zach was already replying. "Ivy sought the answers you are still refusing to give her."

Adrian's gaze swung to me. "Don't do that again," he said in an ominous tone.

"You bet your ass I will," I flared. "My life and my sister's life are on the line, so I have a right to know what's going on. Besides, after the fallout from your mirror omission, you said you'd quit hiding things *and* that you'd apologize."

Zach smirked at him. Actually smirked, and said, "I will enjoy witnessing this." There went another note under my ever-growing list titled Things I Didn't Expect From An Archon.

Adrian gave both of us such a cold glare that I was sure he'd refuse. Then he spoke.

"I'm sorry, Ivy, for not telling you about the mirrors. There's your apology, and here's information you didn't know—because you can see through Archon glamour, you saw me hand blank pieces of paper to the clerk. *He* saw a stack of hundred dollar bills, and we're using the same trick to fly to Mexico because we can't use the Oregon vortex to enter multiple realms through the same gateway anymore."

At my indrawn breath, Adrian went on. "Demetrius will guess that's where we're headed since we were in the Oregon desert when he caught up with us. Zach's here to refill our manna supply, glamour your appearance and remind me that we're on our own once we enter the demon realms. The two sides can't cross into each other's territories, so if we're captured, Zach can't help us even if he wants to."

I was openmouthed by the time he finished, but I quickly recovered. "And you are *what?*" I asked, wanting to know that more than all the other details.

Adrian smiled. "I promised to share secrets and I did. I never specified which ones."

Zach smirked again, and this time, it was directed at me.

"I'll remember that," I replied, giving Adrian a look that promised retribution.

If he thought I'd give up my quest to find out what he was, why he acted so hot and cold around me or what Demetrius had meant when he said that every moment "the bond" would strengthen between us, he was dead wrong. Now, the real trick would be to make sure that none of us ended up *really* dead before I got my answers.

I turned my back on Adrian, giving Zach my full attention. "You're going to change how others see me? Fine. I've always wondered what it would be like to be a blonde."

chapter eleven

The airport teller's name was Kristin. I handed her two blank paper stubs and a stack of equally blank Post-it pages, hoping I didn't look as guilty as I felt.

"One round-trip ticket to Durango, Mexico, please," I said.

Kristin looked at the blank stubs and pages. I tried to smile, but my face froze. Adrian swore that she and everyone else would see a driver's license, a passport and lots of cash in the Post-it note pile. All I saw was my imminent arrest, if the Archon glamour didn't hold up.

After what might have been five seconds but felt like ten years, the teller snapped up the two stubs from the pile, starting to type with crazy quickness on her keyboard.

"Anything to declare?" she asked.

Yes. I'm a total criminal right now. "Uh, nope."

The next flight to Durango had two stopovers, and only first-class seats available. I looked at the Post-it pages. Damned if I knew what monetary denominations they were supposed to be.

"Take it," Adrian said softly from behind me.

"Sold," I told the teller, pushing the pile toward her. If I didn't have enough pretend money in it, I'd get more from Adrian or play up the dumb blonde stereotype as an excuse for not being able to count.

After more brisk typing, the teller handed me the two blank stubs, most of the blank pages—my change, I supposed—and a ticket with the fake name I'd chosen for myself. Adrian bought his ticket, then we checked our bags and proceeded to our gate.

That's when my last shred of denial ripped away. Some tiny part of me must've still been clinging to the idea that everything I'd seen was a hallucination, just like countless doctors over the years had assured me. But after a TSA official ran our blank stubs through a computer that authenticated them as valid IDs, the truth was undisputable.

I wasn't experiencing a psychotic break with another equally crazy companion. The fact that even computer systems were fooled by Archon glamour proved that this was nothing short of a supernatural phenomenon. Archons—*angels*—were real. Demons were, too, and I was going to enter into their world to find a weapon so Adrian and I could kill them.

To say I was in way over my head was an understatement.

This time, I was the one who brooded in silence over the next couple days of layovers and long flights. When the plane finally touched down in Durango, I'd come to the same realization I had in Bennington over two weeks ago.

I had nothing left to lose. My whole family had been taken from me, and I didn't have someone special waiting back at college. Truth be told, there had never been anyone special. I used to blame my lack of romantic enthusiasm on the medication I took, but now that I knew the pills were placebos, I had to admit the problem was me. I even kept my roommate and my other friends at arm's length, so while they'd miss me if I never came back, it wouldn't leave a big hole in their lives. Sure, we had fun hanging out, but no matter how many parties we went to or how many nights we stayed up talking, part of me hadn't really been there. I think they must have sensed that because while I didn't lack for friends, I'd never been anybody's *best* friend. That took the kind of trust and honesty I'd only shared with Jasmine. With everyone else, I was too busy pretending not to catch glimpses of things only I could see, or worrying if I was living the college life the way everyone expected me to. Most days, I worked harder at faking "normal" than I did on my grades, friendships or the few-and fleeting relationships I'd had. So while I was scared shitless, the only person who'd really care if I didn't make it was Jasmine, and my doing this was her only hope of surviving.

It kinda sucked seeing how little my life mattered in the big scheme of things, but then again, that was also my biggest advantage. People with nothing to lose were dangerous, and since I was taking on demons, I needed to be as dangerous as I could.

As we disembarked, Adrian grasped my arm, the contact sending a familiar shiver through me. He was the only guy who'd made me feel everything I'd been missing all these years, and for reasons he refused to discuss, he wanted nothing to do with me. Figured.

"I know I deserved it, but are you done paying me back for all the times I've given you the silent treatment?" he asked.

I looked at him, taking in his height, muscular build and devastating good looks that were invisible to everyone but me. Then I spoke the first words I had in over a thousand miles.

"Yeah, I'm done, and more important, I'm ready."

We spent the night in a hotel in Ceballos, one of Durango's smaller towns. Adrian spoke fluent Spanish, which helped with checking in and getting dinner. Jet lag and my new resolve ensured that I slept well, and in the morning, I found out that we weren't driving to the entrance of the demon realm alone. Two guys approached us as soon as we entered the hotel parking lot, exchanging back-slapping man-hugs with Adrian.

"Ivy, this is my friend Tomas," Adrian said, indicating the tough-looking Hispanic man with a scar curving from his neck down to his upper arm.

"Hola," I said, wishing I'd taken more than two years of Spanish in high school. Tomas accepted my outstretched hand, shaking it firmly.

"Hola, senorita." Then his stoic features cracked, and he flashed a wide smile at Adrian. *"La rubia es caliente! Hora de que empieces a salir de nuevo, mi amigo."*

"It's not like that," Adrian said in English, though I'd translated enough to get the misassumption. "Ivy and I aren't dating. We're…friends."

I stiffened at his pause. No, we weren't besties, but did he have to make it obvious that I was an unwelcome acquaintance? Something reckless stirred in me. Adrian might not want me around, but he wanted some things from me. Plus, I might die before sundown and I wasn't sure I'd really lived during the past twenty years. Time to change that.

I gave Tomas a wide grin as I wrapped my arms around Adrian's midsection.

"Don't mind him, he's in denial over how crazy he is about me," I said glibly. "You should've seen him rubbing my ass the other night. It's like he was trying to polish it shiny."

Adrian gazed at me in disbelief. Tomas choked back a laugh, and the guy I hadn't been introduced to yet let out a low chuckle.

"Looks like you have more on your plate than just demons, Adrian," he drawled, his accent sounding Mediterranean.

Adrian's hands flexed on my back, as though he was having trouble deciding whether to push me away or mold me closer. His gaze had changed, too. Disbelief turned to something darker and infinitely more enticing in those silvery sapphire depths.

"You have no idea what you're toying with," he said, the growled words barely audible.

"What if I want to know?" I replied, and shivered as his grip on me began to tighten.

I'd started this as a game, but it felt very serious now. His stare burned into my eyes with more than the lust I'd called his bluff on. Secrets, promises and lies seemed to swirl together, drawing me in and warning me away at the same time. When he pulled me closer, those warnings collapsed under the explosion of sensation as he pressed against me, and when his hand coiled through my hair, pulling my head back with a strong, possessive grip, I didn't just shiver. I shuddered.

"Do you and your *friend* want to postpone our trip until tomorrow?" an amused voice asked.

Adrian released me as suddenly as if I'd become scalding. Maybe I had. My whole body felt feverish, and if my heart beat any faster, I might be in danger of a coronary.

"We're leaving now," he said in a strained voice. "Get in the black Jeep, Ivy. I'll be right there."

I would've argued if I didn't feel like I needed a moment to compose myself. I walked toward the black, open-topped Wrangler that had four machine guns in the back. No seats, though, and the front ones must be for Tomas and our as-yet-unnamed companion. Looked like Adrian and I would be standing.

Adrian. The thought of how close he'd come to kissing me made that feverishness sweep through me again. Why did he keep pulling away at the last minute? Was it the secret he thought was too terrible to reveal? He wasn't a demon or a minion, and he worked with an *angel,* so how bad could it be?

Adrian's arrival with the two men cut my musings short. He jumped into the back of the Wrangler, grasping the bar that the machine guns were strapped to.

"This is Costa," Adrian said, indicating the handsome young man with the wavy black hair and dark brown eyes. "Get in, Ivy."

I climbed into the back, accepting Adrian's hand up. He held mine a second too long, as if reluctant to let me go. I felt the same way, though I grasped the metal railing between the seats when Adrian did. Was it me, or did something *happen* when we touched? Something more than lust, although I had that bad, too. Could this be the supernatural bond Demetrius had spoken of? If so, he was right. It was getting stronger.

"Hi, Costa," I said, trying to refocus my attention. "You mentioned demons, so I take it you know what we'll be doing?"

Costa snorted. "Yes, though I wish you didn't have to. No one leaves the dark realms the same way they entered them."

Tomas gunned the Jeep, and bracing to stay upright made me almost miss the look on Adrian's face. From the way his features tightened, Costa wasn't referring to different exits. Adrian had told me the demon world was awful, as if I couldn't figure that out for myself. From his expression and Costa's words, maybe I hadn't prepared enough. I drew in a deep breath. *Think about Jasmine,* I reminded myself. If she could survive being trapped in one, I could survive searching however many I needed to in order to save her.

"I'm tougher than I look" was what I said.

Adrian's hand brushed my back, the brief caress wordlessly promising that I wasn't doing this alone. Then he nodded at Costa, supporting my statement. I held on to that as tightly as I did the metal bar that kept me from being vaulted out of the car from Tomas's crazy driving. Jasmine needed me, and Adrian believed in me. I wouldn't fail either of them.

I couldn't.

chapter twelve

The vortex we were headed to was located in a section of desert called *La Zona del Silencio,* or the Zone of Silence. I found out why they called it that after Tomas turned off the highway and started driving on the barren terrain. After a hundred yards, the radio station he'd been blasting abruptly went silent. Costa held out his cell, showing me the screen going blank as though the phone had powered down on its own.

"Technology doesn't work here," he stated. "Most people don't know why, but it's the vortex. It's one of the bigger ones on the planet, so it drains everything around it."

Our surroundings reminded me of where Demetrius had attacked us. Like that sliver of Oregon desert, the endless landscape of sand was interrupted here and there by cacti and other scrub. It had more mountains, though, sometimes narrowing the path Tomas drove through. Every so often, Adrian would call out directions. He seemed to know exactly where he was despite the lack of roads or signs. I tried to pay attention to our route in case I needed to come back in the future, but after half an hour, I gave up. "Turn left at the rock" wouldn't work because all the damn rocks looked the same, and once you've seen one cactus, you've seen them all.

Finally, after my muscles ached from hours of the Jeep's rough jostling, Adrian told Tomas to stop. Then he jumped out of the back, unloading his bulky duffel bag with him.

"We're here?" I looked around, squinting in the bright sunlight. "I don't see any older, rotted versions of what's around us." Plus, the only landmark for miles seemed to be an oblong piece of rock sticking out of the ground.

Adrian flashed me a challenging look. "You can sense hallowed ground. I can sense gateways to the dark worlds."

I jumped down, too. "How can you do that?"

His smile was dangerous and beautiful, like the caress of sunshine right before it became a burn. "A gift of my lineage, same as your abilities."

Wasn't that a not-so-subtle warning? If sensing demon realm gateways was one of his "gifts," he was letting me know that he wasn't the last descendant of Mother Teresa's line. Still, why should his family tree weigh so heavily on him? Our previous conversation replayed in my mind. *Did my ancestor do something terrible to your ancestor?...No, Ivy, it was the other way around...*

Did Adrian keep pushing me away because he felt guilty for what his ancestor had done? If so, could his big, awful secret actually not be about *him,* but about his long-dead relative?

"I don't know who my biological parents were," I said in an even tone. "Or who their parents were, and so on. I do know it has no bearing on who *I* am, beyond genetic leftovers like hair color, eye color, and apparently, an ability to sense hallowed objects and see through supernatural glamour. Same goes for you. Regardless of who your ancestor was, your decisions make you who *you* are, and aside from being a dick sometimes, you can also be pretty great. Maybe, if you dropped whatever your ancient relative's baggage is, you'd like who you were, too."

Adrian's expression was as hard as the grayish rock behind him, but Tomas gave me a thumbs-up, and Costa started to smile. Guess I wasn't the only person to think that Adrian's biggest issue might be Crap Family syndrome.

"I wish I believed you, Ivy," he said roughly. "But believing you is part of the fate that I can't allow to happen, for both our sakes."

Without waiting for me to respond, he opened the duffel bag and tossed a ski jacket, thermal pants and gloves at me.

"Put these on."

I gestured at the scorched landscape, as if he hadn't realized we were in the middle of a desert with high noon approaching. "Are you serious?"

"These, too," he said, adding a pair of fleece-lined boots to my pile.

I gave him a level look. "Either you're trying to kill me, or the realm we're about to enter is really cold."

"They're all cold," Tomas said, accompanied by a grim snort of agreement from Costa.

I was shocked. "You two have been in one?"

"We were trapped and Adrian pulled us out," Tomas said, only to be cut off by Adrian's, "Now's not the time."

I marched over to Adrian and jabbed my finger in his chest.

"You told me there was no way to get Jasmine back without this mysterious weapon, but you got *them* out of a demon realm?"

"Ivy," he began.

"Don't! You said the only thing I could trust about you was your hatred of demons. If you want me to find that demon-kill-

ing weapon, you're going to tell me *right now* why you could rescue Tomas and Costa, but you can't help me save my sister yet!"

I planted my feet, my glare promising that I wasn't moving
until I had an answer. Tomas and Costa looked uncomfortable, and Adrian looked angry enough to deck both of them,
but all he did was let out a sharp sigh.

"I wasn't lying when I said we needed the weapon to save
your sister. The only reason I was able to save them without
it was because I took them with me when I left."

My scoff was instant. "A bunch of demons just let you waltz
out of their realm with two of the humans they'd captured?"

"Yes," he said, his tone now flatter than a polished mirror. "I grew up in that realm, so they were used to me doing
whatever I wanted in it."

I don't know why the words hit me like a punch. Adrian
had told me that Demetrius took him when he was a child. I
guess I'd just assumed minions had raised him in this world,
and Demetrius had…checked in on him frequently.

"You were raised in a demon realm," I said, my anger
changing into something else. "And they trusted you, so you
must've, um—"

"Lived just like they did," he supplied, an icy bleakness filling his tone. "Still think I'm pretty great?"

I didn't know what to think. Part of me was appalled and the
other part was weeping. How old had Adrian been when Demetrius yanked him out of this world and raised him in a demon
one? If he'd been very young, would he even have known that
everything he saw—or did—was evil if it was all he'd ever seen
of "normal?" Maybe finding out was what had made him switch
sides and work with Zach. Maybe that was why he hated demons with such pathological single-mindedness now.

And maybe his twisted upbringing, combined with whatever his ancestor had done, made Adrian feel like fate had doomed him. In some ways, I couldn't blame him.

"I still think you are what your decisions make you to be," I said at last. "I also think if these guys made it out of a demon realm, then my sister can, too, so let's do this."

With that, I pulled the ski jacket over my tank top, slipped the thermal pants over my shorts, replaced my sandals with the knee-high fuzzy boots and put on the gloves. Finally, I released my long brown hair from its ponytail. If it was cold enough to warrant ski wear, my ears would need the covering.

All Adrian did was toss the now-empty duffel bag into the back of the Jeep.

"You're wearing that?" I said, gesturing to his long-sleeved T-shirt and regular jeans.

A diffident shrug. "I'm used to the cold."

I left that alone, forcing a smile as I glanced at Tomas and Costa. "See you guys soon, hopefully."

I didn't get a chance to hear their response. Adrian wrapped his arms around me, walked us rapidly toward the tall, oblong rock and then plunged us through it.

I've always loved roller-coaster rides. The wild exhilaration of being propelled through turns and loops so fast that your face felt heavy and your body molded to your seat was second only to the rush of relief when the ride was over. Being transported through a gateway into a demon realm was sorta like that, only with a lot more noise and nausea. It took a few moments to settle my heaving stomach once we were on the other side, and during that time, I was grateful for the icy air. Then I opened my eyes and realized I still saw…nothing.

"Adrian?" I said, panic setting in when rapid blinking didn't make the blackness disappear. "Something's wrong. I'm—"

"You're not blind," he said, his deep voice almost as comforting as his hand closing over mine. "Sunlight doesn't exist in demon realms. That's why they're so cold, too."

I'd never been in total darkness before. It wasn't just frightening and disorienting—it was dangerous. For all I knew, we were standing on the edge of a cliff. Even if everything around us was flat, I couldn't judge the length of my steps because I couldn't see the ground. When I tried to walk, I ended up staggering.

Adrian's arm went around me, clasping my left side to his right one.

"Close your eyes and concentrate on moving with me," he said, the confidence in his tone easing my fears. "Don't worry. I can see where we're going, and I'm not going to let anything happen to you."

We began to walk, first in hesitant steps while I learned to trust the feel of his body instead of my sight, and then at a normal pace. Surprisingly, it did help to keep my eyes closed. Since I wasn't trying to see, I focused on his smooth strides, the flexing muscles that preceded a change in his direction, and the reassuring way he instantly adjusted his hold to support me if I faltered.

It didn't take me long to be grateful for the parka, boots, gloves and pants, too. Even with them on, the cold seemed to seep into my bones, but just like the darkness, it didn't appear to bother Adrian. He didn't so much as shiver in his light clothing, and his hand felt warm in mine. How many years had it taken for him to adapt to this dark, frigid wasteland? Once more, my heart broke for the child he'd been. Even without demons, growing up in a place like this would have been awful.

After what felt like an hour, Adrian paused. I did, too, of course, sniffing at the new, fuel-like smell in the air.

"You can open your eyes," he said. "The town's up ahead."

At first all I saw was a black-and-gold spotted blur. After a few blinks, my eyes adjusted, and I made out a blaze of light in the distance, showing lots of smaller structures surrounding what looked like a wide, soaring building.

"Thank God," I breathed, so glad to be able to see that I didn't care if I was looking at a demon town.

"Don't say that. It's a real giveaway that we don't belong."

Adrian's face was hidden by darkness, yet his tone made me imagine that he said it with one of his wry smiles.

"Good point, but aren't we avoiding the town?" I asked, whispering in case someone was out in the blackness with us.

"Can't. What's known of the weapon's location is that it was hidden in a wall, and the only walls are in town."

"Is that all we know, or do the demons know exactly where it is?"

He snorted. "No. If they did, they would've used it for themselves a long time ago."

"Why didn't the demon that hid it do that?"

Adrian paused, seeming to choose his words, which meant I'd just be getting part of the truth again. "As it turns out, only a few people can activate the weapon's true power. Minions can't, and neither can the average demon. Zach said that the demon who hid it was on his way to tell a more powerful demon about it when Zach killed him."

"Wait. You said demons could only be killed with the weapon *Zach didn't have*," I emphasized.

A shrug I felt but couldn't see. "Archons don't need it to kill demons, and other demons don't need it to kill their own. The rest of us do, which includes you and me."

Figures. "Couldn't Zach have gotten its location before he silenced its hider forever?"

Another pause, longer this time. My temper flared. "Could you for once just answer me with the *whole* truth?"

"Fine." His tone thickened. "For all I know, Zach did find out where the weapon was. Even if he didn't, his boss knows, yet here we are. Know why? Because neither of them really cares if we live or die trying to find it."

His brutal analysis stunned me. "But that's...they're...they're on the *good* side," I sputtered.

His laughter was like glass grinding together. *"They* win or lose this war, Ivy. Not us. We can only depend on each other, because to Archons and demons, we're just pawns that they move around for their own purposes."

"But Zach's your friend," I argued softly.

"You don't understand Archons. They're not fluffy beings sprinkling supernatural happy dust everywhere they go. They're soldiers who've been relegated to the sidelines until the pesky issue of humanity has been settled. Frankly, I think Zach's reached the point where he doesn't care what happens to our race, as long as he finally gets to fight."

What Adrian described couldn't be true. Good couldn't give a complicit shrug to evil, and the faith of billions of people from every race, background and creed couldn't be worthless to whoever the Archons' "boss" was.

"You're wrong," I said, still softly but with an undercurrent of iron. "We *do* matter to them. It just might not look that way sometimes, from our side of the fence."

The harshness was gone from Adrian's laughter, replaced by a despairing sort of anger.

"That's why I still hide things from you, Ivy. If you can't accept the way the board's set up, you're not nearly ready to learn the endgame yet."

"Maybe you're the one who's not ready," I replied, my sense of resolve increasing. "I get why. You've had it bad for so long, all you see is darkness even when the lights are on."

"Bad?" His voice changed, becoming a whisper that seared me even in the frigid temperature. "You don't know the meaning of the word, but you're about to find out."

chapter thirteen

I had braced myself, but no amount of mental preparation
would've been enough. At least, when I finally did throw
up, it matched the reaction any human would have at seeing how demons lived inside their own world.

At first, the town reminded me of a medieval fiefdom, with
the overlord's manor overlooking the serfs' much cruder lodg-
ings. In this case, wigwam structures were laid out in tight
clusters along the lowest part of the hill. Smoke billowed from
their open tops, reminiscent of pictures I'd seen of sixteenth-
century Native American life. Very few people seemed to be
in the wigwam village, and the ones we passed looked away
when they saw Adrian. They were also skinny to the point
of appearing wasted, and their clothes consisted of shapeless
leather tunics that couldn't have been nearly warm enough in
these frigid temperatures.

"This area is for laborers, the lowest level of human slaves,"
Adrian said tersely. "Next are overseers' and merchants' quarters."

Those must have been the plain but sturdy huts that dotted the hill about a hundred yards higher than the wigwam village. Torches were interspersed among the narrow paths between them, and their interiors glowed from what I guessed were fire hearths. They looked like ancient Southwestern pueblo houses, with the addition of leather flaps covering the doorways and windows to keep the heat in. Once more, no one attempted to stop us as we walked through. In fact, anyone we passed seemed to avoid eye contact with Adrian, and he strode by as though he owned the place. I practically had to run to keep up, and since the hill was steep, it was quite a workout.

After we ascended about three hundred yards, we reached gray stone gates that surrounded what was clearly the town's epicenter. Torches lined the exterior of the gates, but I smelled fuel and heard the unmistakable hum of generators, which explained how this area appeared to have electricity. The added lighting made it easier to see, and once I did, I stared.

This wasn't a mini city located at the top of a hill. The city *was* the hill. The closest thing I could compare it to was a gargantuan pyramid. The base had to be a mile long, with courtyards I couldn't fully see from my lower vantage point. Massive balconies with elaborately carved stone columns showed people milling around inside the pyramid, and one entire side of it seemed to house a huge stadium.

Further up, the corners had huge faces carved into them. One was a lion and one was an eagle, with the predators' mouths open as though about to devour their prey. The very top of the pyramid blazed with so much light that it looked like a star had landed there. I couldn't make out much detail, though. It had to be as high up as the sphere on the Empire State building.

I was so awed that I didn't realize someone had come up to us until I heard Adrian speaking in that poetically guttural language. My gaze snapped to his left, where a dark-haired, muscled man now stood. It wasn't the metal breastplate over his brown camouflage clothes that caught my attention, although *that* fashion mistake should never be repeated. It was the man's face. Light rolled over his eyes like the passing of clouds, and inky black wings rose and fell beneath his cheekbones, as if he had a tattoo that could magically appear and disappear.

My staring seemed to annoy him, so I looked away. He said something sharply to Adrian and then grabbed my wrist hard enough to bruise me. Adrian moved with that lightning quickness, putting Camo Guy in a headlock with his arm bent at the wrong angle before I could even say, "Let go."

"I told you, she goes straight to Mayhemium," Adrian said, speaking English this time. "And if you delay me again, I'll rip your head off."

I didn't know if it was Adrian's dangerous tone or how quickly he'd broken Camo Guy's arm, but he grunted something that must've been an agreement. Adrian let him go, smiled as though they'd exchanged a friendly hello, and then half dragged me through one of the openings in the wall.

Lots of stone steps later, we reached the pyramid's lower courtyards. At first glance, it looked like an average street market. Vendors hawked various wares inside their booths, food cooked on open grills, and people milled around, either buying or window shopping. But every other person had that strange roll of light over their eyes, and when I got a closer look at some of the vendors' wares, my legs abruptly stopped working.

"Keep moving," Adrian whispered, half lifting me so it wasn't obvious that shock had frozen me where I stood.

I forced my suddenly numb limbs to keep working. It helped that Adrian took us quickly through the market section and into a side alcove that had a drain in the floor. Even though his large frame blocked most of my view of the courtyard, I still couldn't stop the grisly images from replaying in my mind.

Along with a few slabs of cow and pig, food vendors also sold human body parts. For customers who wanted fresher meat, their human selections were slaughtered on the spot.

"Why?" I choked, unable to say more because words couldn't make it past the bile in my throat.

"There's no sunlight here." Although Adrian's tone was matter-of-fact, something haunted flashed across his expression. "That means no grass, grains, vegetation or animals. Minions and pampered human pets get to have regular food imported from the other side, but the slaves have only one thing to eat. Each other."

That bile turned into vomit that I couldn't hold back. At the same time, I was shaking with rage. Now I knew what all the leather garments and doorway flaps were probably made of, too.

Adrian didn't mock me for puking, or tell me to pull myself together. He held back my hair, his other hand moving over my shoulders in a comforting caress.

"We can leave," he said low. "The realm's not going anywhere. We'll come back another day to search it."

Laughter drifted down from one of the pyramid's balconies, its sound an abomination. No one should laugh here. No sound should be made except screams of horror at what was going on in this lightless pit of evil. I wanted to run back to my world as fast as I could and never, ever return, but if I did, I'd be condemning Jasmine to spending the rest of her life in a similar hellhole. I'd rather die than do that.

Resolve mixed with my rage, helping me get control of my stomach. I wiped my mouth with a gloved hand and gave Adrian a look that reflected the new hardness creeping through my soul.

"Take me deeper inside this place. I'm not leaving until I check every frigging wall for that weapon."

I learned more about demon life than I ever wanted to know as Adrian guided me through the pyramid's many levels. First, generators supplied heat as well as light to the massive structure, so my extra clothes were now slung over my arm. Second, the inside looked like someone had taken the Great Pyramid of Giza and pimped it out with modern—albeit barbaric—amenities.

The large stadium section was for gladiator-style fights to the death, a popular form of entertainment here. "Pets," which was how Adrian referred to humans who'd caught the eye of demons, lived above the courtyards. Minions lived above them in condo-styled units, and of course, the best, most luxurious quarters were reserved for the supernaturally sadistic rulers of this realm. Adrian said we'd be avoiding those places unless I sensed something, but so far, I hadn't picked up a hint of anything hallowed in this opulent, stone-and-brick nightmare.

I also found out how Adrian was able to escort me around without arousing suspicion. For one, he spoke the language, and every light-show-eyed guard who stopped us only used that to communicate. For another, Adrian's cover story was that I was a newly arrived "pet" for Mayhemium. From the knowing looks that garnered, whoever Mayhemium was, he had a lot of "pets."

I'd figured out Adrian's final trick after noticing how quickly every human looked away from him when we passed. The only other people they treated that way were guards, and since they didn't all dress alike, that left only one other thing.

"Zach glamoured your eyes to shine like the guards' eyes,

didn't he?" I whispered once we had a moment alone in one of the pyramid's many stairways.

The barest smile cocked his mouth. "That's right."

"Why do theirs do that?" Also whispered, but wheezier. I must've climbed two miles in steps by now.

"Part of the perks of being a minion. Along with increased strength and endurance, demon marks give them the supernatural version of *tapetum lucidum*." At my raised brow, he added, "The extra layer of tissue in animals' eyes that allows them to see in the dark."

That explained the odd shine, but... "You don't have that, and you see as well as they do." *And move faster,* I mentally added.

I couldn't read the look he threw me. "I've already told you why."

Right, his mysterious lineage. He might've told me some of the whys, but he hadn't spilled the "what" yet. The more secrets he revealed, the more I burned to know his biggest one.

"That's the gift that keeps on giving, then," I said, trying not to sound like I was probing, which I was.

His jaw tightened until I swore I heard cartilage crack. "I'd give anything not to have this lineage." Sapphire eyes seemed to burn as they swept over me. "Especially after meeting you."

If we weren't inside a demonic version of the Luxor hotel, I would've demanded that he elaborate. He'd already told me more since we'd arrived than he had in the week leading up to it, but "bad timing" didn't begin to cover our current situation.

Of course, that meant it was about to get worse.

The hairs on the back of my neck rose before I saw her. Apparently, my "hallowed" sensor could also pick up on the presence of pure darkness, because with one glance, I knew the woman coming down the staircase was a demon.

It's not that she had "Evil!" stamped on her forehead, or obvious supernatural indicators like Demetrius's shifting shadows. Maybe it was the way she moved, as if every muscle instantly coordinated with the others, turning her walk into a graceful, predatory glide. Maybe it was her hair, each wavy lock either midnight black or a burnished copper shade. Her pale skin was also telling, but it was her face that sealed my suspicions.

No one could be that incredibly, perfectly beautiful unless they'd had a million dollars in plastic surgery or had made a deal with the devil, and my money was on Option B.

Even Adrian couldn't tear his eyes away, which hurt in ways I didn't even want to acknowledge. Yes, she was gorgeous, but did he need to stop walking and stare like he'd been transfixed? He hadn't been affected enough to pause in his stride when they were slaughtering people in the courtyards!

I either made a sound, or my instant hostility caught her attention because dark topaz eyes slid over me as she passed. Just like with Demetrius, I fought the urge to wipe my clothes, as if her gaze had left a tangible trail where it landed. She said something in what I now referred to as Demonish and Adrian responded, his voice much raspier than normal.

He couldn't even talk right around Her Evil Hotiness? I quietly seethed, but when she disappeared down the stairwell, Adrian let out a sigh that almost blew the lid off my temper.

He was actually *sighing* after her. Guess when he said he hated demons, he meant only the males or the ugly ones.

"How much more ground do we have to cover?" I whispered acidly, hating him and hating myself more for caring.

His attention snapped back to me. "You still don't sense anything?"

Only your hard-on for evil incarnate. "Nothing."

"Then we're done. You sensed the burial ground at half the distance from what we've covered, so it must not be here."

Good, we could leave. Not soon enough for my tastes, either. This realm wasn't where the weapon had been hidden, I'd already have nightmares from the horrors I'd seen, and now I wanted to punch my only ally in the face. Lose-lose all around.

We made it out of the pyramid without incident, and I looked down as we exited through the courtyards. No one stopped us at the stone gates, and we navigated the pueblo-like village with nary a word spoken in acknowledgement. Once we'd cleared the edge of the wigwam village, however, our luck ran out.

"Hondalte," a commanding voice ordered.

Adrian paused. I did, too, schooling my features into a blank mask despite the hairs standing up on the back of my neck. When I turned around, I saw that my demon radar hadn't been malfunctioning. The lanky, blond-haired man approaching us had two tall, dark arcs rising out of his back.

Not arcs, I realized when he drew nearer. Pitch-black wings. Then he spoke, causing my stomach to flip-flop in fear.

"If she is a new pet for me," the winged stranger said in English, "tell me, why are you leaving with her?"

chapter fourteen

"My lord Mayhemium," Adrian said, bowing formally. "I have discovered that this one is too flawed for you."

The blond demon came closer. I tried not to stare, but he had *wings*. Were they real or a type of illusion, like Demetrius's ability to transform into shadows and other people?

"What is so flawed about her?" Mayhemium asked, and my skin felt like it was trying to crawl away as his gaze slid over me.

"I have crabs," I blurted out, saying the first gross thing that came to mind.

The single glare Adrian shot my way said that I wasn't helping. "She's mentally defective," he replied, his tone implying that it should be obvious. "I'm taking her to Ryse's realm. He doesn't mind less-than-superior pets."

Mayhemium's gaze swept me again. From his expression, Zach had glamoured me into looking as gorgeous as Adrian's disguise was plain. Then the demon waved an imperious hand.

"I'll take her anyway."

Adrian let go of my arm and stepped away. I tried to conceal my shock, but I wasn't that good of an actress. Yes, we were deep in enemy territory and outnumbered by a thousand to one, but was he really going to let Mayhemium take me?

The demon thought so. My breath sucked in at the gleam that appeared in those inhuman eyes. Now I knew what death looked like when you stared it in the face. Then Adrian straightened, abandoning his subservient posture.

"I never liked you, Mayhemium," he said in a tone so flat, he sounded bored. "At least you're so arrogant, you came alone."

Before the last word left him, he hit the demon, moving so fast all I saw was his usual blur. Mayhemium stared at him, something inky leaking out from the side of his mouth.

"Adrian?" he asked in disbelief.

"Ivy, leave," Adrian ordered, urgency now replacing the flatness in his tone.

Mayhemium's head whipped around, and he stared at me with understanding that turned into unbridled savageness. "The last Davidian," he hissed.

Adrian punched him so hard, I expected a dent to appear in the demon's face. It didn't, but more incredibly, Mayhemium shattered, his body transforming into dozens of large crows that flew straight up before diving in a furious arc toward me.

My arms rose to shield myself, but Adrian was suddenly blocking them, his large body absorbing the stabs from beaks sharpened into knifelike points. With lightning-strike quickness, Adrian snatched the largest crow out of the air and then crushed it in his fist. Mayhemium materialized at once, howling in apparent agony, his long black wings now broken.

"Think I didn't remember how to neutralize your trick?" Adrian's purr dripped viciousness as he punched the demon hard enough to knock him over again. "What's wrong? Can't fight without your wings?"

Mayhemium snarled something in Demonish that turned Adrian's face into a mask of rage.

"No," he spat. "I'll never do it."

"You will," Mayhemium roared. "It's your destiny!"

"Not today." With that, Adrian landed a kick that snapped the demon's leg when he got up again. When Mayhemium bent low and staggered, Adrian smashed a knee into his face, crunching bones with an audible sound. Then Adrian's fist drove through the demon's neck, briefly disappearing up to his wrist before he yanked it and a handful of something pulpy out.

Yesterday, the sight would've made me gag, but after touring the pyramid, all I wanted to do was cheer, especially when Mayhemium fell and didn't get back up.

Adrian strode over, yanking my arm with a hand now coated in what looked like motor oil.

"What part of 'leave' did you not understand?" he snapped.

"The part where I left you alone with a pissed off demon," I replied, feeling dazed. "Is he dead?"

"Of course not." Adrian propelled me into the darkness, running so fast I had trouble keeping up. "For the tenth time, humans can only kill demons with the weapon we don't have yet."

"You're not human," I panted, my strides no match for his.

"I'm as human as you are," he said, shocking me. "And you need to run faster. He'll wake up soon and send every minion in this realm after us."

"I can't...run faster." I could barely talk, I was huffing and puffing so much from our frantic pace.

"Yes, you can." He hauled me closer, his body a guide in the stygian darkness. "We're the last of the two most powerful

lines in history, and our ancestors passed down all their supernatural abilities to us. If you try, you can do everything I can
do, except sense demon gateways. It's in your blood, so *use* it."

The source of his incredible abilities was also in *my* blood?
Impossible. I wasn't superwoman; I was the girl who'd hated
gym class because of all the times I'd gotten picked last for
teams.

"I'm running as fast…as I can," I gasped out.

He only yanked harder on my arm. "Not yet, and you need
to. I can protect you from a few demons, but not all of them.
Do you know what will happen if they catch you? Death
will be the best part. Before that, they'll hurt you worse than
they've hurt anyone else. Rape won't be enough. Torture
won't be enough—"

"Stop!"

"—and they'll make you watch as they do the same to your
sister," he continued ruthlessly. "You'll die knowing that everything she suffered was your fault, so *run,* Ivy!"

Something snapped in me. I'd already failed Jasmine by
leaving her in that B and B when I should have stayed until
I found a way to get her. The last time I'd seen my sister, I'd
been running away, and she had no way to know that I was
coming back for her—

"That's it," Adrian yelled, his grip on me loosening. "Faster,
Ivy, you can do it!"

I didn't feel any change in my body. My legs didn't work
harder, my lungs didn't suck in more air, but I was somehow
ahead of Adrian, running flat out into the impenetrable darkness. Once again, I flashed to that day at the B and B. Mrs.
Paulson had attacked me, and I'd made it into my Cherokee
without knowing how. Right now, I did. I must've run just
like this, with a speed no human should have, but I somehow did.

Was Adrian right? Had ancient legacies and inherited abilities been simmering in me this whole time?

He drew even with me, his hand a brand on my chilled flesh, guiding me in directions I couldn't see. At some point, I'd dropped the ski gear, but I was glad I didn't have it. All that padding would've hindered me, and the cold spurred me on. In my mind, it was now tied to this place, so I hated it. I ached to be back in the sunshine where it was warm and demon-free, and all I had to do to accomplish that was to run faster.

So I did, my legs pumping with the same velocity as Adrian's. When he grabbed me and I felt the body-bending force of hurtling through one realm into another, then found myself face-down with a mouthful of hot sand, I smiled.

We were back in the Zone of Silence.

Adrian didn't give me time to celebrate by kissing the ground, which I wanted to do. He also didn't pull me back through the gateway so we could search another demon realm through the vortex's version of a revolving door. Not with Costa and Tomas waiting here like sitting ducks. Instead, Adrian hauled me up into the Jeep, barking something to Tomas in Spanish that had the brawny Mexican and the handsome Greek scrambling for their machine guns.

"*Vamonos!*" Tomas shouted, starting the Jeep.

Adrian practically flung me into the back, jumping in after me and grabbing the third gun. To my surprise, he shoved it into my hands, barking out quick instructions.

"Hold it tight. It'll still fire if you drop it, then you'll blow your own head off. Stay down, but if anyone gets too close, shoot them until you see ash."

He grabbed the last gun, hooking his other arm through the railing behind the seats. I did, too, after Tomas's rapid acceleration almost pitched me out the back. I'd just gotten a good grip on both the automatic weapon and the metal bar when a stream of people hurtled out of the oblong rock behind us.

"Incoming!" Adrian yelled, and started firing. Costa did, too. The noise was like explosions going off in my ears, but when the minions began running after us as if they had rockets strapped to their asses, I didn't care if I'd go deaf.

They moved like Adrian did, and they were armed, too.

Adrian shoved me down at the first hail of bullets. The back of the Jeep shuddered, but the rounds didn't penetrate. Now that I was eye level with it, I saw how thick the back door was, and that extra metal plating couldn't have come standard.

"Didn't I tell you to stay down?" I heard Adrian snap, then another barrage of gunfire stole his voice. The Jeep bounced madly from Tomas's speed, but Adrian and Costa held on to the rails as they fired and ducked in a frenetic display of violence and defense.

"You gave me a gun, let me help!" I protested.

"No," Tomas yelled, whipping the Jeep around so fast that I hit my head on its side panel. "Stay down! You're who they most want to kill!"

Me? Then I remembered Mayhemium's look of loathing, and what he'd hissed right before Adrian hit him. *The last Davidian.* Did the demons want me dead because I was the only one who could locate a weapon that could kill them?

It didn't take long to get my answer. Despite the hail of gunfire Adrian, Costa and even Tomas leveled at the minions, they kept trying to get to where I crouched. My little corner became dented from all the bullets fired at it, and every so often, minions would hurtle themselves into the Jeep kamikaze-style. Adrian threw them out with his incredible speed, but I was soon covered in blood, bruises and cuts. And they kept on coming, until I was convinced that the whole realm had emptied in their attempt to kill us.

Or kill me, specifically.

When Tomas had to slow down to get through the tight passage between the mountains, five minions managed to jump onto the Jeep. Adrian got clobbered by three of them, and Tomas and Costa sounded like they were in their own life-and-death struggles. Their bulky machine guns were a hindrance in a close-contact fight, but I still had mine. I got up, raising it with grim determination.

Out of nowhere, another minion grabbed the barrel and used it to yank the gun from my hands, delivering a brutal kick to my midsection at the same time. I fell back into the corner, and for a split second, our eyes met. His were cerulean blue, and he grinned as he raised his own gun. Unarmed and wedged between the door and the seat, there was nothing I could do to save myself.

A knife suddenly slammed into the top of his head, twisting with vicious force. My would-be killer abruptly went cross-eyed and dropped his gun. I snatched it up, clutching it but not firing. Adrian was now right in front of me, and I didn't want to hit him, plus my would-be killer looked really, really dead.

Adrian yanked his knife out and the minion began to fall. As he did, his body transformed, turning dark as pitch and then dissipating altogether. What landed on the blood-spattered floor wasn't a man. It was a pile of ashes that coated me when the Jeep bounced from Tomas's wild acceleration as we finally cleared the mountain pass.

Adrian knelt, one hand roughly cupping my face while the other searched me for injuries.

"Thank God you're okay," he breathed.

For some reason, hearing Adrian thank a deity he mostly seemed to despise shocked me as much as seeing my would-be killer disintegrate before my eyes. I stared at Adrian, the ashes covering me and then the horizon. No more leaping, murderous minions appeared, and since Costa and Tomas had stopped firing, I assumed we were finally in the clear.

But with the sun hanging lower into the sky, we wouldn't be clear for long. Night was coming, and with it, demons.

chapter fifteen

We didn't go back to our hotel in Ceballos. Tomas drove straight to an empty, ancient-looking monastery, and we passed through the gates right as the last rays of sunlight disappeared. I staggered into the abandoned sanctuary with relief so intense, it felt like a cheap high. Who knew that entering a church would be my new favorite thing?

"Hide the Jeep," Adrian ordered. "How're we on ammo?"

"Nearly out," Tomas said, running a red-splattered hand through his hair. "I'll make a call, try to get more."

"Costa." Adrian threw the bag of manna at him. "Here."

The curly-haired man winced as he reached up and caught it. "Thanks. Bastards got me."

When Costa lifted his shirt and I saw two oozing holes in his abdomen, I ran over to him. "You've been shot!"

Mentally defective is right, I immediately chided myself. Talk about stating the obvious.

"Let me help you," I added, tucking my shoulder under

Costa's arm so he could use me as a crutch. Adrian shook his head, muttering something unintelligible as he left the gutted sanctuary. I led Costa to an alcove, seating him on the groove.

"You know what you're doing with that?" Costa asked, sounding pained yet amused.

"Scoop 'n slap, right?" I replied, digging my fingers into the mushy substance. Out of everyone, my hands were the cleanest, but I still left bloody smudges in the bag.

Costa grunted. "That's it." Then he visibly braced as I held my manna-smeared hand over the first entry wound. "Do it."

I pressed it against the bullet hole, wincing in empathy as his whole body jerked. After a few minutes, his harsh breathing eased, so I pulled my hand away.

No more blood oozed from the hole, which was growing smaller before my eyes. After another minute, it disappeared entirely, leaving a smooth, shiny patch of skin in its place.

"One to go," I said, reaching for more manna.

"Did your hands get shot, too, Costa?"

The question startled me. I hadn't noticed Adrian return, but there he was, standing where the doors would have been, if the sanctuary entrance still had them.

Costa lifted one shoulder in a shrug. "Only a fool turns down attention from a pretty girl."

Adrian's expression hardened even more than his current scowl, which made no sense. First, having your bullet wounds treated could hardly be counted as flirting, and second, why would he care even if Costa *was* flirting?

"I'm trying to help," I said, placing manna over the second bullet hole, which effectively silenced Costa. "I didn't prove too useful with a gun, but this, at least, I can do."

Adrian's stare went from my face to my hand on Costa's abdomen and back again. "Oh, I'm sure he appreciates it."

After those quietly growled words, he disappeared. Costa's

brow rose. I lifted my free hand in a "don't ask me" gesture. Maybe his rudeness was just another side effect of having been raised by demons.

"I don't think he likes you touching me," Costa said, his mouth curling. "Adrian, acting jealous. That's a first."

"He's not jealous," I muttered, wiping my hands on my shorts after I confirmed that his wound had healed. "He keeps reminding me that he can't wait to get away from me."

"That's not about you." Something dark flitted across Costa's expression. "That's about him."

Tomas returned, stopping me from probing more. "Jeep's hidden," he announced, "and more guns are on the way."

Relief swept through me. Who knew that guns would be my *second* favorite thing after hallowed ground?

"What're the odds the demons won't find us until we get those guns?" I asked, hoping for a high percentage.

"Fifty-fifty," Tomas replied, dashing that. "They know you can't have gotten too far by sundown, so they'll have minions search every hallowed site within a hundred miles."

"Right, they want me dead because I'm the only person who can find a demon-killing weapon," I said wearily.

"That's not—" Tomas began, then shut his mouth at the warning look Costa gave him.

"Not what?" I asked, suspicion replacing my fatigue.

"If Adrian hasn't told you, he must have a reason," Costa said, landing himself right after Demetrius on my shit list.

"Yeah, because he's pathologically secretive," I snapped. "I'm getting sick of being the only person who doesn't know what's going on, so one of you had better talk."

Tomas exchanged another look with Costa, then he leaned back against the wall.

"You know what it was like for us in the realms?" he asked

in a conversational tone. "We were beaten, forced into canni-
balism, worked almost to death…and that was on a good day."

Sympathy tempered my anger. "I am so sorry," I said, meaning every word.

Tomas's dark brown stare held mine. "Don't be. We survived. Know how Adrian was treated before he started fighting demons? Like a prince." He paused, letting that sink in.
"Anything he wanted, he got. He didn't even have to ask.
They practically worshipped him, and when demons want
to shower someone with adulation, *crèeme,* they make it rain.
Beautiful women, more gold than Fort Knox, power to rule
any realm he entered—"

"Why?" I whispered, stunned.

"Because of his lineage, they believe he's going to do something that will make demons unbeatable in their war against
Archons."

It's your destiny! Mayhemium had roared at Adrian. Demetrius had said something similar when he caught up with us.
Even Zach had told Adrian he couldn't escape his fate, but
Zach was an *Archon,* so he couldn't believe Adrian was destined to help demons win the war against them. If he did,
why wouldn't Zach kill Adrian as a preemptive strike? The
demons sure wanted to kill me, and all I could do was find
one ancient weapon.…

I sucked in a breath, realization shattering me. "It's the
weapon, isn't it? Adrian said if the demons knew where it was,
they'd have already used it for their own purposes. I didn't
think it through at the time, but that means it must do a lot
more than just kill demons."

Tomas's mouth thinned into a straight line. Costa got up,
dropping a hand briefly on his friend's shoulder.

"You've heard of David and Goliath?" Costa asked evenly.
"Thousands of years ago, a shepherd boy killed a giant with

nothing more than a slingshot and blind faith, thus David's fame was born. You are the last Davidian, so in your hands, that ancient slingshot has the one-time power to overcome any and all odds. In short, whatever you point it at, it will defeat."

That sounded too good to be true, so there had to be more. "What can the demons do with it?"

Costa's smile was grim. "Goliath was no ordinary giant. He descended from demons, and some of his originating blood-line lives on. If one of *those* demons gets the slingshot, they get a one-time ability to overcome unbeatable odds, too. So with it, demons think they can win the war against Archons in a day."

My head was starting to pound, probably from trying to process information that was too incredible—and horrible—to believe. If I hadn't crossed through to a different realm today or seen multiple examples of supernatural phenomena all my life, I would have called Tomas and Costa crazy.

Unfortunately, I knew they weren't.

"Is Adrian descended from Goliath's line?" was what I asked. "Is that why the demons think he's their savior? Because if he gets the weapon, he can use it against Archons?"

Tomas and Costa exchanged another look, then Tomas let out a deep sigh.

"No, Ivy. Adrian's the last of another line."

"Whose?" I asked in a steely voice, my glare daring them not to tell me.

"Get out, both of you."

Adrian's voice cut through the silence. Like before, he'd come in without anyone noticing. Tomas and Costa rose at once, leaving without another word. When I saw the expression on Adrian's face, part of me wanted to follow them, but the rest wanted the truth so much, I didn't care about the consequences.

"Whose line are you the last of?" I said, refusing to back down. "Tell me now, or I leave that weapon lost, and after what I just heard, 'lost' is probably where it should stay."

He smiled, the seductive curve of his lips not taking away from the lethal hardness in his jeweled gaze. His jaw was shadowed from not having shaved recently, and that hint of darkness only made his high cheekbones look more pronounced, giving an edge to his already unforgettable features. Even in his bloody, torn clothes, I'd never seen him look more gorgeous, and for the first time, I was also afraid of him.

"Haven't you guessed?" he asked, his voice caressing the words like silk draping across daggers. "Who in history committed such a heinous act that it made his name forever synonymous with betrayal?"

"I don't know," I said, backing up as he came toward me with slow, stalking steps.

"Yes, you do."

A rough, throaty whisper, and then he was in front of me, his arms a cage that blocked me in while the wall behind me made retreat impossible. Despite my fear, I shivered as he leaned down, his mouth only inches from mine and his hands sliding to rest on my shoulders. The last time we'd been this close, he'd almost kissed me, and God help me, I still wanted him to. My feelings for him defied logic, sanity or safety, and judging from the intensity in his gaze as he wound one hand through my hair, it was possible he felt the same way.

Then his mouth lowered, but not to my lips, though they parted in reckless anticipation. Instead, he kissed my cheek, whispering his darkest secret at the same time.

"I'm the last descendant of Judas, and like my infamous forefather, my fate has been, and always will be, to betray the children of David."

chapter sixteen

I felt like I couldn't breathe. His mouth was still pressed to my skin, caramel-colored hair like rough silk against my forehead, breaths teasing my ear with soft heat. Add that to his revelation, and the wall was the only thing holding me up.

"Adrian," I began.

"Don't." His hand tightened in my hair. "Everything that's happened since we met only proves how entangled in our fates we already are. Judians and Davidians have always been drawn to one another, but then Judians betray and destroy Davidians. Thousands of years and countless betrayals later, we're the only ones left."

His hand stroked from my shoulder to my face, moving over it in a caress that made my skin burn.

"Maybe being the last of our lines made what we feel for each other so much stronger. I'm not just drawn to you, Ivy. I've wanted you since the first time you touched me. It was as if you reached inside and claimed something that had always been yours." He drew back to stare at me as if he was trying to memorize my features. "That's why I thought you had to be a minion. Nothing but dark magic had ever felt so powerful, and when I touch you, it's a thousand times worse. You're the light I can never have…and I'm the darkness you'll never succumb to."

His hand dropped, leaving my skin feeling cold. "That's why it would never work between us, so now you understand why I need to get away from you, Ivy. Before I betray you like everyone else in my line has betrayed Davidians. I refuse that part of my fate, and it's not just to spite Demetrius anymore. It's because I can't stand the thought of hurting you."

Before my next breath, he was standing in the sanctuary entrance, the night surrounding him like a cloak.

"So do what your ancestors weren't able to," he rasped. "Save yourself by never believing you can save me."

Then he was gone, leaving me with questions I had no answers to and emotions I couldn't seem to control.

Tomas sat in the sanctuary with me, his cell phone screen providing a small circle of light. Adrian and Costa were on the roof, watching out for any unwelcome visitors. Even if Adrian wasn't the only one who could see in the dark, he still wouldn't have stayed down here. His decision to avoid me didn't take into consideration my wishes on the subject.

For now, I'd let him get away with that. My emotions got in the way when Adrian was near, so this gave me a chance to separate fact from feeling. Unfortunately, that hadn't helped.

Fact: Adrian had lived like a demon for many years. Feeling: with how he'd been brought up, he wouldn't have known it was wrong. Fact: he felt doomed to repeat the mistakes of his ancestors. Feeling: to hell with them, everyone was responsible for their own choices. Fact: I didn't want to be betrayed. Feeling: Adrian wouldn't do it. Fact: I shouldn't fall for a borderline psychopath with demonic daddy issues. Feeling: something special was brewing between me and Adrian, and it had nothing to do with Adrian being the last Judian or me being the last Davidian.

The sound of a car interrupted my thoughts. I ran over to the window, but Tomas said, "Don't worry, it's my friends."

"How do you know?" I couldn't see anything except headlights.

"Because they just texted me, 'Don't shoot, we're here.'"

Okay, then. Tomas went to tell Adrian and Costa, and I stayed in the sanctuary, watching through windows that hadn't seen a pane of glass in decades. A worn Chevy pulled into the monastery, two people in front and one in the back. They got out, speaking Spanish so rapidly I only caught the names Tucco, Danny and Jorge. They'd brought a bunch of weapons, though, and that made them a welcome sight.

Adrian was in the middle of checking the scope on a rifle when he paused, staring into the distance. "Are there more of you coming, Tucco?"

"No, *por qué?*" the shorter man replied.

Adrian cocked the rifle. "Take positions on top of the church," he said curtly. "We've got company."

I didn't see anything, but I believed him. So did the others. They scrambled to unload the rest of the guns, then at Adrian's command, parked the truck in front of the sanctuary. Now the vehicle blocked the largest entrance to where I was, although the windows were big enough for someone to get through.

Adrian proved that when he vaulted through one, angling his big body sideways to fit.

"Here," he said, pressing a small caliber gun into my hand. "This'll be easier for you to use. It's cocked and ready. All you have to do is pull the trigger."

"And not get it yanked away," I said grimly.

Adrian flashed me a smile. "Second time's the charm."

I hoped so. "Adrian, before you go—"

"No matter what happens, stay here," he said, cutting me off. "They can't cross hallowed ground. The gun's for emergencies, but Tomas'll be with you. Stay down so the minions don't see you. We'll be on the roof, keeping them from getting too close."

"No," I protested, but he was already gone. Tomas jumped through the window Adrian had just vacated, his dark gaze flicking to me as he accepted a bundle of automatic weapons from Costa.

"You want to help, *sí?*" At my vigorous nod, Tomas gestured to the weapons. "I'll show you how to change the magazines. When I run out, you replace them."

In the short time it took me to learn, three cars began bouncing across the desert terrain toward the monastery, their headlights the only illumination for miles.

"Any chance they're lost tourists?" I asked with a fake chuckle.

Tomas shrugged. "Could be members of a local drug cartel."

"Oh, let's hope."

When they were close enough to notice the truck blocking the entrance, the vehicles screeched to a stop. A barrage of gunfire from the roof cut off the instant chatter of Demonish, dashing any chance that these were drug runners looking to hide their stash.

As instructed, I stayed low while the minions returned fire. Then again, these ocher-colored walls were already in bad shape; I doubted they'd stop bullets for long. Maybe we should've tried to hide. As soon as I thought it, I rejected the idea. Would minions sent on a murder mission by demons really be content to shine a flashlight around and then call it a night?

"This one's out," Tomas said, dropping one rifle and snatching up another. Quickly, I replaced the magazine, trying not to flash back to the last firefight when I'd been almost killed. Easier said than done with the rat-a-tat-tat-tat! of gunfire going off. If I lived through this, I'd never be able to watch a war movie without risking a PTSD attack.

Right now, I channeled my anxiety into replacing Tomas's ammunition as fast as he needed it. The pile of magazines seemed to be shrinking at an alarming rate, and the sanctuary walls were beginning to look like Swiss cheese from the hits they were taking. Every time a bullet penetrated, a small cloud of stone dust puffed out. There had been so many, the air was starting to get chalky.

Worse, it sounded like fewer guns were firing back from the roof. I tried not to think about what that meant, or drive myself crazy wondering if Adrian was okay. Every so often, a shout would rise above the other noises, but I couldn't tell who made it. The roof had stone arches, carvings and a bell tower to hide behind, but if they were sustaining as much damage as the sanctuary walls, things were getting dire.

And we were down to only two clips of ammo.

"How many minions are still out there?" I asked Tomas, needing to shout to be heard above the gunfire.

"Four more carfuls just pulled up," he yelled back.

Four! An irrational urge to start screaming built, but I choked it back with forced optimism. We'd survived a minion attack before. If we hung in there, we'd survive again—

Tomas spun around, clutching his chest. Horrified, I saw a new hole in the wall right where he'd been standing. I barely managed to catch him before he crumpled, crimson leaking out between his fingers.

I set him down and rushed across the room to retrieve the manna Adrian had left. Something burned in my leg, but I ignored it, zigzagging to avoid more bullets on my way back.

"No," Tomas groaned, coughing up blood with the word.

I tore open the bag and, pulling his hands away, clapped a large glob of manna onto his chest. He coughed up more blood, then his lips stretched into a grisly imitation of a smile.

"Doesn't work…mortal wounds."

My eyes welled, causing his features to blur. "You're not dying," I insisted, pressing another handful to his chest.

"Can't save…me." His breathing became labored, and blood continued to stream through my fingers, soaking the manna.

"Don't talk," I said, desperately trying to stem the flow. "You need to save your strength."

Tomas stared at me, and for a second, the agonized haze left his vision and his eyes became clear.

"You need to save Adrian," he said distinctly. Then his eyes rolled back, and his body convulsed before he went limp.

"Tomas!" I screamed.

No response. His chest didn't rise for another breath, and the gush of blood between my fingers slowed to a trickle. I didn't need to check for a pulse to know he was gone. Slowly, I lifted my hands from his chest and sent a single glare upward that wasn't directed at the men on the roof.

Why? I thought furiously. *He was fighting for Your side! Don't You even care?*

No response again, not that I expected any. Maybe Adrian was right and we were nothing more than collateral damage to both sides. Fine. If the Archon's boss wouldn't do anything to help, I would.

I picked up Tomas's gun, barely noticing how hot the metal was from his repeated firing. Every part of me was consumed by guilt and rage. I'd stayed down like they told me to, and

Tomas had died. No more. I'd fight and live, or I'd fight and die, but either way, I was fighting.

I braced the barrel against a hole in the wall like Tomas had done and started firing. For the first few rounds, my aim was terrible, and I hit the cars the minions hid behind instead of them. Stone exploded near my face as they returned fire. I ducked low until it stopped, then began firing again, aiming for the flashes of light I'd glimpsed from the minions' guns.

I didn't hear a yelp, but one of their weapons abruptly went silent. I felt nothing except grim satisfaction, which surprised the small part of me that hadn't been irrevocably changed by the past two weeks. I kept firing, scooting over when the wall became too pocked with holes for sufficient protection. I'd just replaced the magazine clip with the last full one when a thunderous boom shook the sanctuary.

Sand rolled in like a fast-moving fog. Between that and the sudden glare of headlights, I was momentarily blinded, but the noise and the shuddering ground kept me moving. I ran toward the back, keeping low, which was a good thing. The sickening rushes of air over me had to be gunshots I barely avoided.

"Ivy!" I heard someone scream before a frenzy of gunfire drowned out the sound. Then another, more ominous noise swelled. Metal screeched, stone groaned, and the ground shook like I was in the middle of an earthquake. Frantically, I blinked the sand out of my eyes, finally able to see enough to realize the sanctuary was crashing down around me.

chapter seventeen

I ran for the window, pain exploding over me as I was pelted by chunks of the roof. Then I dove through it right as the walls folded, releasing a thick cloud of crushed stone from the tremendous impact. My knees and arms tore, but I forced myself to keep moving through the rubble. Through the chalklike fog, I saw something dark rush toward me. I raised my arms before realizing I no longer held a gun. Sometime during my mad dash to escape the collapsing sanctuary, I'd dropped it.

I tried to run—and was grabbed before I made it a step. Then I recognized the large body I was pressed to. Felt rough, hot hands race over me, seeking out signs of injury. I hurt everywhere, but the pain faded at the knowledge that Adrian was still alive. I threw my arms around him and, for a blissful second, felt him hug me back with equal vehemence. Then Adrian thrust me behind him fast enough to make my teeth rattle.

"Hondalte!" a voice rang out.

Stop, I mentally translated, recognizing the Demonish word from our time in the realm. The thick cloud dissipated, revealing the cause of the sanctuary's demise. One of the minions had rammed their truck into the side of the building, taking down the gunfire-weakened walls. What I saw when I peeked around Adrian looked equally ominous.

Half a dozen minions were silhouetted against the vehicles' headlights. Demetrius stood in the middle, his black hair merging into the shadows that trailed behind him like a cape.

"Adrian, enough," the demon said in an annoyed voice. "Move aside. I have no wish to hurt you."

"Sure you don't," Adrian mocked. "All those bullets aimed my way were just you trying to say hi."

Demetrius's gaze raked over him. "Those were to limit the damage you inflicted on my people, but you, more than anyone, know why we want you alive. In fact, Mayhemium is being punished for not instructing his people to take care with you earlier."

I hadn't thought a demon was capable of telling the truth, but right now, I believed Demetrius. For starters, six guns were trained on us, yet at the demon's command, no one was firing. As for Adrian, blood dripped down him from multiple wounds, staining his clothes and turning his hair auburn, but when I'd held him, he had felt whole. Sad that I was learning to tell the difference between seriously injured and moderately hurt.

"Ah, but if she's dead, then you don't need me anymore," Adrian countered.

Good point, and a very frightening one. I glanced down. We were still on hallowed ground, from the faint luminescence drifting up, so Demetrius couldn't get to us. Of course, with all the guns pointed our way, he didn't need to.

"You're still my son," Demetrius said quietly. "Give us the Davidian, and I will gladly welcome you home."

Adrian's whole body tensed. "Stop calling me that," he said, each word vibrating with hatred. "And you're only getting Ivy over my dead body."

Demetrius sighed, resignation flickering across his pale features. "If you insist on dying for her, so be it." Then his black eyes gleamed. "I will, however, raise you back up so you can fulfill your destiny."

Adrian's breath hissed through his teeth. "You don't have the power to."

The demon's laughter sent shivers of revulsion through me. "All your overdoses, son? I already have. Many times."

Six guns rose with lethal purpose. Amidst a surge of fear, I also felt sheer resolve take hold of me. I couldn't save myself, but no one else was dying for me tonight.

I shoved Adrian aside as hard as I could. Whether it was adrenaline or the determination of a last wish, I actually succeeded in knocking him over. Right as his shocked gaze met mine, multiple loud cracks sounded. I tensed, waiting for the pain...and then a cool, familiar voice spoke.

"Is this a bad time?" Zach asked dryly.

Shock froze me with my muscles still bunched and eyes mere slits from the process of squeezing them shut. It took a second before I registered that I was not, in fact, dead. I wasn't shot, either, unless you counted my leg, but that was from earlier and felt like a flesh wound, anyway.

Bullets were lined up in front of me, though, close enough to reach out and pluck them from the air. They hung as if someone had pressed Pause on a remote control, and I stared at their hollow points in morbid fascination. Then another series of loud cracks sounded.

My firing squad fell in a row, their bodies dissipating into

ash as soon as they touched the ground. Not even their clothes
or shoes remained. Only their guns were left, the sand absorbing the impact as the weapons dropped with muffled thuds.

"Archon." Demetrius's voice was a barely controlled growl.
"You should not be here."

What do you do when you have a demon staring down an
angel while the ashes of dead minions blew between them?
You get out of the way, of course.

I slunk sideways, clearing that path of bullets in case they
suddenly reactivated. Adrian got up, grasping my arm and
moving me toward the shattered sanctuary. Zach didn't look
at either of us. His piercing dark gaze was focused on the
demon, whose shadows stretched and grew ominously large
behind him.

"You should leave," Zach stated in a mild tone.

I was in full agreement, but he was talking to Demetrius.
The demon let out another growl, his shadows increasing even
more. Then they began to spin, forming into multiple funnel
clouds that whipped up the sand and caused the cars nearest
him to slowly slide and spin.

"The Davidian is mine," Demetrius hissed.

"Uh, time to go, Adrian," I said nervously.

"Our cars are smashed," was his grim response.

"Stop the theatrics, Demetrius," Zach said, still in that calm
tone. "You can't defeat an officer of the Most High."

"If that's what you are," the demon responded with luxuri-
ant hatred. "I know all the officers, because once, I was one,
yet none of them are named Zacchaeus." Then he cocked his
head as if curious. "You could be concealing your identity behind that name and your human shell, but if you are what you
claim, why not smite me along with my servants?"

"Those weren't my orders," Zach replied indifferently.

Why not? I wanted to yell, but kept backing away with

Adrian. We were now even with the ruined sanctuary, the desert spreading out like a blank canvas behind us.

"Orders." Scorn dripped from Demetrius's tone. "Don't you ever weary of those?"

Zach's mouth curled into the faintest of smiles. "Some days."

"Then free yourself," Demetrius commanded. "Live under your own rule as we do, my brother."

Then he said something in a language that reminded me of Demonish, if you took out all the harsh syllables and replaced them with lyrical exquisiteness. Zach replied in the same language, and I almost closed my eyes in bliss. Nothing had ever sounded so beautiful. Of course, if he was accepting Demetrius's offer, we were both dead.

"Do you know what they're saying?" I whispered to Adrian.

He kept backing us away. "Demetrius said his people would soon claim this realm, and he urged Zach to join them. Zach refused."

That had pissed off the demon, clearly. I watched with dread as Demetrius's funnel clouds grew into what looked like F-4 tornados, tossing up debris from the crumpled sanctuary. One of the minion's cars flipped over, setting off an alarm.

"Are you able to run, Ivy?" Adrian asked, his voice barely audible over the wind and whooping car alarm.

I felt like I didn't have the energy to crawl, but if my life depended on it? Yep. "What about Costa and the others?"

"They're dead," Adrian replied flatly.

Despair made me stumble. I didn't even remember all their names, and they'd died because of me. How many more would die if I kept going after that weapon to save my sister?

"Go now," Adrian urged, releasing my hand.

What about you? I was about to ask, then light crashed around us, briefly illuminating everything with noonday clarity. I saw arms and legs amidst the rubble, the back end of the truck that had demolished the sanctuary, piles of ashes blowing away and every nuance of Demetrius's shocked expression as his wall of tornados abruptly dissipated.

Zach's hand dropped, but light still pulsed beneath his skin, as if his veins had been replaced with streaks of electricity. "Leave, Demetrius," he said in the sudden silence.

"Who are you?" the demon almost whispered.

Zach's stare didn't waver. "This is your final warning."

Demetrius disappeared, taking the wispy remains of his ruined shadows with him. I would've let out a triumphant whoop if I wasn't so upset by the senseless loss.

"Everyone else is dead," I said, my tone as flat as Adrian's. "Why didn't you show up before, Zach?"

"I wasn't sent," he replied, the answer making me want to scream. "Besides, not all are dead. Some are asleep."

With that, he walked over to the rubble and grasped a dirty, limp hand. Costa came up from the rocks with a gasp, his gaze darting around as if expecting an attack.

"Don't be afraid," Zach stated. "You are safe."

And uninjured, judging from how easily Costa moved once he was free from the rocks. I stared, disbelief turning to amazement. No way had he only been "asleep." He still had bullet holes in his shirt, not to mention he'd been buried under a stone building; yet now, he looked in better shape than me.

One glance at Adrian's face confirmed it. He stared at Zach while his expression changed from shock to expectancy.

"Wake the rest of them up," he said with barely contained vehemence.

Zach didn't reply, but he did go over to another motion-less body part and then pulled up a perfectly healthy Tucco.

"What happened to the minions?" Tucco asked, shaking the dust and debris out of his hair.

"Ashes," Adrian responded in a terse tone.

"Bueno," was Tucco's reply, followed by, "Where's Tomas?"

"In the sanctuary," I said, my voice catching on the next word. "Asleep."

"Not asleep. Tomas is dead," Zach corrected, no emotion in his tone.

Adrian strode over, gripping Zach by the collar of his pullover sweater. "Wake. Him. Up," he said through gritted teeth.

Zach's handsome features stayed in that serene mask. "He is dead," he replied, spacing out the words like Adrian had. "Neither your demands nor your anger can change that."

"But you can save him," I burst out, rushing over to grip the Archon's sleeve. *"Please,* save him."

Zach looked at Adrian and me before brushing our hands aside. "His time had come, as with the other two. It is done."

Then he walked away, adding, "There are others you can still save, if you haven't given up. Tickets are waiting at the Durango airport. Whatever you decide, don't remain here. Demetrius will soon find his courage and return."

As Zach disappeared, one of the formerly silent cars revved to life. The four of us stared at it for a moment, and then, by unspoken agreement, climbed inside.

I didn't know if the rest of them were motivated by survival instinct, but I knew why I got into the car, and it wasn't just because I wanted away from the sanctuary of death behind us. I might be angry, confused and in desperate need of a shower, but I still wasn't ready to give up.

chapter eighteen

Adrian used the last of the manna he'd stuffed in his pocket to heal our injuries on our way to the airport. Tucco got off on our first layover in Mexico City. Costa, Adrian and I continued to our plane's final destination of Miami, Florida. I'd learned on the flight there that Costa and Tomas lived in Miami, and they'd journeyed to Durango to help Adrian after he called them. Now only Costa had survived to make the trip home.

Their house was a former church located only two blocks from the beach. It even had a steeple with a cross on top. When Costa showed me around, I realized that he and Tomas had closed in that soaring, pointed ceiling, turning it into the house's second floor. That was where I stayed, in Tomas's old room, and for the first day, all I did was sleep.

The second day, I went to the beach. I wasn't trying to work on my tan, but the sun, heat and tropical scenery made it the exact opposite of the demon realm, and I gratefully soaked up the differences. Already, I couldn't stand the cold or dark.

I'd kept the lights on when I slept, something I hadn't done since I was child, and if the air conditioning dipped too low, a feeling of dread washed over me.

Costa said that no one left the realms the same way they entered them. Adrian had warned me, too. They were both right.

I stayed at the beach the whole afternoon, moving under the shade of the pavilion when my skin began to redden. Late October in Miami felt like June in Virginia, but the beach wasn't crowded, probably because it was a Thursday. Back at WMU, Delia and the rest of my friends would be making their weekend plans. They knew which bars had a strict ID policy and which didn't, plus there were always parties on or around campus. I'd joined them on the classes-parties seesaw for the past two years, but it almost seemed strange to realize I'd be doing that again if I went back home. I'd often had to fake my enthusiasm for going out, and that was before I knew the freaky things I saw were real. Now? I couldn't pretend to be impressed by some drunken guy pulling off a keg stand. Kick a demon's ass, *that'll* impress me.

Speaking of guys, a few hit on me throughout the day, which would've been flattering under regular circumstances. These were anything but. For starters, they were hitting on my blond disguise, not *me*. More importantly, when I wasn't thinking about Tomas's death, my sister's imprisonment or the awfulness of the realms, I thought about Adrian. Flirting with cute strangers was the last thing on my mind.

Three of the guys took my rebuff like men and went on their way. The fourth, however, was being a little bitch about it.

"Come on, sugar, have *one* drink with me," he urged.

"Again, no," I said, not adding "and I'm not your sugar" only because simple phrases already seemed too much for him.

He grinned, showing off nice teeth. He wasn't bad-looking,

either, with his short black hair and a leanly muscular build, but even if I was looking for a date, he wouldn't be it. Years ago, I'd dated another guy who didn't understand the word *no,* and I'd ended up breaking an empty beer bottle over his head on prom night. *That,* he'd understood.

Mr. Pushy grabbed my hand, tugging on it with that same smug grin. "Bar's right up the street. You'll love it—"

Being snatched backward and flung to the sand ended his grabby sales pitch. Adrian stood over him, his foot grinding into the guy's back. Somehow, I wasn't a bit surprised.

"You've been spying on me all day, haven't you?" I said. "I told you I needed some time to myself, Adrian."

He glanced down at Mr. Pushy. "Good thing I didn't listen."

I rolled my eyes. "Like I couldn't handle him? If nothing else, you should've known that I'd be able to out*run* him."

"...'et me...up," the guy said, his words garbled, trying to spit out enough sand to talk.

Adrian hauled him up, though a hard cuff almost sent Mr. Pushy sprawling again.

"Get lost," he said curtly.

The guy looked at Adrian with surly confidence, reminding me that he only saw the disguise. Not the hulking, six-six man who'd ripped the throat out of the last person who touched me without my consent.

"I should kick your ass," the guy muttered.

"You should run while your legs still work," I told Mr. Pushy. To Adrian I said, "He's not worth the police report, so don't do whatever you're thinking of."

Either the guy sensed the danger in Adrian's glare, or he suddenly remembered another girl who wanted to go to the bar. Whatever it was, with another mutter, he left, still brushing sand off himself as he climbed up the pavilion staircase.

Once he was gone, Adrian and I stared at each other. Moments ago, he'd been poised to strike; now he looked almost hesitant, like he didn't know what to say.

"Costa's making dinner," he told me, as if that had anything to do with why he was here. "It'll be ready in half an hour."

My annoyance began to evaporate. I'd seen Adrian look angry, vengeful, bitter, confident, lethal and seductive, but this was different. He almost seemed…shy. Was it because I'd busted him for spying on me? If so, he must not have been doing it only out of concern for my safety.

"So what's for dinner?" I asked, my voice soft.

He smiled. "Burnt moussaka, probably. Costa loves to cook, and I don't have the heart to tell him that he sucks at it."

I laughed. "Thanks for the heads-up. I'll play along and clean my plate, too."

Adrian chuckled before he looked away. The sea breeze blew his longer bangs back while the setting sun turned his blondish-brown hair into different shades of red. His shirt molded to him from the wind, and his shorts showed off those shapely, muscular legs.

"You did really well in the realm," he said, still not looking at me. "I meant to tell you that before, but…"

"Everyone died and Zach only brought a couple back," I filled in, grief chasing away my other thoughts. "Thank you, by the way. I didn't get to say that before, either. I wouldn't have made it out of there alive without you."

Or out of the desert, the monastery, the other desert, Bennington… Because of Adrian, I was turning out to have more lives than a cat.

He looked at me then, sadness making his eyes appear a deeper shade of blue. "Did Tomas… Was it quick?"

I drew in a shuddering breath, remembering that awful wound and Tomas's last words. "It was quick."

He nodded, returning his attention to the water, but I

glimpsed the grief he was trying to hold back. I moved closer, sliding my hand into his without even thinking about it. His fingers curled around mine, and the sense of rightness I felt hit me like a wrecking ball. Had I fallen so hard, so fast?

"I'm glad you were with him," he said, his tone faintly hoarse. "Dying's hard enough. Doing it alone is worse."

I couldn't imagine all the death Adrian had seen growing up in the demon realms. I'd suffered so little by comparison, and some days, I still felt like I couldn't take it. Today had been one of those days. All the warmth and sunshine I'd tried to soak up hadn't put a dent in the icy darkness rising inside me. But holding his hand did, and that scared me as much as I silently marveled at it.

"Do you really think I'm strong enough to keep searching the realms until I find this weapon?" I asked, my voice barely audible as I spoke my greatest fear aloud.

His hand tightened on mine. "I know you are," Adrian said, turning to look at me once more.

It wasn't the words, though I'd needed to hear them. It wasn't even his voice, though it vibrated with surety. It was his eyes. I'd never read so much from a person's eyes before, but Adrian's seemed to spill all the secrets he still refused to tell me. In those sapphire depths, I knew he meant what he'd said. I might not believe in me, but he did, and right now, it gave me hope that we would make it through. All of us.

I reached out, trailing my free hand down his arm. "Thanks," I said softly.

He stepped closer, brushing my hair back, and I closed my eyes. I felt so safe with him, which he'd say was the last thing I should feel. Still, if nothing but betrayal loomed ahead, how could Adrian be the only person I trusted? And how could he be the only person who made me feel alive if he was destined to be the death of me?

"I believe in you, too," I told him, not opening my eyes. "You'll beat your fate. I know you will."

He let out a strangled sound, and my skin felt cold from how fast he let me go. When I opened my eyes, I wasn't surprised to see only surf-soaked sand in front of me.

Once again, Adrian had vanished, but like all the other times, he wasn't really gone. Whether by destiny or by choice, neither of us could completely walk away from the other.

Not yet.

chapter nineteen

The next morning, I awoke to a strange man sitting on the end of my bed. His back was to me, and I would've screamed if I hadn't recognized his faded blue hoodie. Good thing I'd caught myself. Adrian and Costa would've run in with their guns drawn.

"What are you doing here?" I asked Zach.

The Archon set down a picture of Tomas as a boy with his father. Family pictures occupied most of Tomas's room. I hoped looking at them made Zach feel guilty. He could've saved Tomas, but he'd chosen not to for reasons I still didn't understand.

"I am here to glamour your appearance," Zach replied, ignoring the thought I knew he'd heard. "Adrian has chosen the next realm for you both to search, and demons will be more watchful of blond women."

I ran a hand through my hair, remembering that only Adrian, Zach and I saw its deep brown shade. As for my face, well, I hadn't seen that clearly in almost two weeks. Not being able to look in a mirror without risking a demon attack cut back on any feminine urges to check my appearance.

"Don't overdue the hotness factor this time," I said. "We might have made it out of that realm without a fight if Mayhemium hadn't gotten a hard-on over my glamoured looks."

Zach nodded. "I will make appropriate changes."

Then he placed his hand on top of my head. Like last time, I didn't feel anything, but when he said, "It is done," I knew I now looked completely different. Pity I couldn't see my disguises. When I looked at my reflection in shiny surfaces, it still looked like the "real" me.

"Okay." I got out of bed, put on a robe and went to the door. "I'm making coffee. Don't suppose you want any?"

The side of his mouth twitched. "I'm trying to cut back."

Had he just cracked a joke? I looked sharply at him, but that twitch was gone and his expression was back to its normal, placid mask. Deciding I had more important things to worry about, I left the bedroom.

"Zach's here," I announced on my way to the kitchen.

Costa's door flung open, and he stared at me, shock creasing his features. "Ivy?" he asked with disbelief.

I waved a hand. "I know. Zach gave me a makeover, so minions and demons don't recognize me from my old disguise."

"They sure won't," Costa croaked, his lip curling in a way that said Zach had taken my admonition seriously by beating my new appearance with an ugly stick.

I gave a mental shrug. I was shallow enough to care if Adrian saw me that way, but he didn't.

Speaking of Adrian, his door opened as we passed. He'd been in the process of pulling on a shirt, which gave me a glimpse of his muscled chest and ripped abs before the loose material covered them. I swallowed, glancing away. With a mind-reading angel in the house, now *really* wasn't the time to dwell on how much Adrian affected me.

"Zach." Adrian's voice was brisk. "We need more manna, plus a new appearance for me, too."

Costa said something in Greek that had Adrian whipping around to stare at me. Then he let out a snort of amusement.

"Nice," he told Zach, the edginess gone from his tone.

Had Zach given me Halloween-style warts, too? I lifted my nose and started making coffee. Some of us were too mature to worry about things like unattractive fake appearances.

"Where are we going this time?" I asked.

Zach remained standing, but Adrian and Costa sat at the kitchen table. I pulled three cups out from the cabinet. None of *us* were trying to cut back on our coffee habit.

"Roanoke, North Carolina," Adrian replied.

Not another desert, at least. "There's a vortex there?"

"No." The edge was back in Adrian's tone. "No more vortexes."

I turned around, still holding my empty coffee cup. "Why?"

"Demetrius now knows the weapon is hidden in a demon realm," Zach answered for him. "He'll expect you to try vortexes, since they are the most efficient means of entry into their realms."

Adrian's shrug conveyed, *What he said.* Costa still seemed to be reconciling my new appearance with who I was, but I was focused on the information no one had told me before.

"You mean the demons didn't know the weapon had been hidden in one of *their* realms before they caught us looking for it?"

"That's right," Adrian said, with a sidelong glance at Zach. "It'll be a race to see who finds it first, and you can bet they'll be searching their worlds from top to bottom."

"Do you know where it is?" I asked Zach bluntly, remembering Adrian's accusation about the Archon.

As if he knew the source of my question, Zach gave Adrian a measured look before he responded. "No."

Archons don't lie, I reminded myself. Then again, I only had an Archon's word on that, so it wasn't exactly unbiased.

"But your boss knows," I prodded. "Right?"

The faintest smile curled Zach's mouth. "He would not be much of a 'boss' otherwise."

"How about we save a lot of lives by having him tell us where it is, then?" I asked, barely holding back my sarcasm.

Zach gave an infuriating shrug. "If that were His will, you would already know its location."

The coffee cup in my hand shattered. I yelped, both at the pain and the clattering sound as pieces hit the floor. I hadn't been aware of tightening my grip, but in my anger, I must have. Adrian started forward, but I waved him back with a frustrated swipe of my hand.

"Sorry," I muttered to Costa, bending to pick up the pieces. To Zach I said, "Then your boss sucks. It's to *his* benefit that I find the weapon before the demons do, but instead of helping, *he's* grabbing popcorn to sit back and watch."

"Get used to it," Adrian said dryly.

"Isn't that what *you* would rather do?" Zach replied, his gaze flashing as it swept over me. "If your sister's life wasn't tied to this weapon, would you risk yourself searching for it?" Before I could respond, he started in on Adrian. "And if it wasn't the key to your vengeance, would you risk your fate to help her? No," he answered for both of us. "Therefore, sit judgment on your own sins before you presume to judge others'."

Now I was glad I'd broken the thick glass cup. Otherwise, I might have thrown it at him. "There's nothing wrong with wanting to save my sister's life," I almost snarled.

"Untold thousands are trapped in the dark realms. If hers is the only life you care about, something is very wrong," Zach responded at once.

"That's out of my control and you know it. If I could save all of them, I would!" I snapped back.

Absolute silence fell. For a second, it seemed like the traffic noise outside Costa's house vanished, too. Adrian closed his eyes, anger and resignation skipping over his features. Light briefly gleamed in Zach's gaze, and he stared at me with such intensity that a wave of foreboding swept over me.

Something significant had just happened, and as usual, I was the only one who didn't know what it was. Also per usual, none of them were going to tell me about it.

Whatever. I'd get it out of them eventually. I threw the last of the shattered cup into the trash and then ran my hand under the tap, washing the cut one of the shards had made.

"When do we leave for Roanoke?" Costa asked, breaking the loaded silence. "And before you argue, Adrian, I *am* going with you. Tomas died fighting for Ivy's chance to find that weapon. I'm seeing this through until she does. Then my best friend can finally rest in peace."

I'd started this to rescue my sister, but in a short amount of time, the stakes had grown much larger. Now more than Jasmine's life hung in the balance. So did Adrian's revenge, Tomas's justice and Costa's tribute to his friend, all hinging on my ability to find and successfully use a supernatural weapon, if the demons hunting us didn't kill us first.

No pressure, right?

Adrian's gaze moved to Zach, and the two men exchanged a look I couldn't read. Whatever it was, it wasn't happy.

"Did you bring my car?" Adrian finally asked.

An oblique nod. "Of course."

Adrian went over to the now-full coffee pot, downed a

steaming mug like it was a single shot and then flashed the rest of us a grimly expectant smile.

"We leave in an hour."

chapter twenty

A glimpse inside Adrian's trunk explained why we were driving to North Carolina instead of flying. It looked like an NRA gold-member kit, with row upon row of handguns, regular rifles and assault rifles. We barely had room for luggage, not that I had much to bring. Aside from the clothes and basic hygiene items Zach had gotten me, all I owned was a lipstick, gum and face cream, all stuffed inside a tiny, clear travel bag.

I took that bag out to put my lipstick on during our first pit stop. Costa wasn't the only person who stared as I contorted my head in order to see a distorted reflection in the chrome from Adrian's empty side mirror. Not that I cared. I wasn't doing this to look prettier for Adrian, Costa or even myself. I did it because it was my last link to a semi-normal life. Everything else had been turned upside down or taken away, but this small feminine ritual was my silent promise that one day, if I survived, I'd get it back. No matter how long it took, or what I might change based on truths I now knew.

"That looks…disturbing," Costa said when I was finished.

I smacked my lips at him, unperturbed. "I'll get better at doing this without a mirror. Now, pass me the rock and gloves. I'm hitting the ladies' room before we leave."

"Uh, I don't think—" Costa began, only to be cut off by Adrian's "Don't. This I have to see."

I gave them a questioning look as I accepted the gloves and rock I'd need to smash the mirror. That turned to suspicion when they followed me into the gas station, not even pretending to browse as they watched me enter the bathroom. Jeez, had I screwed up my lipstick *that* badly?

This time, I glanced under the stalls before I broke the mirror. No one, good. After I kicked the worst of the shards out of the way, I answered nature's call. I was in the process of washing my hands when the door opened and a squeal startled me.

"That was already broken," I began to lie, only to be interrupted by the heavyset African-American woman saying, "You are in the *wrong* place, Grandpa!"

What? As I goggled at her, the woman's gaze dropped to my lips, then to the glass on the floor.

"You okay, sir?" she asked in a less scandalized voice.

"I'm not a man," I protested, then stopped at the sudden burst of laughter from inside the store. Uh-oh.

Costa's look of disbelief when he first saw me. Adrian's amused comment of "Nice" to Zach. Both of them following me to the ladies' room. This woman calling me "sir" and "Grandpa."

"I look like an old guy, don't I?" I asked resignedly. "An old guy wearing lipstick, no less."

Concern pinched her features. "Is someone here with you, sir? Or is there someone we can call?"

"Yeah." My voice was wry. "Call the angel with the warped sense of humor, because this is all his fault."

Now she *really* looked concerned, but I brushed by her, saying, "Fun's over, sonnies. Time to take Grandpa for a ride!" to the two grinning guys waiting for me.

Way back when, Roanoke Island had been the site of a Colonial-era settlement that mysteriously disappeared. Today, parts of the island drew visitors by marketing that event. Take Festival Park, a tourist attraction complete with a structural re-creation of the Lost Colony, a play about it, several Elizabethan-styled games, and people wandering around in sixteenth-century costumes.

Costa didn't drop Adrian and me off here so we could join the festivities. In the glimpses I caught of the demon realm, the north side of Roanoke Island was surrounded by ice instead of water, with barren earth replacing the pretty oak and myrtle trees. Some of the pre-Colonial huts from Festival Park were there, though, looking not much different from the ones that duplicated the village in the former Lost Colony.

"It's like the realm swallowed this place," I murmured to Adrian, glad someone else could see what I did.

"That's exactly what happened," he responded, his voice low. "Realms start out as duplicate reflections of our world, with everything we build here getting mirrored there."

"Everything?" I tried to absorb the staggering thought that demon realms had duplicated the entire world.

"As reflections," Adrian stressed, leading me into the trees behind the Visitor's Center. "They're not tangible yet. That only happens when demons get powerful enough to absorb an area. When they do, the place, along with everyone in it, gets sucked into a new realm in the demon world. So in effect, they swallow it. Then what's left in our world is an empty shell."

For a second, I closed my eyes, thinking of the two versions of the bed-and-breakfast Jasmine was trapped in. "But that shell can be rebuilt."

"It can." Adrian looked around, his mouth curling. "Absorbed places carry negative imprints of what happened, even if people don't understand why they don't want to build there. Festival Park is at the back end of the demon realm. The main part looks just as beautiful in our world, but it isn't crawling with shops and hotels like these sections of Manteo."

He was right. The part of Manteo we'd rented a room in had nearly wall-to-wall bed-and-breakfasts, inns, restaurants and stores. Compared to that, the place where the former Lost Colony had been located was largely undeveloped.

"So what was our version of Mayhemium's realm, before he swallowed it?" I asked, no longer whispering since we were a hundred yards into the woods by now. "It looked like bigger versions of the Sun and Moon pyramids in the Avenue of the Dead."

He gave me a tight smile. "You know your history."

"It's my major," I said, remembering that the ruins of Teotihuacan were thousands of years old on our end. The demons had had plenty of time to keep building on their side of the realm. By comparison, the colony at Roanoke had been recently swallowed, and it was far less impressive than sucking in the third-largest pyramid in the world.

"Why'd the demons want this place?" I wondered.

Adrian gave me a jaded look as he held back a low-hanging branch so I could duck under it.

"Same reason every conqueror wants more territory. The person with the most usually wins."

Duly noted. "And you think the weapon might be here, why?"

He stopped in front of a tall tree stump that had been halved, as though a lightning strike long ago had split it in two. The dark wood rising up behind him reminded me of

Mayhemium's wings, and I shifted uncomfortably. What horrors would I discover in this new realm?

"It's led by a weak demon," Adrian said. "All I know of the demons from Goliath's line is that they're very strong. That rules out the weapon being hidden in one of their realms. Otherwise, the demon who stole it would've just given it to that realm's ruler instead of hiding it while looking for someone who could wield it."

I stared at him, incredulous. "You're saying that Mayhemium was a *weak* demon?"

His snort was contemptuous. "Oh, yeah. Total pussy."

"Sure. Because who can't transform into dozens of killer crows, am I right?"

His mouth quirked at my shrill tone. "You freaking out, Ivy?"

Yes. If Mayhemium was the demon-lite version, we were so screwed! "I'm just…absorbing this."

That quirk deepened. "Sorry, time's up. Here's the door."

With that, he grasped me and then dropped us backward into the V in the tree stump. Instead of hitting the long-dead wood, the realm-piercing roller coaster started, leaving me with a familiar sensation of nausea when it spit us out into a dark, freezing version of Festival Park.

This time, lights from the realm's residents were close enough that I didn't feel like I'd been struck blind. Of course, it also meant that we were stopped by a minion before we'd been here less than five minutes. The slide show of white in his eyes matched the furs he wore over his leather-and-metal outfit, making him look like he'd gotten it at a Viking surplus store.

I'd heard enough Demonish to know that he said a variation of "Stop! Who goes there?" to Adrian, but his reply was lost on me. It seemed to satisfy the minion guard, and the way he barely looked at me made me glad for Zach's old-man disguise.

"What was your excuse this time?" I whispered when the guard was far enough away not to overhear us.

Adrian's mouth tightened. "I told him you were food."

Right, because that, forced labor and forced sex were the only things demons imported humans into their realms for. A sick sort of rage swept over me. *Jasmine*. Despite Adrian's assurance that the demons were treating her better than anyone else, I couldn't help but wonder what horrors she'd gone through while I was fumbling around looking for this weapon.

I forced those thoughts back. They only led to more rage and feelings of helplessness, which wouldn't do my sister any good. Finding the weapon would, and to do that, I needed to concentrate on abilities I was just learning to use.

We passed some old wooden huts that were covered by a thick layer of ice. Human slaves occupied them, and it was all I could do not to give away my warm jacket, boots and gloves when I saw them shivering in their paltry coverings. I couldn't, of course. That would be announcing myself to the minions and demons here, and though there were a lot less of them than in Mayhemium's realm, there were a lot more innocent bystanders on our side of Festival Park. Costa waited with our arsenal in the parking lot, but starting a firefight at a tourist attraction was the last thing we wanted to do.

After the wooden huts, we walked along what seemed like a mile-long line of igloos. The igloos made sense, I supposed, since ice was the only material in large supply here, and demons had absorbed this realm before anything substantial was built. Light inside made the igloos glow, and while I was sickened by all the trapped people they denoted, I was grateful for the extra illumination. Did I mention I'd come to hate the dark?

"Sense anything?" Adrian asked.

"No," I replied, and he grunted as though he'd expected that. Guess the last place he thought the weapon was hidden was in the wall of a slave hut.

About three miles into our hike, I had a question, too. "Why are demon headquarters so far away from realm entrances?"

Adrian shot me a slanted look. "Tactical advantage. They want to see an army coming, if someone's after their realm."

"Demons fight each other for control of the realms?"

Adrian's mouth curled into a sardonic grin. "Humans don't have a monopoly on land grabs, Ivy."

Guess we wouldn't. Compared to all the demons' other cruelties, snatching each other's kingdoms seemed almost a benign activity.

After ten minutes of brisk walking, a castle came into view. The walls glowed with different colors, faint but ethereal, reminding me of a small, multicolored version of the Emerald City in *The Wizard of Oz*. When we got closer, I saw the gates were adorned with ice sculptures that looked like mermen and mermaids. A long staircase bordered by ice-carved waves led up to the castle, and the front doors resembled huge seashells.

More guards were stationed around the gates. In addition to metal, some of their weapons seemed to be forged from ice. It was as though we'd stepped into a demonic version of Poseidon's Frozen Paradise, and the more I stared, the less I wanted to remember. I hated that it was so beautiful when I knew what horrors lurked beneath the exquisite exterior.

After exchanging a few words with one of the guards, Adrian took us around to the back of the castle. There, we were stopped again, and Adrian relayed the same cover story as before. One of the guards shook his head as he gave me a rough cuff, and I didn't need to know Demonish to guess

that he was disparaging my proposed edibility. I hunched my
shoulders and tried to look terrified while I hoped Adrian's
darkening expression didn't mean he was about to deck the
guard. I still hadn't sensed anything, but we hadn't entered
the castle, and I wasn't leaving until I'd given it a supernatural once-over.

Thankfully, Adrian didn't do anything violent, and we were
finally allowed into the back of the castle. The narrow hallway looked more igloo-like than Icy Emerald City, but I guess
fanciness wasn't required for the slave entrance, although the
floor was a pretty shade of deep pink—

Adrian's grip on my arm tightened until it should have been
painful, but I barely felt it. The floor of the room we entered
resembled a layer of rubies. The reason for that became abhor-
rently clear as I saw a cloudy-eyed minion mop up a pool of
blood, its crystallized stain adding another layer of red. The
blood came from a nearby ice slab, where another leather-clad
minion carved out sections from the body lying on it.

This wasn't the slave entrance. It was the slaughterhouse.

Mopping Minion said something in Demonish to Adrian.
He responded in a harsh voice, dropping his hand from my
arm, but I wasn't focused on him.

A bound, naked boy lay on the floor. At first, I thought he
was dead, too. Then his gaze slid from the dripping slab to
me, and the absolute hopelessness I saw in it shattered me. He
wasn't silently begging for help. As he watched the butcher-
ing going on above him, his blank, empty stare said he knew
nothing could save him from being next.

Without the slightest hesitation, I drew out the gun Adrian
had given me and fired. The butcher went down, clutching
his chest. I kept shooting as I advanced, part of me marveling
at the quiet, cough-cough sounds the gun made. That silencer
Adrian had screwed onto the end really worked as advertised.

I stopped shooting only when the butcher's body turned into ash. Adrian looked at the black ashes on the ice, at the slack-jawed minion who'd stopped mopping, and finally at me.

"Shit," he said simply.

chapter twenty-one

Mopping Minion opened his mouth. Before he could scream, Adrian's punch to the throat cut him off. Then Adrian gripped him in a brutal headlock that ended with a jerk, a snapping sound, and the minion dissolving into a pile of ashes on the floor.

"Move, Ivy," Adrian ordered. "We don't have long until someone finds them."

With the same eerie calm I'd felt when I shot the butcher, I put my gun away and knelt next to the naked boy.

"Give me your knife," I said to Adrian.

He frowned but passed it to me, and I cut through the plastic that bound the boy's hands. He blinked once, but said nothing, even when I took off my parka and wrapped him in it.

"Ivy," Adrian said in a warning tone.

"We're taking him with us," I replied, kicking off my boots.

Pity creased Adrian's expression. "I wish we could, but—"

"We're taking him *with us,*" I repeated, almost spitting out the last two words. "I don't care if it's more dangerous. I don't care if he'll slow us down. He's coming or I'm not."

"You'd risk your sister's life to save him?" Adrian asked harshly.

I shoved my boots onto the little boy's feet. He couldn't have been more than twelve, so they were too big. Tightening the laces would have to do.

"I can't save Jasmine right now," I said, my voice calm from the absolute certainty I felt that this was the right thing to do. "But I can save him. Don't pretend you don't understand. Costa and Tomas are proof that you do."

Adrian muttered something in Demonish, but picked the boy up, throwing a hard glance at my now-bare feet.

"Put the boots back on. I'll carry him."

"He's freezing and I can manage," I argued.

"We do it your way, all of us die," Adrian said flatly. "Put the boots back on, then shut up and do what I say."

I bristled, but our survival outweighed pride, so I took the boots off the boy and put them back on. He still didn't say anything. Maybe he was in a state of catatonic shock.

"Now, activate your power and search the castle from right here," Adrian ordered.

I tried to clear my mind enough to concentrate. It didn't work, probably because I was in a small icebox with two piles of minion ash on the floor and a chopped-up body less than five feet away.

"I need to get out of this room," I said.

Adrian's sapphire gaze seemed to burn into mine. "Not an option, and we're running out of time."

I tried again, closing my eyes, but I still couldn't concentrate on anything except the carnage around me. I was standing on layers of frozen blood, for crying out loud.

"Adrian," I started to say, but his sudden grip on my throat cut me off.

"Maybe you don't understand," he said, fingers slowly tightening. "You need to search this castle *right now,* and you're not moving from this spot to do it."

I grabbed his wrist, digging my nails into his skin. His hand only tightened more, until my throat burned from the pressure. He didn't even need to shift his grip on the boy to throttle me, and the child watched us with dull, empty eyes. Panic filled me as I couldn't get in more than a few thin, insufficient breaths. My chest started to heave in urgency, trying to force in air that Adrian wasn't allowing me to have.

Stop! I thought, unable to say anything. My nails ripped into Adrian's wrist, yet that ironlike grip didn't lessen.

"Still can't utilize your power?" he asked, staring into my eyes with pitiless determination. "Then I'm going to choke you unconscious and leave this kid behind while I carry you out instead. You can't look for the weapon anyway, or can you?"

My gasp of horror caught in my throat. He wouldn't do that…would he? Had I been wrong about him? Was he every bit the monster he'd warned me about?

"The only way you'll stop me is to access your power and search this place," he went on. "And, Ivy? I can feel it when you do, so don't bother trying to fake it."

I'll never forgive you! my gaze swore, but then his grip loosened and air rushed into my lungs, claiming all my attention. My second deep breath was ambrosia, quelling the frantic clenching in my chest. The third took away my panic, and the fourth had me closing my eyes as I sagged with relief—

An invisible flare ripped out of me, like I'd fired off a sonar ping that somehow made no sound. With it, I *felt* the castle and nearby grounds as though I'd managed to scour them in an instant. At the end of it, I knew, with a certainty as strong as my decision to take the boy, that the weapon wasn't here. Nothing hallowed was. This was a frozen wasteland of evil.

With a measured look, Adrian let me go. Red drops blended into the ruby-colored floor as blood dripped from his wrist where my nails had ripped into it.

"I'm sorry," he said stonily. "We couldn't take the boy into the castle without getting caught, so I had to do something extreme to make you access your power from here."

"How's this...for extreme?" I rasped, then slapped him as hard as I could, anger tapping into strength I normally didn't have. Adrian's head rocked sideways, and when he turned to face me, a red handprint was already swelling along his cheek.

"I deserved that," he said, still in that flinty voice. "Now, let's get out of here."

I was furious at him for choking me into near-unconsciousness and threatening to leave the boy, but I filed that away under a rapidly growing list titled Paybacks To Come. I did shake his hand off when he led me toward the exit, and my glare warned him not to touch me again as I followed him down the pink-floored hallway.

Before we reached the door, Adrian took my gun out of my parka, replaced the empty clip with a full one, and then handed it back to me.

"We might have to shoot our way out," he said, mouth curling with the dark anticipation he always showed before a fight. "But this time, don't fire unless I do."

I bit back my caustic reply because talking made my throat hurt more. Besides, we might not live through this. If we did, though...Paybacks.

"Don't fall behind," Adrian warned, and then exited the castle, running at a crouch in the opposite direction from where we'd come in.

I followed, keeping low like he did. As soon as I was outside, glacial air seemed to pummel my upper body, my thin sweater no protection against the realm's frigid temperatures. At once, my teeth began to chatter, the wind making it worse as I ran as fast as I could to keep up with Adrian's form-blurring sprint. Even as I shook, I comforted myself by thinking of how warm the boy would be in my parka. It was made to withstand subzero temperatures, and right now, that was what it felt like outside.

No guards chased us, which was a happy surprise. Maybe it was because we'd run right into the wall of darkness that bordered the rear of the castle. Nothing and no one seemed to be out this way, and as I abruptly fell on the hard, slick surface, I realized why. Adrian had led us out onto the island's frozen coastline.

I scrambled to my feet, ignoring the jabs of pain from whatever I'd bruised. At least I hadn't lost the gun or shot myself from the impact. I couldn't see in front of me, but the glittering castle behind me was all the motivation I needed to keep running toward where I'd last spotted Adrian. Despite my best efforts, I fell again, cutting my elbows and forearms on the uneven ice. Grudgingly, I had to acknowledge that Adrian had been right. I wouldn't have been able to run ten feet on this without boots. My feet would've been cut to ribbons.

Something large and dark rushed out of the blackness toward me. I lifted the gun, only to hear a familiar voice growl, "I *told* you not to fall behind!" before Adrian grasped my arm.

This time, I welcomed his grip as he propelled us farther onto the ice. If the town was close enough for me to use its light to see, then we were close enough for the guards to spot us. Adrian didn't have my visual handicap, of course. He drew me next to him while he moved with his usual breakneck speed, keeping us well inside the blackness while we ran parallel to the coast. By the time he slowed to a stop, I was gasp-

ing so hard that I was almost hyperventilating, and icy trails
had frozen on my cheeks from wind-induced tears.

"Be very quiet," he ordered. "We have to go back on the
island to reach the gateway."

I tried to squelch my noisy breaths by sucking in air through
my nose instead of my mouth. It only made me sound like a
winded horse instead of a winded human. Adrian rolled his
eyes, keeping low as he ran across the ice to the mainland.
Deciding that meant speed was more important than silence,
I followed him.

Light from nearby igloos meant I could see the figure that
strode toward Adrian when he reached land, the guard holding out his hand in the universal gesture for "stop."

"Hondal—" the minion began, but didn't finish the word.
Two short coughing sounds later, the guard dropped like a
stone. When I caught up to him, I glimpsed a gaping hole in
his forehead before his body dissolved into ashes. In an attempt
to cover the evidence of what had happened, I kicked at the
ashes, hoping they'd blow away before someone found them.

"Ivy!" Adrian hissed, waving his gun impatiently at me.

I dashed toward him, my thighs burning from running
while trying to stay low. A few minutes later, Adrian stopped.
I didn't see anything, but I braced myself when he clasped me
to him and then threw the three of us backward.

We tumbled through the gateway into our world, coming
out at the base of the split tree trunk. My relief at the embrace of warm temperatures was cut short when I saw how
dark it was.

"What?" I rasped. It still hurt to talk, damn him. "We've
only been in the realm two hours, and we entered it at noon!"

Adrian pulled me to my feet after adjusting his grip on
the boy. "Time moves differently there," he said, leading me
through the woods. "Sometimes faster, sometimes a lot slower.

Costa told me he and Tomas waited two days in the desert for us in Mexico."

Two days? That seemed impossible, but then again, so did everything associated with the realms—myself included. I'd shot someone in cold blood, and I didn't feel the slightest bit bad about it. In fact, it was the only memory I wanted to keep about the glittering, icy realm.

"Something's not right," Adrian muttered, his pace quickening. "That was easy. Only one guard stopped us, and I expected to kill at least half a dozen minions on our way out."

We were lucky, I almost said, and then I paused. We were *never* that lucky. I looked behind us, seeing nothing except trees and darkness, but that didn't mean we were alone.

"What's the plan?" I whispered.

"Get more guns," he replied grimly. "Now."

We ran past the now-closed Visitor's Center to the parking lot. Adrian's car was still in the back, and Costa stood next to it, an overhead streetlight revealing the automatic weapon he'd set on its roof. That wasn't what made Adrian stop, yanking me to a halt with him. It was the woman next to Costa, her arm almost casually draped over his shoulder, head cocked in apparent curiosity as she looked us over.

I recognized her at once. Those long, ebony-copper locks were unforgettable, not to mention that dazzlingly perfect face and the pale skin she was showing off in her low-cut dress. Full red lips drew back into a chilling smile as topaz eyes flicked over me, Adrian and the boy he held.

"So," the gorgeous demon from Mayhemium's realm said, her voice as sensual as her appearance. "Which of you three is the Davidian in disguise?"

chapter twenty-two

"I am," Adrian stated.

My gaze swung to him in disbelief. Adrian flashed the demon a hard little grin as he let the boy slide from his grip, stepping away from him once he slumped on the ground.

"No, he's not," I snapped hoarsely. I was going to tear Adrian a new one later for choking me, but no way was he sacrificing himself now. "*I'm* the Davidian!"

The demon's gaze gleamed as she looked between Adrian and me, seeing nothing except an old man and an unfamiliar young one due to our Archon glamour.

"Who's a noble liar, and who's the would-be savior?" she mused aloud.

"I'm not a liar," Adrian ground out as if offended.

"You lie your ass off all the time!" I countered, words coming easier due to my anger. "Here's a surefire 'Who's the girl?' test—give him to the count of three to name a brand of tampons."

Adrian shot me a furious, if disbelieving, look. The demon

laughed throatily, her features softening into something that resembled affection when she looked at Adrian. Then they turned flinty as she looked at me.

"Ivy, isn't it?"

Her accent held the harshly musical cadence that denoted her first language as Demonish. I hated hearing that accent from anyone except Adrian, and I put all my revulsion toward her kind into my gaze as I stared back at her.

"Ivy," I repeated, wondering if I could shoot her before she hurt Costa. "So unpleasant to meet you."

Bloodred nails dug into Costa's shoulder. He let out a yelp, which only caused the demon to jab them in deeper.

"Don't, Obsidiana," Adrian said quietly.

I was wondering where I'd heard that name when the demon inclined her head. "Give me what I want, and I'll release him."

"You know I can't," Adrian said, still in that low, resonant voice.

Obsidiana managed to make an evil chuckle sound sexy. "Oh, but you can, my love."

My love? I almost got whiplash from how fast I looked at Adrian. "You *didn't* tap a demon," I gasped out.

The way his expression closed off said that he had, and a lot. *Now* I remembered where I'd heard her name! Demetrius had said that Obsidiana missed him when he'd urged Adrian to come back home. From the way Adrian had stopped dead when we ran into her in Mayhemium's realm, part of him had missed her, too.

I could guess which part, and it was all I could do not to kick it. "*Me* you keep pushing away, but a demoness is good enough for you?" My glare was withering. "Nice."

"With how plain Demetrius said you were beneath that disguise, I'm not surprised" was Obsidiana's smug response.

Hey, I'd been hot as a glamoured blonde! Besides… "Beauty fades, but Evil Bitch is forever," I snapped.

Obsidiana flung Costa to the ground. Adrian grabbed her before she reached me, his arm like a vise around her neck.

She stilled at once, her topaz gaze sliding up to look at him. "You would harm me? Over her?"

She actually sounded surprised, and I'd heard people refer to feces with more respect than the way she said "her." I told myself it wasn't jealousy or spite that made me hope he ripped her head off. She was evil.

"I can't let you hurt her," Adrian said grimly.

Obsidiana seemed to sag in his arms. "When I heard someone had killed two of my people, I knew you'd come to my realm. That's why I came alone to see you." Her voice deepened with apparent distress. "It wasn't even to capture the Davidian! I thought if you would finally speak to me, you'd let go of your anger. Does nothing matter to you except this fruitless quest for revenge? Don't you love me at all anymore, *benhoven?*"

"Does this answer your question?" Adrian's arm whipped back, snapping her neck with an audible sound. If she were a minion, she'd start turning into ashes, but all she did was go limp. I glanced away when he ripped something pulpy out of her throat. I hated Obsidiana, but my gross quota had already been exceeded today.

"Why do you do that?" I asked, busying myself by helping the boy up.

"Keeps them out longer," he replied, dumping Obsidiana's limp form in the grass. "Demon physiology is different. Their version of a heart is in their neck."

The vindictive glow I felt was *not* because he'd metaphorically ripped Obsidiana's heart out, I assured myself. It was because now we had more time to get away.

"Costa, are you okay?" Adrian asked, striding over to him.

A groan was his response. Adrian lifted him up, depositing Costa in the passenger seat. Then he cranked the driver's seat forward so I could climb in behind it.

"Is he okay?" I asked, half lifting the boy to the car.

"Just a concussion. A little manna, and he'll be fine," Adrian said. It didn't escape me that he sounded pissed, as if he had a right to be. When we were all loaded into the car and driving away, he started in on me.

"Why did you bait Obsidiana?" Adrian demanded. "Were you *trying* to give her more reasons to kill you?"

What was I going to say? That I'd been so insulted over the bitch's comments and learning about their past relationship that I'd almost forgotten my life was in danger? Ah, noooo. That was too stupid. And humiliating.

"I did it *to* bait her," I said, widening my eyes for increased innocent effect. "I was trying to get her to charge me so she'd let Costa go!"

Adrian's stare said he wasn't buying it. Time for another tactic. I tossed my hair, letting out a scornful laugh. "You really think I care that you used to get it on with her, or anything else I said? *Please.*"

Costa muttered something in Greek as he pressed a handful of manna to the gash on the back of his head. Whatever it was, Adrian let out a snort of agreement. When he looked at me, his expression was less stern, but no less intense.

"Unlike me, you're a terrible liar, but since we didn't have a better plan, I'm glad what you did worked."

Did that mean he believed I'd been faking jealousy? Or did it mean he knew I was lying now? Asking would only show how much I cared, so I focused on the boy. He was slumped in his seat, most of his body tucked into the parka except his feet. He still wasn't reacting to anything going on around him.

Was it shock, or did he have something physically wrong that we couldn't see?

"We should take him to a hospital," I stated.

"That'll do more harm than good," Adrian said, with a sardonic glance back at me. "Remember being told you were crazy your whole life? What do you think they'll tell him, once he starts talking about demons, minions and different worlds?"

I winced. "True, but he needs the kind of help we can't give him while we're looking for the weapon. Besides, he might have family that's worried sick about him."

"Next time we see Zach, I'll ask him," Adrian said, his tone roughening. "He always knows about kids' families."

I tried not to let that statement affect me, but it did. *Your real mother didn't leave you because she was running from the police,* Zach's voice whispered across my mind as if he were here. *She did it to save you, just like your dream revealed....*

I forced those thoughts back. One monumental crisis at a time, thank you. Until I found this weapon, it didn't matter why my birth mother had left me beside that freeway. If I was the last Davidian, then whatever her reasons, she was dead. Gone forever, just like my adoptive parents I hadn't even been able to say goodbye to because that detective tried to kill me before I could give them a proper burial....

"Ivy." Adrian's tone was urgent. "What's wrong?"

I swiped under my eyes, only now realizing that I'd started to cry. "Nothing."

"Bullshit," he said emphatically.

"Just a little post-traumatic stress." I forced a shaky laugh. "I'm still not used to narrowly escaping death, okay?"

His gaze repeated the same thing—bullshit. Okay, so maybe I *was* a terrible liar. I pretended not to notice him staring at me as much as he could without wrecking, and busied myself by tucking the boy's feet under my legs so they'd be warm.

Then an idea struck me, exciting me so much that I reached over the seats to grab Adrian's shoulder.

"Drive to Bennington! We snuck the boy out with our disguises, so we can use them to get Jasmine out, too!"

Costa gave me a pitying glance, and I felt as well as heard Adrian's sigh.

"Remember I told you that your sister will be the best-treated human in all the realms? She'll also be the most guarded. Bennington might not be Demetrius's main realm, but he'll expect you to try that. I guarantee he's given an order that if anyone unfamiliar shows up, they're to be detained."

My brief hope crashed. Adrian was right. The demons had no intention of making this easy on me, so either I went in with the ability to kill them all, or I died.

Or both. No one had said that, but no one needed to. Having the weapon didn't mean I'd suddenly be bulletproof, so finding it didn't guarantee victory. It only gave me a chance at it.

"You're going to be okay," I told the boy, giving him the assurance I so badly wished someone could give to me.

A slow blink was his only response. Either he still wasn't processing what was going on, or he didn't believe me. I patted his leg, wishing I could tell him I knew how it felt to be surrounded by people and yet still be on your own.

I couldn't fix that for myself, but I could fix it for him. Then I'd keep trying to save Jasmine while trying not to get killed by demons, and maybe somewhere along the lines, reclaim my own life, too.

Dreams were beautiful things to have, weren't they?

chapter twenty-three

We left North Carolina and drove to a Catholic seminary in Washington, D.C. Adrian knew two of the priests who met us around the back of the large church complex, which was Surprise One. Surprise Two was him telling them that the boy had been rescued from a demon realm. The priests didn't accuse Adrian of being crazy, either. Instead, one of them hurried to take the boy back into what they called the "house" section.

"Are demon realms an open secret to priests?" I whispered to Costa while Adrian continued to talk to the other priest.

Costa grunted. "No. These two know about them because Adrian saved them from a demon kidnapping a few years ago."

I don't know why that surprised me. It was how we'd met, and Adrian had said he'd been "retrieving" people for Zach for a while. Guess I never expected to meet anyone he'd rescued, let alone find out that they were priests.

I was too tired to swap rescue experiences with the two Fathers, which was why I was relieved when Adrian came back to tell us that the seminary had rooms for us tonight, too. Even more wonderful than that, it had leftover pizza and a microwave. I devoured several pieces, then showered and flopped onto the narrow bed in a room that reminded me a lot of my college dorm. Just with a lot more crosses and pictures of saints and popes.

I was almost asleep when my door opened. No locks meant relying on the honor system, but since Adrian hadn't knocked, he must not be in an honorable mood. Situation normal, then.

"What are you doing here?" I demanded wearily.

He'd showered, too, the dampness making his hair look darker than its usual honeyed shades of blond. I refused to notice how that same dampness caused his shirt to cling to him. I was still too mad.

He shut the door behind him. "I'm sorry for hurting you," he said, actually managing to sound as though he meant it.

Which time? I thought, but touched my throat as if the bruises there were the only damage he'd inflicted on me today.

"Did you know choking me would work to activate my abilities?" I asked, my tone grating. "Or was it a lucky guess?"

His stare reminded me of ancient sailors' legends of sea serpents. On the surface, all I saw was roiling blue, but every so often, glimpses of the monster appeared beneath.

"Demetrius wanted me to be the strongest Judian ever, so he did whatever was necessary to hone my abilities. Like throwing me into the gladiator rings at thirteen. Lesser demons fought there, too, and if a ruler wanted to show off, he or she jumped into the fight. Demetrius didn't let anyone kill me, but he let them beat me within an inch of my life enough times that I learned what he wanted me to know—the fastest, most efficient way to use my abilities. So, no, I wasn't guessing. I was counting on you being just like me in that regard.

I hated hurting you, but it was the only way you could search the castle without getting caught with the boy."

Since the minions' ashes must've been discovered right away for Obsidiana to beat us back to our realm, he was right. We would've gotten caught taking the boy with us to search the castle. If I'd known him throttling me would make my powers flare that way, I would've demanded that he do it. I'd take bruises any day over abandoning a child to a demon realm.

"And Obsidiana?" I hated that I couldn't stop myself from asking, so I tried to hide my motivation behind a fake laugh. "Now I know why you stopped in your tracks when you saw her in Mayhemium's realm. Must've been weird to run into your old girlfriend, but you should've told me who she was. It's not fair to keep finding out from other demons where they used to rank in your life."

His jaw clenched, and I thought he'd leave as he'd done so many times before. Instead, he began to pace.

"I stopped in my tracks that day because I was worried that Obsidiana would sense who I was through my disguise. Demetrius always can, and if she had, she would've realized who you were, too. As for why I didn't tell you about her, it's because she means nothing to me. The whole time we were together, she lied to me just like the rest of them did."

"About what?" *Your supposed destiny?* I thought but didn't say out loud.

He gave me a measured look. "Tomas told you what it was like for me in the realms before I walked out."

"Girls, gold, power, adulation…" I forced another insincere laugh. "Your basic hedonistic fantasy."

"He didn't tell you why I hated Archons back then. My earliest memory was of them trying to kill my mother and me."

"What?" I gasped.

His mouth twisted. "Judas's descendants are a threat to Archons, so eliminating the line means eliminating the threat. Throughout history, demons have tried to do the same to David's descendants. They nearly succeeded several times, most recently with the Holocaust."

"I'm Jewish?" That should've occurred to me before....

"Possibly. David's line started out that way, but over thousands of years, beliefs changed, even if genealogy didn't."

"Back to Archons trying to kill you," I said, filing the other away under Future Musings.

Those beautiful features hardened. "All my life, I've had nightmares about my mother and me being chased through the tunnels. My mom said I was remembering when I was five and Demetrius saved us from Archons trying to eliminate the Judian line. I was brought up believing we were only safe in their realms. Since the demons gave us everything we wanted, it took a long time before I even asked to see the world we'd come from."

"But when you did, how could you go back?" I said, voicing the question that had been eating at me. "You would've seen how evil the demon realms were by comparison."

His jaw tightened. "They thought of that, so they hid the uglier aspects from me for as long as they could. After I discovered them, they took me to places in the human world that looked the same. Like Darfur, where hundreds of thousands of people have been slaughtered while the world gives a collective shrug. Or South African diamond mines, where laborers are regularly worked to death, or all the countries with unchecked human trafficking, and of course, the countless sweat shops around the world." His sigh was bitter. "Seeing those things made it easier to believe what the demons taught me—that the only difference between them and humanity was more opportunity."

"Bullshit," I said at once. "Yes, atrocities exist here, too, but so do people who try to fight them. For every horrible example you gave, you can find a thousand more of people helping other people, even from several continents away."

Adrian's expression softened. "I know. When I started sneaking out to explore on my own, I saw that, too. The first time I encountered children at a playground, I watched for hours." Brief smile. "Someone called the cops, but that made an impression, too. Strangers came to protect the young of other strangers. I'd never seen that before, and for the first time, I understood what I'd become. A monster."

"Is that when you left?" I asked softly.

He threw me a jaded look. "That's when my drug addiction began. I couldn't leave because I was afraid the demons would retaliate against my mother, and she said she'd never leave while Archons were after us. So instead, I escaped through every mind-altering substance I could find. Of course, I couldn't snort enough, shoot up enough or smoke enough to forget all I'd done. I thought my bloodline kept me from overdosing, but after what Demetrius said the other week, it might've been him. I wanted to die, though. That's why I kept sneaking out of the realms, hoping Archons would find me. One night, I got my wish."

"What happened?"

His smile was jagged. "I was puking in an alley behind a bar when light suddenly exploded all around me. You've seen what Zach looks like when he shows his true nature, so I knew what he was. He said, 'If you're ready, come with me.' I thought he meant ready for death, so I did. He didn't kill me, though. He took me to the old Shanghai tunnels in Portland."

"Why?"

His expression became haunted. "My dream was always the same—Mom and I were running through the tunnels, trying to get away from the monsters. She was screaming at them to leave me alone, and I was so tired, but I kept going because she was terrified. We were almost at the end when a black cloud swallowed her. At the same time, the exit got really bright and a voice told me to keep running. Then my mom came out of the cloud, picked me up…and that's when I'd wake up."

He paused, his mouth curling down. "That night, in the same tunnels, Zach showed me what really happened."

After I'd seen what Demetrius could do, I'd already guessed, but it still made me ache to hear Adrian say it.

"What came out of the darkness that day was Demetrius, not my mom. He'd killed her, but he used her appearance to trick me into staying in the realms while he molded me into someone who hated Archons as much as demons did. I didn't think to question why I never saw my mom and Demetrius in the same room, and everyone played along, pretending he was my mother when they knew she was dead. All so when I met the last Davidian, I wouldn't hesitate to fulfill my destiny and betray him." He met my eyes. "Or her, as it turns out."

My throat felt tight, both from unshed tears at the merciless manipulations Adrian had been put through back then, and the pain he still carried now. No wonder he'd reacted with such horror when Zach told him who I was. I was the destiny he'd been groomed for, and then rebelled against by turning his back on the creatures that raised him.

Well, I didn't believe in destiny. Fate couldn't override free will, and just because Adrian's ancestors were betrayers didn't mean he was doomed to be. He'd already had several opportunities to hand me over to the demons, yet instead, he'd fought them with all the power they'd assumed would be to their benefit. No matter what anyone thought, his choices determined his destiny, not the other way around.

Now to convince Adrian of that.

"If your fate was already sealed, Demetrius wouldn't have

worked so hard to mold you into a monster." My voice was raspy from all the emotion I held back. "He must know your destiny is still up to you. Same with Zach. He helped you back then, and he keeps looking out for you now—"

Adrian's laugh stopped me. For a moment, it sounded so ugly, it could've come from a demon.

"Zach showed me *everything* that happened in the tunnel that day." Something sharper than pain edged his tone. "He was the light I saw at the exit. Ever since, I've wondered if Zach could've stopped Demetrius from taking me if he'd wanted to. That night at the Mexican sanctuary, when Zach decimated Demetrius's shadows in seconds, I finally got my answer."

Shock made me stammer. "But that…that's…"

"Indifferent at best, cruel at worst?" Adrian supplied with another ragged laugh. "I know, but Zach'll say he was only following orders, so that means his boss doesn't want me to beat my fate. No, I'm supposed to play my part like a good little Judas, but screw them. Once Demetrius is dead, I'm gone, both from your life and theirs. It's the only way I can pay them back for what they allowed Demetrius to do to me."

I didn't know what to say. Everything he'd been through was made more awful by the knowledge that it had all been preventable. Zach should've stopped Demetrius, with or without "orders." He also should be supporting Adrian now, not telling him to resign himself to a fate he clearly didn't want. Couldn't they see how hard Adrian was trying? Didn't they even care?

If they didn't, I did. I might not be able to do anything about their former betrayals, but I wasn't helpless. I got out of bed and took Adrian's hand, tightening my grip when he tried to pull away.

"You're right," I said huskily. "We'll find the weapon, use it to save Jasmine *and* kill Demetrius, then we'll walk away from each other. Both sides can choke on their expectations of your fate. They don't know how strong you are, but I do, and I trust you, Adrian."

He jerked his hand away. "Ivy, don't—"

"I trust you," I repeated, gripping his shirt so he either had to stand still or risk me ripping it off. "There's no danger of you betraying me while we're working to get this weapon. I can always trust your hatred of demons, remember?"

Some of the tension eased from his shoulders as I used his own argument to make my point. "Yeah, but you still don't understand your full part in this—"

"I do," I interrupted grimly. "Tomas and Costa said that only a Davidian or a demon from Goliath's line can bring out the weapon's true power, which means I have to be the one to use the slingshot, and I'm not even that good with a gun."

He stared at me, emotions flickering across his face too rapidly for me to translate. Then his jaw flexed, and his expression hardened into one I recognized well.

Pure, unadulterated determination.

"I'll teach you how to use a slingshot," he said, his voice rougher. "With practice, you can do anything."

"Then we have a plan," I agreed, smiling because I had another plan. One that involved showing Adrian he didn't have to walk away from me when this was all over, but for now, I'd keep that to myself.

Demetrius had said the bond between us would grow every moment that we spent together. Demons were liars, but my heart knew *that* much was true. Already, I cared about Adrian more than I'd cared about any other guy, and he'd admitted that he was powerfully drawn to me, too. By the time we'd found the weapon, killed Demetrius and rescued Jasmine, I intended to convince Adrian that he wasn't doomed to betray me. Everyone else might have given up on him, but I hadn't, and I'd use every bit of our supernatural bond to show him he shouldn't give up, either.

Now to break down the wall he'd erected around himself, one stubborn brick at a time.

chapter twenty-four

Adrian was right. Zach didn't even need to look at the boy before he told us that his name was Hoyt, and his family was dead. I was a little skeptical, but Adrian believed Zach. When I asked him why, he reminded me that Zach had told Adrian the exact time and place that minions would attempt to kidnap me. How Zach knew these things, I still didn't know, but according to Adrian, the Archon had never been wrong.

It was all I could do not to ask if Zach had taken the day off when my sister was kidnapped. I didn't because I'd bet Zach's response would contain the word "orders," and I didn't trust my reaction to that. Until I had the weapon, I needed Zach, plus punching him in the face might be the last mistake I ever made. In this case, ignorance wasn't bliss. It was necessity.

Costa was taking Hoyt to Tomas's family in Phoenix. They'd agreed to shelter the boy, and the long drive would give Costa a chance to share his own realm experience. Hoyt still wasn't speaking, but I held out hope that, with time, he'd be able to recover mentally, physically and emotionally.

I had to believe that, for Hoyt's sake, and for Jasmine's.

This time, Zach glamoured me into looking like a young guy with shiny, cloud-rolling eyes. Having both Adrian and I pose as minions came from our being zero for two on finding the weapon, and two for two on getting caught. Not an auspicious start, but if at first you don't succeed and demons haven't killed you…well, trying again was a given.

Collinsville, Illinois, was the proud owner of the world's largest ketchup bottle. It was also home to over a hundred man-made earthen mounds. Such quaint distinctions should've meant the city wasn't a hotbed of demonic activity, but guess again. Tourists visiting the Cahokia Mounds only saw lots of little green hills and one big one amidst a tranquil park, but I saw a bustling populace in a dark, glacial world where the little mounds were a lot bigger, and the big one was a gargantuan pyramid.

"I gotta ask," I said, following Adrian to the realm gateway, "what's with demons and pyramids?"

"Ego," he replied succinctly. At my raised brow, he elaborated. "The first demons were Archons who rebelled against their boss because they wanted to be masters instead of servants. After they were sent to the dark realms as punishment, they built their kingdoms there, using force to get the worship they craved. Pyramids, castles, towers…they're the demonic version of bling, so whoever has the biggest and best wins."

"And they realm-snatch from each other to get more." I nodded as if it made perfect sense.

The look Adrian gave me made me wonder if I'd missed something important. "Not just from each other. Every chance they get, they absorb more of our world into theirs."

"You never mentioned how," I reminded him.

A shrug. "If you believe in M theory, they do it by manipulating gravity to force contact between two dimensional layers, creating a new interdimensional bubble."

He sounded like a physicist. "Laymen's terms, please."

"When a vacuum gets switched on, it sucks whatever's closest into a lint bag, right? When they get enough power, demons use gravity like a vacuum's On switch to activate an area's natural geographic instability, crashing one multiverse into its reflective duplicate. Once the gravitational layer restabilizes—in essence, the vacuum getting turned off—everything in the new lint-bag realm is trapped."

"So gateways are like the hose that runs from the sweeper to the lint bag," I mused, adding, "Why do you always grab me when we go through them? Couldn't I make it through myself?"

A smile ghosted across his lips. "Try it," he said, gesturing to an empty space to his right.

I gave it a doubtful look. "Nothing's there. All the other realm gateways had markers."

"All the others?" He snorted. "You've only seen two. More than half the gateways aren't marked, Ivy. That's why they're so hard to find unless you can feel them."

I didn't feel anything, and all I saw next to Adrian was air and grass. "You're sure it's there?"

Another snort. "Even if I hadn't been through this one before, I'd still be sure. Think you could *not* notice jamming your finger into a light socket? That's what gateways feel like to me."

Wow, my abilities must be weak. I had to concentrate like a fiend to sense a hint of something hallowed, and Adrian felt dark objects like they were electric shocks. Then again, he'd had years to hone his abilities. I'd just found out about mine less than a month ago.

I squared my shoulders. Time to exercise some supernatural muscle! I focused on the space Adrian indicated, and then flung myself forward like I was diving into a pool.

Face-plant. Ow, ow, ow!

Adrian's chuckle penetrated the part of me that wasn't seeing cartoon birdies fly over me in circles. My body vibrated from the impact, and I now knew that dry grass tasted like uncooked spaghetti with dirt sauce.

"Not funny," I groaned.

He knelt next to me, still chuckling as he offered me a hand up. "If you saw the air you caught before you hit the ground, you'd disagree."

I flipped over, glaring as I swatted his hand away. "Payback's a bitch. Remember that."

"I'm trembling."

He pulled me to my feet. Even as I swore revenge, part of me savored his unfettered amusement. Adrian rarely laughed unless it was in derision, bitterness or challenge. Seeing him do it with only mischief tingeing his features was like seeing a diamond in the sunlight versus glimpsing it in shadows.

I shouldn't, but I stared anyway. No wonder Obsidiana had wanted him back enough to risk coming after him alone. I hated the hell-bitch, but I couldn't fault her for her taste.

Adrian's laughter died away, and he glanced at our hands, as if just realizing that he still held mine. Our eyes locked, and his words from before replayed in my mind.

I've wanted you since the first time you touched me…. Nothing but dark magic had ever felt so powerful, and when I touch you, it's a thousand times worse….

My grip started to tighten, but he pulled away, a familiar hardness turning his expression into an impenetrable mask. His gaze flared, though, and his hands clenched into fists as he drew in a harsh breath. His expression might be statue-like, but in those seething sapphire eyes, I caught a glimpse of the wildness he held back, and it made me shiver.

If Adrian ever freed the part of him that wanted me, would I be able to stand it? Or would I love every second of being overcome? Only concern for my sister kept me from testing both of us by throwing myself into his arms and forcing him to feel what he kept telling himself he couldn't have.

His muscles bunched, as if on a primal level he sensed the reckless passion growing in me. Maybe he did. Maybe it was more than our bond that made me throb in places he'd never touched, as though demanding to feel his hands, his mouth, on me there.

Adrian spun around, his coat unable to hide how his whole body had suddenly tensed, as if he'd been zapped with the electric shock he'd alluded to before.

"Let's go," he said hoarsely. "Places to be, minions to kill."

My hands trembled as I drew on my thick winter parka and gloves. I already had on the insulated pants and boots.

"First, tell me why I can't get through the gateways on my own," I asked, stalling so I'd get a second to compose myself.

He half turned to show a smile like uncut crystal—beautiful, yet jagged around the edges. "Same reason as everything else— bloodlines. You need minion, demon or Judian blood to cross through the barriers that lead to the dark worlds. You don't have that, so by wrapping myself around you, I'm essentially covering you with my blood to get you through."

That explained so much. No wonder demons didn't bother to station guards at every gateway. Even if the humans they captured managed to navigate the pitch-blackness to find them, they couldn't cross through them to get back to their world. Once in a realm, they were hopelessly trapped.

My jaw tightened. Not Jasmine. As soon as I found that

weapon, I was coming for her, and with Adrian's help, she *would* see the sun again.

"I'm ready," I said, my tone now only slightly breathy.

He didn't look at me when he pulled me to him and then dropped us into the gateway I hadn't been able to see, let alone penetrate. As soon as we finished tumbling through the invisible membrane linking our realms, he let me go. I blinked, my eyes adjusting to the darkness that seemed to seep inside my soul, chasing away my desire while hardening me with purpose. If the weapon was here, Jasmine's awful captivity would be over. All I had to do was stay strong, focus and find it.

Light from the town reflected off the icy ground, adding an eerie, faint luminescence that kept me from being totally blind. Still, it was dark enough that I couldn't see Adrian's face. Only the bulk of his large body next to me. The tall silhouettes around us must have been trees, frozen into place from the cold. I couldn't see more than the widest part of their outlines; their branches, if they had any, were invisible against the darkness that hovered above us like a malevolent spirit.

Adrian leaned down, his warm breath in stark contrast to our frozen surroundings as he spoke near my ear.

"Anyone stops us, let me do the talking."

Since I didn't speak Demonish, I'd already planned on that. I was about to tell him the same when his whole body froze with such suddenness, it was as if he'd been transformed into stone.

"Ivy, don't move," he whispered in a low, vehement voice.

I tried to will every part of me to similar stillness, but I couldn't stop my eyes from darting around or my chest from rising as my heart sped up and my lungs responded with a demand for more oxygen. What was out here that was so dangerous, Adrian was playing statue instead of reaching for his gun?

My answer was a hissing sort of growl that raised every hair on the back of my neck. It sounded like a feral wolf that had just found a meal, and somewhere to my left, an answering, howling hiss shattered the dark in answer.

"Adrian," I whispered, terror skittering through me.

Fast as lightning, he was behind me, his arms like twin bands around me. "Close your eyes," he ordered, his voice barely audible. "It can't hurt you if you don't move."

I slammed my eyes shut. I'd seen people butchered plus demons transform into deadly clouds and crows, but if Adrian didn't think I could handle whatever this was, I'd believe him. The growls came closer, and with a sudden vibration in the ground, I felt something big land right in front of me. Reeking breath came in pants that hit my face like light slaps. I fought a fresh surge of panic as I realized I was standing, yet the creature was still eye level with me. What *was* it?

Its hiss turned guttural before I felt something slimy and wet flick across my face with the quickness of a snake's tongue. Fear-driven revulsion would've made me immediately swipe at the spot if not for Adrian's warning.

It can't hurt you if you don't move.

I didn't know how that could be true. The thing had licked me; it *knew* I was here! Not a muscle on Adrian twitched, though, and after that disgusting lick, the creature didn't do anything except wheeze in that weird, hissing way. I mimicked Adrian's stillness, keeping my eyes shut and willing my breaths to be soft and shallow. Then a new, ominous vibration shook the ground. Another creature had landed right behind us.

More reeking breath filled the air with the stench of old garbage and rotted fish. A hissing snarl blasted out, loud as a trumpet and so terrifying, my knees felt like they turned to Jell-O. Only Adrian's grip kept me standing perfectly still as something massive bumped my body, like a shark testing its prey. I squeezed my lids tighter, fighting a near-overwhelming urge to go for my gun. I felt beyond helpless, beyond vulnerable. If Adrian's arms hadn't been wrapped around me, a tangible reminder that I wasn't facing this alone, I might have started shaking.

Then a roar blasted in front of my face, so loud it seemed to reverberate inside me. My heart pounded as something sharp grazed the top of my head, parting my hair with multiple hard points. I didn't need to open my eyes to know what it was. The creature's gigantic fangs. My guts twisted with terror and resignation. One snap of those jaws, and it would all be over.

It can't hurt you if you don't move!

I couldn't tell how long I frantically repeated Adrian's promise, but the fangs on my head eventually vanished. Then, with two sets of vibrating thumps, the space around us felt less oppressive and I knew the huge, hulking beasts had gone. I still didn't move or open my eyes, though. Not until Adrian lifted me up, ran, and I felt us tumbling through the gateway back into the light and warmth of Collinsville, Illinois.

Grass hit me in the face from our hard landing, but I didn't care. Instead of standing up, I started to swipe at my cheek hard enough to bruise, and still it felt like the slime from the creature's tongue remained. I wanted to wash my skin with scalding water, but I couldn't. All I could do was keep rubbing my face with my gloved hands.

"What were those things?" I whispered, still too traumatized to speak in a normal tone.

Adrian knelt and grasped my wrists, forcing me to stop my rough grooming. His face had shiny trails on it, too, showing I hadn't been the only one the creatures had licked.

"Hounds," he said evenly, "which means we have a problem."

I started to laugh. Not the exhilarated, yay-I'm-alive kind, like when I'd survived Demetrius's first attack, but wild cackles that hovered between derangement and despair.

"A problem? You *don't* say," I gasped out. "I thought huge demonic dogs would only be a minor nuisance."

Adrian smoothed the hair out of my face, his hand lingering to cup my chin.

"'Hound' is a nickname. They're not dogs. They're ancient reptiles the demons selectively bred until they made the most vicious thing on four legs. Can't see, taste or smell for shit, though, which is why you're safe if you don't move. If you do, they're trained to tear you to pieces."

I stopped laughing, but that didn't mean I felt more stable. "I vote we skip this realm and only search ones without demonic, man-eating reptiles."

"It's not that simple," he said, still in that infuriatingly calm tone. "They weren't supposed to be there, so the demons must be amping up their security. They know you've searched two realms for the weapon, Ivy. Looks like they're trying to stop you from searching a third."

The suck never seemed to end. "But now that we know they're there, can't we just bring bigger weapons and kill them?"

"Hounds are almost as difficult to kill as demons," Adrian responded, a hint of grimness making me wonder if he spoke from experience. "Plus, they're cold-blooded, so they have to keep returning to their handlers to warm up, which means it wouldn't take long for one of them to be missed."

Crawling into the world's largest ketchup bottle and not coming out was starting to sound like a great idea. "Now what?"

He gave me a level look. "Now we talk to Zach."

chapter twenty-five

We used most of our remaining Archon-glamoured sticky notes for gas money to return to Costa's house in Miami. Once there, we waited. And waited.

By the fourth day, Zach was still a no-show despite Adrian repeatedly trying to reach him. I tried, too, mostly by folding my hands, glaring upward and thinking multiple variations of *Where are you, Zach? I know you can hear us!*

Costa wasn't around, either. At least he'd called, saying he was staying a few more days with Hoyt at Tomas's family's house. With no one actively trying to kill me and our realm-searching put on hold, I had nothing to do except brood. I couldn't even enjoy the sunny warmth of South Florida. If I wasn't feeling guilty over Jasmine languishing in her captivity, I was being tormented in another way.

For the past three nights, I'd fallen asleep listening to Adrian pace. He spent his days in the outdoor carport, claiming that he needed to work on his car. Bullshit. The Challenger was in mint condition, and he could only wax and detail it so many times before it was obvious that he was just avoiding me.

Tonight, I was finding out why.

I got out of bed, hearing his pacing come to an abrupt halt when I opened my door. Too bad. I was done playing the avoidance game. He wasn't, though. By the time I came downstairs, he was nowhere to be seen and his bedroom door was shut.

Quietly, I went to his door and tried the knob. Locked. My mouth curled. He was the one who'd taught me not to give up that easily when something needed to be done.

I grabbed the car keys he'd left on the counter and went out the front door. I'd barely slid them into the Challenger's ignition when Adrian came flying out of the house after me.

"Where do you think you're going?" he demanded, yanking open the passenger door after he tried mine and couldn't get in. I waited until he'd shut it, then I hit the lock button.

The sound was like a gun going off in the sudden quiet. Adrian stared at me, knowing better than anyone that he was now trapped. He was the one who'd rigged the Challenger so that the only exit was through the driver's side when the doors were locked.

"I'm not going anywhere," I said evenly, "and neither are you until we have a little talk."

"What are you doing, Ivy?" he asked, his voice very low.

"Ending our stalemate," I responded, leaning back into the leather seat. "For the first few days, I thought you were avoiding me because I'd done something wrong. Then I realized it wasn't my fault, so now I want to know why."

He looked away. "I haven't been avoiding—"

"Ooh, lies, looks like we'll be here awhile," I mocked. "Seriously, Adrian, Costa's house is on hallowed ground and it doesn't contain a single mirror, so I'm totally safe. Yet aside from getting groceries the first day, you haven't left once. If you can't stand to be in the same room with me, why is it that you can't stand to leave me alone here, either?"

His hands slowly closed into fists. "Let me out, Ivy. Now."

"Not until you give me a straight answer," I countered.

He looked at me, anger sharpening the gorgeous lines and hollows of his face. "I'm warning you, don't push me."

"Or what?" I flared. "You have nothing to threaten me with! The only reason I can stand to keep going is because I don't have anything to lose, so pushing you doesn't scare me—"

I didn't see his hands flash out, but suddenly, they were in my hair as he yanked me to him, his mouth scorching mine. I gasped in shock, and his tongue slid past my lips, claiming mine with a passionate desperation that sent heat rocketing through me.

My shock vanished. So did my questions. Desire hijacked my emotions, leaving nothing except a surge of blistering need. I kissed Adrian back, opening my mouth in a silent demand for more. Hints of alcohol flavored his kiss, but beneath that was his taste, infinitely more intoxicating, and I responded as if it was my drug of choice. I moaned as my head tilted back from the force of his kiss. Then he pulled me across the seats until I was on top of him, his strong grip molding me against every muscled inch of his body.

"This is why I stayed away," he growled against my mouth as his hands started to rove over me with knowing, ruthless passion. "Can't be near you without wanting you. Can't stop myself anymore—"

His words cut off as his kiss deepened, until I could hardly breathe from the erotic thrusts and delves of his tongue. I'd been kissed before, but never like this. He wasn't exploring my mouth. He was claiming it.

And I couldn't get enough. All the feelings I'd had to fake with other boyfriends came roaring through my senses, shocking me with their intensity. My heart pounded while my body felt hypersensitive, making each brush of his skin, lips and tongue dangerously erotic. I needed more of his kiss despite barely being able to breathe. More of his hands moving over me with sensual urgency, and more of the hard, muscled body I could feel but not touch because of how tightly Adrian held me against him.

I moaned when his lips slid down to a spot on my neck that made every nerve ending jump with exquisite anticipation. They jumped again when he pushed up the back of my pajama top, his hands now roaming over flesh instead of fabric. Everywhere he touched seemed to burn with a need so intense, it left me aching, and when he sucked on my neck, a blast of pleasure reverberated straight down to the throb between my legs.

"All I think about is you. Every day, every minute…you," he muttered hotly.

I was so lost in sensation, the words barely penetrated, especially when his mouth slanted over mine with carnal hunger. Before, my hands had been trapped against his chest, but I forced them free, gripping his head while I kissed him back. His mouth was addictive, and the sinuous flicks of his tongue had me arching against him in wordless, primal need. Desperate to feel him the way I'd secretly fantasized, my hands left his head to slide down his body. Our cramped space limited my exploration to his shoulders, arms and sides, but I wanted to touch him so badly, I didn't care. Muscles bunched and flexed as he reacted to the feel of my hands on him. His body was so hard, but his skin was sleek and smooth, as if someone had stretched heavy silk over stone. Touching him while he kissed me made my mind reel from desire, and when my hand grazed his taut, flat stomach, a tremor went through his whole body.

He broke our kiss to pull my pajama top over my head, groaning as he flung it aside.

"You're so beautiful, Ivy."

His hands on my bare breasts ripped a cry from me. My skin felt too tight, too sensitive, and when his mouth closed over a nipple, the pleasure was so intense, it was almost painful. I gripped his head without thinking, my gasps turning into groans that caused him to hold me tighter. His mouth was a brand that seared those unbelievable sensations all through me, making my whole body feel fevered. Every part of me ached for him, but when his hand slipped inside my pajama pants, I couldn't stop myself from tensing even as I cried out at the jolt of pleasure.

His mouth immediately left my breast and his large hand slid up to thread through my hair instead.

"What's wrong?"

Adrian's eyes were darker with passion, making their silver rims more startling, but it was the barely leashed wildness they contained that caused the words to stick in my throat.

"I, ahem… Before we… Ah, I need to tell you something."

I could actually see the moment he guessed what I was having trouble articulating. His eyes widened, and his hands ceased the sensual way they'd been running through my hair.

"You've never had sex before."

A statement, not a question. I still had on my pajama pants, but suddenly, I'd never felt more exposed. My arms crossed over my chest, and for the first time, I was glad I didn't have D-cups because they covered everything.

"Yeah," I mumbled. "Sorry."

"Don't." Adrian's sigh was ragged. "Don't ever apologize for being who you are. You're perfect, and I'm the one who's sorry. Touching you made me forget all the reasons why I have to stay away from you."

That was the last thing I wanted to hear. Frustration rose, covering my previous embarrassment. Was I supposed to go back to pretending that he didn't consume my thoughts as much as I apparently consumed his? Damn my momentary hesitancy that had ruined this!

"I don't want you to stay away," I said. To prove it, I dropped my arms.

His eyes closed while he shuddered as though absorbing a punishing blow.

"Don't," he said roughly. "After you find and use that weapon, I *have* to walk away from you, and I can't do that if we're lovers. I can barely do it now, and I need to, Ivy. It's the only way I can protect you from my fate."

Before I could say anything else, he flipped us until he was on top of me. Then he punched the window so hard that it shattered. His body shielded mine from the instant rainfall of glass, then he opened his door from the outside and left.

For a few dazed moments, I stayed in the passenger seat, clutching the top Adrian had handed me right before he walked away. He loved this car like it was his baby, yet he'd smashed his own window to get away before he lost control and finished what he'd started.

I didn't know whether it was the most romantic thing he'd ever done, or the most insulting.

chapter twenty-six

The next day, Zach showed up with his usual style of no warning. I looked up from my book to see him seated in the chair opposite mine, a book in his hands as if he'd been reading, too.

"Adrian!" I called out, not bothering to say hello. "Zach's finally here!"

"Why do you seem angry with me?" Zach asked, to the accompanying sound of the front door slamming.

"I shouldn't be upset that you took your time getting back to us when we're not able to search for the only weapon that can save my sister?"

Frustration over more than that scalded my tone. Zach didn't get a chance to respond before Adrian came into the room. No surprise, he'd been outside all day. At least he'd given himself a reason to work on his car instead of just pretending to. As for me, I'd been pretending to read so it wasn't obvious that I hadn't been able to stop thinking about what we'd almost done in that shiny black Challenger.

"What the fuck, man?" Adrian asked, summing up his feelings more succinctly than I had.

Zach stood. "I am not a man," he stated crisply. "Nor am I yours to command or to reprimand."

Adrian replied with a burst of the exquisite form of Demonish, the sound caressing my ears like a symphony. Instead of being mollified, Zach was more upset.

"How dare you use the tongue of my brethren, mortal!"

"That's angel-speak?" I asked in surprise.

Adrian threw me a brief glance. "Yes, and I know it because it's what demons originally derived their language from." To Zach, he said, "We didn't have a week to waste waiting for you. You of all people know we're on a countdown."

"What countdown?" I piped up, but both men ignored me.

"I needed time to procure your solution," Zach said, his dark gaze blazing with pinpoints of light. "Did your impatience prevent that from occurring to you, *endante?*"

At the foreign word, Adrian looked more pissed than Zach.

"How about texting a cloud version of 'brb' then?" Acidly.

I got up, the anger between them starting to concern me. We were dead in the water without Zach, so I had to shove my own feelings aside—again—to smooth this over.

"Zach, you've been around forever, but we *are* mortal. Five days might be nothing to you, but with no word and only unbeatable obstacles to dwell on, it's been tough on us."

The Archon glanced my way, his gaze stating that I hadn't smoothed anything over. Okay, time for rough honesty, then.

"For starters, I barely sleep because I keep wondering if this is all for nothing." My voice caught. "No matter what Adrian said about the demons not wanting to lose their leverage, Jasmine might already be dead. Sometimes, I even wish she was. Then she wouldn't be suffering, and I wouldn't have to enter another realm. Then I hate myself for thinking that, so guilt torments me."

I paused to draw in a shuddering breath. "Worse, after last night, I know that I want Adrian so bad, I don't care what happens afterward. Another night alone together and I won't be able to stop myself from going to him, and no matter how much he thinks he has to, I know he won't have the strength to turn me away again."

I made sure to keep staring at Zach as I spoke. If I so much as glanced at Adrian, I wouldn't have been able to admit such raw, personal truths. Guilt over my sister wore me down on a daily basis, so last night with Adrian had used up the last of my willpower. Since he'd resorted to damaging his beloved Challenger rather than wait for me to open the driver's side door, his willpower was on empty, too. Another night alone and it would all be over.

A large part of me wished the Archon would have waited one more day to show up.

Zach stared back at me, his expression turning thoughtful. I still didn't look at Adrian, but I could feel his gaze moving over me, flaring everything it touched. I'd never been so hyperaware of anyone before, and when he let out a low, harsh sigh, I found myself inhaling so I could absorb his breath inside me.

Zach's hand on my head whipped my attention back to him. The Archon closed his eyes as if concentrating, and this time, I actually felt a tingle run through me. Or maybe it was still my body responding to Adrian's unrelenting stare.

After a moment, Zach removed his hand. "This new disguise will see you past the demon's Hounds," he stated.

"How?" Adrian and I asked in unison, but then a car pulled up in the driveway. Adrian let out a sigh of relief this time.

"Costa's back."

Costa parked behind the Challenger. When he got out, I waved at him through the window—and then was slammed to the floor, Adrian's large frame almost crushing me from the impact.

"Don't shoot," I heard Zach say over Adrian's urgent, "Are you okay? Did he hit you?"

I couldn't answer because I couldn't breathe. My hands smacking at his shoulders must've conveyed that, because Adrian leaped off me with the same speed, though he remained crouched in front of me. I took in a deep breath, wincing as my ribs and the back of my head throbbed with pain.

"Why'd you...squish me?" I managed.

Over his shoulder, I saw Costa burst into the room, his gun drawn and his tanned face pale. "Is it dead?" he snarled.

Adrian had Costa against the wall, the gun knocked out of his hand, before I could grunt out a confused "Huh?"

"Why the fuck did you shoot at Ivy?" Adrian demanded.

Costa threw a horrified look my way. "That's *Ivy?*"

"I can explain," Zach said in an unruffled tone. "In order to get past the beasts, I glamoured Ivy to resemble one."

Adrian let Costa go, his gaze sliding to me with disbelief. "She looks like a Hound?"

"Biggest, ugliest one I ever saw," Costa croaked.

"That's rude," I muttered, trying to reconcile the fact that I now looked like one of the demons' guard reptiles.

Costa's mouth curled down. "Make it—*her*—stop hissing."

"I'm not hissing!" was my immediate protest, but Costa winced and backed away a step. "Oh, crap, all he hears is hissing, right?" I asked resignedly.

A strangled sound came from Adrian's throat. I looked sharply at him, realizing he was fighting back a laugh.

"Ivy, stop hissing at Costa," he said with mock seriousness.

So it was all fun and games now that he realized I hadn't gotten shot? I'd never get used to Adrian's mercurial moods.

"You're sure this will get me past the Hounds?" I asked Zach.

He inclined his head. "They've been trained not to attack their own. Glamouring you to look exactly like another Hound is what took me additional time, as first I had to catch one."

"How?" I blurted, watching Adrian's eyes narrow, as well. "You said Archons can't go into demon realms."

"The sounds she makes are seriously disturbing," Costa muttered, but at least he put his gun away.

"We can't, but the demons are stationing Hounds in every realm as a precaution," Zach stated. "Waiting at vortexes for them to appear as they were transported from one realm to another is how I procured the Hound you now resemble."

Zach had spent the past five days Hound-hunting to help us, and we'd both bitched at him as soon as we saw him. No wonder he'd gotten mad. If I were him, I might've left without giving me my new disguise, too.

"Thank you," I said sincerely, "and I'm sorry."

Once again, he inclined his head. "Apology accepted."

Adrian's mouth thinned, but he didn't ante up an apology. From Zach's expression, that wasn't a surprise. Then again, after what Adrian had told me about that day in the tunnels, the person who really owed the other an apology was Zach.

I cleared my throat, knowing that wasn't going to happen, either. "Okay, now that we've got a way past the guard reptiles, let's head to the nearest realm and search it."

Adrian nodded at me and then gave Costa a measured look. "You up for going with us?"

"I am, but Ivy's the problem," Costa said bluntly. "You can't take her out in public. She looks like what would happen if a werewolf humped a Komodo dragon."

I bared my teeth at him, intending it as a joke, but he visibly flinched. All right, so I was horrifying. I'd say I was sorry, but it would only sound like threatening hisses to him.

"And her clothes!" Costa went on. "You can't expect a fully dressed Hound to go unnoticed in the realms."

"You can see my clothes?" I asked stupidly, then waved an impatient hand and said, "Adrian, translate."

"I don't need to," he said, giving me an appraising look. "Your disguises have only ever been skin-deep, so right now, Costa's looking at a Hound in shorts and a tank top."

"And flip-flops," Costa added, shuddering.

I turned to Zach. "Well, *that* needs fixing."

The Archon raised a single brow. "The answer is obvious."

I waited for him to put his hand on my head again, but he didn't. Realization dawned and, with it, incredulity.

"You expect me to enter the realms stark naked? Not only would I freeze, I'd be *naked!*"

Logic failed in the face of the appalling thought. Zach looked unconcerned by my dismay, but Adrian raked his gaze over me in a way that was both foreboding and anticipatory.

"Hounds wear leather straps for easier handling. If we placed some strategically on you, they would cover the necessary parts without drawing undue attention, and as I said, Hounds return frequently to the town to get warm."

I closed my eyes. Either I let my sister rot, or I had to run around freezing demon realms wearing the equivalent of a leather bikini. How had this become my life?

"Let's get the bondage lizard party started, then," I finally said, opening my eyes.

Like it or not, this *was* my life, so I had to make the best of it.

chapter twenty-seven

We didn't go back to the gateway in Collinsville, Illinois. Instead, the three of us drove to Boone, North Carolina so we could access something we'd been avoiding for weeks. A vortex.

Since Hounds were being transported through vortexes, and I now looked like a Hound, Adrian said it was time to chance one. According to him, vortexes were like revolving doors, hitting several realms back to-back. The bigger the vortex, the more realms it could access. Adrian said if Demetrius hadn't stopped us in Oregon, and minions hadn't chased us through the vortex in Mexico, we could've covered all the realms in North and South America through just those two entranceways.

By contrast, the Boone vortex was much smaller, hitting only about a dozen realms. Still, it would take two weeks to reach each of those realms separately, and with my new disguise, limiting travel time was mandatory.

Something I hadn't thought of when I learned that I looked

like a huge, prehistoric dog-lizard to everyone except Zach and Adrian: public restrooms were out of the question. I had to use the bushes along the interstate. If that wasn't humiliating enough, Adrian and Costa had to walk me to and from them so their bodies blocked Ivy-monster from passing motorists' view. When all of us were in the car, Costa would complain that parts of my beastly frame hung over his seat even though my arms and legs stayed completely in the back. And in gas stations or drive-throughs, I needed to have a blanket thrown over me so no one freaked out over seeing a monster in the backseat.

Yeah, I was sick of this disguise already, and the worst of it was about to start now.

We waited until after dark to enter the vortex marked by a tourist site called Mystery Hill. As with other vortexes, people knew there was something off about the spot due to its gravitational anomalies, but little did they know it contained a revolving door to demon realms. I wished I didn't know, either, but that didn't stop Adrian from pulling me through the gateway, which was situated on a concrete slab called the Mystery Platform.

When we tumbled into the shadowy, cold version of the Mystery Hill site, the concrete platform was gone. So were the tourist buildings and the nearby highway. The scent of wood smoke remained, surprising me until I realized there were trees around us. Frozen ones, of course, but if some remained, it made sense that they'd be burned as a heat source.

As expected, we'd been spit out onto the outskirts of the realm's epicenter, so we were alone on the icy hill. For now.

"Okay," Adrian stated. "Stick to the plan, and remember, don't show any fear, either to the Hounds or the handlers."

It was too dark for me to see his expression, but with his enhanced vision, he could see mine as I unzipped my ankle-length parka and let it drop to the ground. Beneath it, I wore only boots, a leather strap across my breasts, and the most uncomfortable leather G-string ever invented.

The blast of cold on my bare skin felt like a full-body punch, knocking out my awkwardness at standing in front of Adrian with almost nothing on. My teeth began to chatter like a windup toy's, and when I kicked my boots off, the ice made it feel as though I was standing on knives. I thought I'd mentally prepared myself, but "mind over matter" didn't exist when you were all but naked in freezing temperatures.

"C-can't do th this," I stuttered.

Adrian pulled me to him, his arms chasing away the cold on my back and his body warming up my front. Without thinking, I stood on the tops of his boots, easing the stabbing pain in my feet. The last time I'd been mostly naked in his arms, he'd overwhelmed me with passion. This time, tenderness seemed to pour from his embrace, soothing parts of my emotions I hadn't even realized were bruised or broken.

"You *can* do this," he said, his words low but resonant. "The otherworldly abilities of legendary warriors, kings and queens run through your veins. With it, you are capable of so much more than I ever will be, but even if you didn't have that bloodline—" his voice deepened "—I'd still believe in you, Ivy."

I let out a laugh that was half gasp, half choked sob. How could he say that? I'd screwed up every challenge thrown at me, and that was *with* his help. Without it, I'd be dead several times over by now.

A growling hiss jerked my head to the right. To our left, another sounded, and another right in front of us.

Ready or not, the Hounds were here.

"You can do this," Adrian repeated, going absolutely still. I disengaged myself from his arms, seeing him keep them in their half circle as though still cradling me. Amidst the smash of cold, my fear at those ominous growls, and the sole-splitting pain in my feet, I also felt a tinge of wonder.

In our time together, Adrian had yanked me up, knocked me down, hurtled me through realms, trapped me against a wall and kissed me until I burned with need, but this was different. When he'd held me, I realized there was more between us than legacies and lust. He was what I'd been missing my whole life, and if he felt the same way, I'd be damned if either of us was going to die before we could do something about it.

I turned around, shaking and all, to confront the lizard monsters who crowded around us.

"Back off!" I yelled, hoping to them it sounded like the meanest, most badass hiss ever.

Then I stared, my mind taking a few moments to process what I was looking at. When I could think again, Costa's description was right. They *did* look like what you'd get if a werewolf and a Komodo dragon had a monster baby. No wonder he'd opened fire at the sight of me disguised as one.

Even on four legs, the Hounds stood almost as tall as me. Their snouts were elongated like a bull terrier, only with lots more teeth, as I saw when their mouths opened impossibly wide. Their front legs were small, but their back ones were massive with muscle, and they were balanced by a thick tail that narrowed into a point at the end. Claws as long as my fingers stabbed through the frozen ground, and though their skin had the leathery look of a reptile, it was also covered by a thin layer of dark hair.

I could see all these things because light radiated from the spots on their backs, giving off an eerie glow, as if the Hounds needed any enhancement to their menace. Forked, thin tongues flicked out of their mouths, and when the biggest of the three came close enough to give me what I hoped was a friendly lick, I forced myself to stand still and not scream.

If we made it through this, I was drinking an entire bottle of Adrian's superstrong bourbon. Count on it.

"B-back off," I said again, making my voice authoritative and firm, which wasn't easy with chattering teeth. One of the Hounds cocked its head, as if trying to translate the sounds from my rapidly clicking jaw. Then it came forward, leaving a trail of slime over my arm as it gave me a lick, too.

"Gross," I muttered, but it was better than them ripping me to shreds. Zach's glamour was fooling them. I knew it worked on demons, minions and humans, but I hadn't been sure about beasts. Oh, me of little faith.

"Okay, guys, let's go into town and get warm," I announced, starting to run toward where Adrian had told me the town was.

One followed me, but the other two stayed back, as if sensing Adrian's presence even though he hadn't moved a muscle.

"Come *on!*" I said, circling back and nudging both beasts, then running toward the town again. Hey, that's what my dog used to do when I was a kid, and he wanted me to follow him. Here's hoping the Hounds lived up to their nickname and understood.

After a few more nudges and circles, during which I was pretty sure the nerve endings in my feet had become frostbitten, all three Hounds finally went with me. I let them lead since I couldn't see in the stygian woods, but I was so eager to get this over with—I was *cold!*—that I had to force myself to slow down to keep from outrunning them. Finally, we reached the realm's epicenter: a mountain-turned-mini-city, from all the lights, terraces, pathways and courtyards dug into the rock.

The Hounds seemed to know exactly where they were going, taking me up a smooth stone bridge that led inside the metropolitan mountain. If I didn't know that forced human labor had built it, I would've been impressed by the stone city. As with other demons' headquarters, it had electricity, heat and beautiful architectural touches. I also saw jewels artistically embedded into parts of the rock, which reminded me of Adrian's ego comment. Whoever ruled this realm wanted to show off their wealth, and studding jewels in the wall of your mountain castle was certainly one way to do that.

Looking like a Hound meant that I ran past the guards without once being stopped. We streaked through the courtyard with everyone stepping aside to get out of our way, and as the Hounds led me down a stone hallway past that, the air grew noticeably warmer. When we arrived at the end of the hallway, it was almost humid. Once inside the dimly lit room, I understood.

The Hounds jumped into a large, steaming pool cut into the rock, immersing themselves up to their eyes. The water smelled atrocious, but I jumped in, too, telling myself I was just doing it to avoid suspicion.

It was a lie. That steam sold me. It could've been hot mud, and I would've still dived right in. After a few painful minutes where my feet and hands felt like they were on fire as circulation returned, I stopped shaking and my teeth quit chattering. Another few minutes, and I felt focused enough to concentrate. Here was as good a place as any to search the castle with my hallowed-radar.

I'd just begun to do that when rolling noises echoed through the nearby hallway. I tensed, but the Hounds next to me began to wiggle in what could only be called joyous expectation.

Moments later, two minions bearing lightning-like marks in their skin pushed wheelbarrows into the room. The Hounds leaped from the water, jostling each other for position as the contents were dumped into a corner. Then they fell on the pile like hungry pigs at feeding time, and what they'd been given to eat was as revolting as it was expected in a demon realm.

I looked away, rage scalding me with such intensity that it flared my abilities. They pulsed outward, covering the castle with the same sonar-like efficiency as before, and my supernatural ping returned with nothing at the end of it.

The weapon wasn't here.

I got out of the water, still looking away from the Hounds. My anger made my near nudity irrelevant as a minion looked my way, not that he'd see a girl in a belt bikini anyway. He seemed surprised that I wasn't joining the feeding frenzy, but then came toward me while holding out a large blanket.

I stood still as he dried me, speaking in Demonish the whole time. He even used exaggerated vowels and the singsong voice people affected when talking to babies or favored pets. When he was done, he scratched my head and patted my ass as if I'd been a good little Hound.

"I *wish* I was one of them right now," I told him, knowing all he heard were hissing noises. "I'd bite your head off."

He replied with the Demonish version of what was probably "Whoooo's a grumpy guuurl?" and patted me again. This time, I bared my teeth at him.

"Touch my ass one more time and I'm clubbing you with the nearest femur from that pile."

Not that I could, because using a bone like a club was un-Houndlike enough to get the other minion's attention. Also, I needed to seize my chance. With my search complete and the other Hounds occupied, now was the perfect time to return to Adrian.

I ran out of the Hound-spa, glad there weren't many turns to remember to get out of the castle. Once again, no one attempted to stop me, and when I was dashing down the hill

on my way to where I last left Adrian, something else occurred to me.

I could see where I was going. Not great, as the several times
I tripped proved, but I wasn't blinded by the darkness, and I
was far enough away from the lights of the mountain castle
that I should've been. My abilities were growing at an incredible rate. Was it because I was finally using them, or was it the
virulent seesaw of emotions that kept kicking them into hy-
perdrive? Between my feelings for Adrian, my guilt over Jasmine, and the rage that demon realm atrocities brought out in
me, I wouldn't know a moment of calm if it bit me in the ass.

"Ivy, over here!"

I adjusted my course at Adrian's directive, now noticing him
next to the cluster of dead trees. He'd remained so still that
he'd blended in at first glance. Once I reached him, I almost
hurtled myself into the ankle-length parka he held out and
yanked my boots on fast enough to leave skid marks.

"It's not here, let's go," I panted.

We ran the short distance to the gateway, but before he
dropped us through it, he paused.

"Are you up for doing another realm now?"

My body felt like a Popsicle and I never wanted to see another Hound feeding trough again, but I didn't hesitate.

"Yes."

I'd find this weapon, and not only would I save my sister,
I'd kill every damn demon and minion in the realm she'd
been trapped in.

chapter twenty-eight

I made it through seven realms the first day, and finished the other five two days later. A stint with hypothermia was responsible for the delay, but it wasn't just manna combined with Adrian and Costa treating it that got me past it so quickly. I was changing. I could feel it in the muscles I'd never had before, and in the hallowed-hunting sensor that was easier and easier to utilize. I'd searched the last realm without even entering the main building, and despite keeping that to myself, Adrian had sensed the changes, too.

That's why he said it was time for me to learn how to use a slingshot.

Because of my hideous disguise, we went into the Pisgah National Forest to practice. Costa came with us in case we needed an extra trigger finger, if minions happened upon us, though I doubted it. We were out in the middle of beautiful nowhere, with tall trees, waterfalls and bubbling creeks as far as the eye could see. Compared to demon realms, the forties temperature was also downright balmy, but it seemed to keep park visitors at bay. Good thing, too. Forget innocent hikers—if Bigfoot were real, he'd crap himself at the sight of me.

After Adrian set up a target, Costa sat on a fallen tree stump to watch. I stood next to Adrian, frowning when I saw the long, braided rope he pulled out of his duffel bag. Was *that* a duplicate of the infamous weapon? In my head, David's slingshot looked like a Y-shaped branch with stretchy material wound around the opposing ends. Not what resembled a skinnier version of a child's jump rope.

"What am I supposed to do with that? Hang the demons with it?" I wondered.

Adrian grinned, taking a stone from the bag and placing it in the small section of rope that split into two pieces. Then he began to spin the rope in a lasso-like circle, increasing the speed until it made a low, whirring sound. That turned into a crack as he snapped it forward. I didn't see the stone release, but one of the glass bottles he'd set up thirty feet away suddenly exploded, spewing beer over the branch he'd set it on.

"Wow," I said, impressed. "You nailed that like you were using a sniper rifle. How long have you been practicing?"

His grin vanished. "When I met Zach and learned about my mother's death, I researched the slingshot David would've used, then made sure I knew how to use it. Zach didn't bother telling me until recently that only a Davidian or a demon from Goliath's line can utilize the slingshot's true power."

Somehow, I wasn't surprised. It could be that Zach hadn't cared enough to relay the information before, but I thought the Archon might've had another motivation.

If Adrian had known he couldn't use David's slingshot to kill demons, he wouldn't have learned how to use the ancient weapon. Because he had, now he was teaching me. Was that Zach's plan? To keep Adrian near me at every opportunity so he'd be unable to avoid his fate?

If so, I intended that plan to backfire, and I knew how to do it because Adrian had told me himself that touching me was his weakness. So I deliberately brushed against him when he showed me which finger the loop went on and how to hold the rope. His lips tightened, but he acted as if he didn't notice. Then he took my wrist, moving it to mimic the far faster manner I'd need to perfect to get the stone to fly out.

"First you spin the rope to build up momentum," Adrian said. "Then you aim and snap it when you let go. Try it."

I did, and the stone dropped near my feet instead of slinging toward the target. Legendary bloodline or not, clearly I wasn't a natural.

"That happens to everyone the first time," Adrian said evenly. "Try again."

I did three more times, and got the same results. My spirits sank. No wonder Demetrius had said he wasn't afraid of me. I couldn't hit the broad side of a barn, let alone him or any other demons guarding Jasmine.

"Here." Adrian pulled me to him, his body so close that I could feel his heart beating. Then his hand covered mine, though he spread his fingers so he didn't impede the rope. "We'll do it together. Move when I do, Ivy."

We began to spin the rope, first in slower circles, then fast enough to hear that whirring noise. My sense of despair diminished because it was easy to move with Adrian. So easy. His arm shadowed mine while his chest was a muscled wall that teased my back. Every time I adjusted my stance, his thighs brushed the backs of mine, making my breath catch. He was so big, so powerful, yet his breathing roughened when I leaned into him, and brought my body tighter against his. I'd started the taunting touches to chip away at his self-control, but I might end up being the one who came undone.

"On the count of three," Adrian ordered, voice much hoarser than before. "One…"

I leaned forward and aimed. His body curved, following the movement, and feeling his hips line up with mine almost made me drop the rope.

"Two…"

His breath seared the back of my neck, making gooseflesh spring up. When his jaw brushed my cheek as he adjusted to look at the target, I almost rubbed against him like a cat. The feel of him was more than exciting. It was the stuff obsessions were made of.

"Three!"

I let go when I felt his fingers lift, and the slingshot snapped forward with a crack. The rock didn't hit the beer bottle, but it hit the branch it was on, bouncing off after leaving a gash in the wood.

"Yes!" I shouted, so happy I spun around and hugged Adrian.

His arms tightened until it was hard to breathe, but all at once, I didn't care about breathing. I hadn't hugged him with ulterior motives, yet my whole body seemed to come alive in his embrace. I reared back, suddenly desperate to see him. The ridges and hollows that made up his high cheekbones, full mouth, dark gold brows and straight nose were arresting enough, but it was his eyes that had me transfixed. Molten silver gripped sapphire in the same unbreakable hold Adrian had me in, and the blatant need displayed there made things low in my body clench.

"You can't keep teasing me this way." His voice was so guttural, it was almost animalistic. "I'm not the good guy, Ivy. I'm the bad one who'll take everything and then leave."

My mouth felt dry, but that wasn't why I licked my lips.

"You're wrong," I breathed. "Maybe you were once, but you're not anymore. Otherwise, you'd have already done it."

"Do you two mind?" a disgusted voice muttered behind us. "I know that's Ivy, but I'm still going to have nightmares about you dry-humping a Hound, Adrian."

The mental image caught me off guard, and I burst out laughing. We'd hardly been doing that, though the mere sight of Adrian hugging a Hound would be highly disturbing.

Adrian released me, but his smoldering gaze promised that this wasn't over. I couldn't agree more, though for different reasons. Now wasn't the time, however. We had an audience, and we'd already traumatized Costa enough.

Adrian must've thought so, too. He strode over to Costa, twisting the top off one of the beer bottles he'd brought for target practice.

"This'll help wash away the memory."

Costa took it, muttering something in Greek that had Adrian snorting as if in agreement. I turned my attention back to the target, taking out another stone from the duffel bag.

Now that I knew I *could* operate the slingshot, I just had to learn how to do it better.

chapter twenty-nine

Several hours later, I flopped back against the couch, letting the remote control slide from my fingers. The cabin we'd been staying in boasted a wood-burning fireplace, but the cable channel lineup sucked.

For the fifth time in the past thirty minutes, I glanced at Costa's suitcase. Tonight was our last night in this cozy, remote hideout, and Costa, ever prepared, had already packed. He even had his suitcase by the door, leaving out just the items he'd need to get ready in the morning.

I hadn't meant to spy on him while he packed. I'd been flipping through channels, and his room happened to be to the left of the TV set. His door also happened to be cracked, and it just so *happened* that I saw what he slipped into his suitcase before he hauled it to the door and left with Adrian to get dinner. See? Total accident.

Besides, I reminded myself as I gave into temptation and slinked over to Costa's suitcase, he hadn't told me I wasn't allowed to use his laptop. He just hadn't mentioned it, much like I intended not to mention taking advantage of the cabin's Wi-Fi connection. Okay, if I got caught, the guys wouldn't be happy, but yesterday, Costa had eaten my bag of Fritos without asking permission and I didn't flip out. Why? Because friends shared. Everyone knew that.

I unzipped his suitcase and felt around through the pile of clothes until I came across something hard and flat. Then I slid the laptop out as gingerly as if it were booby-trapped with alarms. Once it was free, I almost ran to the desk where the cabin owners had the Wi-Fi information. As I turned the computer on, I found myself holding my breath. When the screen lit up and I saw that I didn't need a password, I let out a whoop. No security? It was like Costa *wanted* me to use it!

I did follow Adrian's warning not to log in to any of my accounts or contact any of my friends. I desperately wished I could message my roommate to tell her I was okay, but minions could still be scoping out Delia or my other friends. Instead, I Googled "Beth and Thomas Jenkins" to see if my parents' funeral had still taken place, even though I hadn't been there to attend. Not being able to officially say goodbye to them had been tearing at my heart for weeks, but I hoped they'd had a proper burial, at least—

I froze over a headline that had my name along with three words I'd never expected to see: Wanted For Murder. With trembling fingers, I clicked the article beneath.

"*...Ivy Jenkins, daughter of recently deceased Beth and Thomas Jenkins, has still not been found. Jenkins fled the town of Bennington after murdering Lionel Kroger, the detective assigned to her sister's case. Jenkins has a history of abnormal psychosis and should be considered armed and dangerous....*"

I heard a car pull up, but I couldn't stop reading. The article went on to detail how I was also a "person of interest" in Jasmine's disappearance. Worse, it implied that the brakes on

my parents' car might have been tampered with, and noted
that I was the only other person with access to their vehicle.

In short, it accused me of being a mass murderer.

"What are you doing?"

Under other circumstances, Adrian's harsh tone would've
made me flinch. Right now, I was too numb from shock.

"Finding out that I'm a wanted criminal," I said with as
much calmness as I could manage. Then I swung around to
face him. "But you already knew that, didn't you?"

Adrian set down the bag he'd been holding, and I ignored
the delicious aromas coming from it. Costa shut the cabin
door and went straight for the food. He couldn't understand
what I'd asked Adrian anyway. *Thanks again, Hound disguise.*

"I knew," Adrian said, giving me a measuring look. "What
did you think the police were going to say? That you went
into hiding with the last descendant of Judas because the detective assigned to your sister's case tried to deliver you to his
demon master? They had to explain Kroger's death somehow."

I waved an impatient hand. "Fine, but why claim that *I* murdered him? Or make me a suspect in Jasmine's disappearance,
let alone my parents' deaths? Aren't the demons begging for
unwanted attention with this?"

Adrian sighed. "Bennington isn't the first police force
they've infiltrated. They're everywhere, and with their con-
nections, they made sure your picture was plastered all over
the news and internet, turning everyone who sees you into a
potential informant for them."

"But they know I'm disguised!" I protested.

"And now they've made sure you have to stay that way or
they'll catch you," was his inexorable response. "Same as me."

I opened my mouth—and nothing came out except a short,
sharp sound, like a last gasp before dying. Adrian stared at me,
his expression filled with a hard sort of empathy.

"I told you before, Ivy, we don't win this war. Archons or demons do, but either way, there is no going back for us."

I looked away, staring at the online article that had shattered the last of my hopeful illusions. This whole time, I'd kept telling myself that if I found the weapon and saved Jasmine, I could go back to some semblance of my old life. I might not have had the greatest one, what with pretending more than actually living, but it had been *my* life to screw up or improve. Sure, once I was back, I'd have to avoid mirrors and move Jasmine and me from the WMU dorms to hallowed ground, but I could handle that. Eventually, I'd make new friends, maybe finish college online, get a decent job, and—

And what? Go back to pretending that the dark, icy places I'd glimpsed were figments of my imagination? Hope that every new person I met wasn't a minion in disguise? Even if demons hadn't been behind the warrants for my arrest, what did I *really* think was going to happen if I saved Jasmine by decimating one of their realms? That the demons would call a truce and let my sister and me live in peace? No. We'd have to hide for the rest of our lives, and to do that, we'd have to leave everything and everyone we'd ever known behind.

My head dropped into my hands. Adrian was right. Even if I won, I didn't really win. The Archons did, but Jasmine and I were still screwed.

"Is that what you really look like?"

I picked my head up to see Costa staring at my computer, a half-eaten burger still in his hand. I glanced back at the article. My Facebook user pic was next to the part that talked about my abnormal psychosis.

Was I still the smiling girl staring back at me? Right now, I felt decades older, but that wasn't what Costa meant. I nodded, which needed no translation despite my Hound disguise.

Costa let out a wry snort as he glanced at Adrian. "No wonder you've been having such a hard time, bro."

Was that a compliment? I looked at my picture again, trying to see it through the viewpoint of the handsome Greek. Okay, so I probably wasn't as hot as I'd been with my blonde disguise, but my brown hair was thick enough not to need mousse, my eyes were a nice hazel shade and my mouth had a pouty kind of fullness. A guy I'd briefly dated had even called it lush.

Then I caught a glimpse of my reflection in the screen. My hair looked like it had been styled by drunk witches, raccoons would be jealous of the dark circles under my eyes, and if my skin was any oilier, the shine would light up the room. I needed a hairbrush, concealer and lots of pressed powder, stat!

Of course, that wasn't possible. Even if it was, Costa would only laugh at the image of a Hound trying to primp. As for Adrian…the best makeover in the world couldn't fix our issues. Only a broken destiny could, and while I still believed that was possible, Adrian didn't. Not now and maybe not ever.

"I need to see my sister."

Costa didn't react to my statement, but Adrian froze in the middle of picking up a burger.

"Ivy," he began.

"I so don't want to hear it." The words came out as a sigh despite my screaming on the inside. "You want me to embrace the suck? Fine, but I'm also finished with guessing if I'm weapon-hunting for Jasmine, or for you."

He dropped the burger and stalked over. "What do you mean?"

I met his gaze without flinching. "You don't want me entering the Bennington realm without the weapon, but is that because you're worried about extra demon security? Or because you're afraid that if I find out my sister's already dead,

I'll stop looking for it and you'll lose your chance at killing Demetrius?"

Anger suffused his face, flushing his cheeks and turning his eyes into burning gems. "Is that what you think?"

Costa glanced between us. "You two fighting?"

"What's the only thing you told me I could trust about you, Adrian?" My voice was flat from the weight of my desolate future bearing down on me. "Your hatred of demons. So I'm supposed to believe you *wouldn't* string me along about my sister's survival to keep me looking for the one weapon that can kill them?"

Adrian's hands closed into fists while he stared at me. The last time he'd done that, he'd grabbed me and kissed me, but something darker than passion seethed in him now.

"Get your stuff," he said in a voice that vibrated from barely controlled rage. "We're leaving for Bennington tonight."

chapter thirty

"This is a bad idea," Costa said for the eleventh time.

Adrian and I responded the same way we had to his other ten warnings—with stony silence. We were too busy playing our high-stakes version of "chicken" to let Costa deter us. Adrian was counting on me changing my mind about entering the world's most dangerous demon realm, and I was betting he'd refuse to pull me through the gateway when the time came.

We'd see who swerved first.

"Obsidiana's seen your ride, so you can't drive this into town without every minion knowing who you are," Costa went on, not giving up his attempt to talk sense into us. "This is a mint-condition, '68 Challenger, so it's gonna draw some eyes."

"We'll leave it outside Bennington," Adrian replied, the tightness in his tone saying he was still steaming mad.

"And do what with the hulking demon lizard in the back-seat?" Costa shot back, adding, "Sorry, Ivy," as an afterthought.

Adrian didn't even glance my way. "We'll hide her in something else."

Costa cast a dubious look over his shoulder. "It'll need to be something big."

My lips tightened. "Enough with the fat-lizard cracks," I snapped, hoping the hiss Costa heard sounded as pissy as I felt.

"This is a bad idea," Costa muttered once again. Apparently he was going for an even dozen.

"The gateway's inside the B and B, but your sister won't be there anymore," Adrian stated, not glancing away from the road even though he was now talking to me. "The spot where it's located was swallowed recently, after Demetrius took over the realm. She'll be in old Bennington. That and parts of New York got swallowed a long time ago, so that's where his palace is."

"I don't remember glimpsing a palace when I went through Bennington." Then again, I'd been focused on showing Jasmine's picture to hotel and motel employees, not on paying attention to what I thought were hallucinations.

Adrian grunted. "It's there."

Every realm I'd entered had had a grand structure, and Adrian hadn't been wrong about his realm blueprints yet, but something about his tone made his surety sound more...personal.

"You lived there before, didn't you?" I guessed.

His eyes briefly met mine before he returned his militant attention to the road. "For a long time, I ruled it."

Anger shot through me. Of course, he'd failed to mention *that* before.

"You're only a few years older than me, so it couldn't have been that long, Adrian. Unless you were a toddler king."

"If I'm guessing right about where this conversation's going, it's time she knew anyway," Costa muttered, giving Adrian a sympathetic look.

"Knew what?" I asked curtly.

Adrian's hands tightened on the steering wheel. "I told you time moves differently in the realms. Once I was old enough to fight, Demetrius made sure I lived in realms where time almost froze to a stop so he'd have plenty of it to perfect my training. I might only look a few years older than you, Ivy, but I was born in 1873."

My mind froze while doing the math. Adrian couldn't—just could *not!*—be over a hundred and forty.

"No," I croaked.

Costa reached around to pat my head. "I know it's hard to take in. When Adrian got me out and I realized fifty years had passed over here, I had trouble adjusting—"

"How old are *you?*" I burst out before remembering he couldn't understand me.

"Costa's seventy-three, or seventy-four, I guess." Adrian gave his friend a humorless smile. "Forgot your birthday."

Denial still had me in a fierce grip. "But Tomas's family is still alive! We sent Hoyt to them so he could recover!"

"Those were his grandkids, Ivy," Adrian said, sparing another glance my way. "Didn't you notice the old clothing his parents wore in the photographs in Tomas's room?"

I had, but I'd thought his family had just liked to wear more, um, quaint apparel.

"You're really a hundred and forty?" Call me slow, but I needed to hear him confirm it one more time.

"Yes."

I angled my head so I could see him more fully, as if he'd look different now that I knew his true age. He didn't, of course. Same piercing sapphire eyes, curving brows, high cheekbones, sensually full mouth and strong jaw, all making up a face that left gorgeous behind in the dust. Considering that face was on top of a body so built that it could make a superhero jealous, Adrian's looks were unforgettable.

So was this revelation. He hadn't just spent his childhood and teen years living with demons. He'd spent nearly a century and a half with them. No wonder Demetrius had referred to Adrian's working for Zach as a "little rebellion." It barely registered next to the staggering length of time he'd lived in the realms as the demons' prophesied savior.

I understood then, more than I ever had before, the absolute assurance that Demetrius, Zach and even Adrian had that he couldn't avoid his destiny. How could a few weeks of being attracted to me compare with thirteen decades of being groomed to betray the last Davidian? It's not like Adrian was trying to kick a recent bad habit—he'd literally spent a couple of lifetimes training so he could bring about my doom!

And I'd pretty much done everything I could to help him, I realized with a scald of self-recrimination. Even now, I was insisting that Adrian take me to a realm where his demonic foster father and a few hundred of his closest evil friends waited. A realm Adrian had admitted he'd once ruled over, and where he could now return as the conquering betrayer.

All I needed to do was slap a bow on my ass to make myself the perfect, too-stupid-to-live sacrifice.

"Having second thoughts, Ivy?"

Adrian's voice broke through my crushing musings. His accent was as darkly alluring as ever, but it was a *demon* accent. When I met his gaze, those gemstone-colored eyes held their usual mixture of brooding danger, but who was his veiled violence aimed at? The girl he was destined to destroy, or the demons he'd told me he intended to take down?

After all, they wanted the weapon, too. I'd bet Demetrius and the rest of them would consider the minions Adrian had killed as acceptable losses if he delivered the slingshot—and me—to them in the end. What if all the times Adrian had saved me were just so I'd willingly lead him to the powerful weapon that his demonic brethren needed? What if all his claims to care about me were only so I'd run headlong into my own betrayal? In short—what if the only time Adrian had been telling me the truth was when he told me *not* to trust him?

"Yes, I'm having second thoughts," I said hoarsely.

"Tell me she said yes," Costa muttered. "Because this—"

"Is a bad idea," I finished, though only Adrian understood me. "Costa's right. Let's stop off somewhere. I, ah, don't feel so hot all of a sudden."

Adrian shot a suspicious look my way, but my stomach gurgled as if in agreement. Either he heard it or decided not to push me, because he turned off the highway at the next exit.

I drew in a deep breath, trying to force back the clenching in my gut that came from fear, anger, and a very real sense of betrayal. Despite all his warnings, I *had* trusted him. Hell, I'd done more than that. The rest of my ancestors might have been drawn to Judians out of compassion or the belief that darkness could be overcome by light, but I'd allowed myself to fall for Adrian, making me the stupidest Davidian to ever walk the earth.

My teeth ground together. Fine. I might have been the most gullible person in my ancient, illustrious ancestry, but that ended right now. I'd make sure my sister was alive and if so, I *would* find that weapon. I'd just do it without Adrian.

But first, I had to find a way to get away from him.

chapter thirty-one

Adrian rented only one room at the Motel 6. We had enough money and Archon-blessed oil for more, so I guessed he intended us to just grab a few hours' sleep before we hit the road again.

The single room worked for me, but for different reasons. I'd come up with a plan. Not a great one, but I couldn't think of anything else in the short time I had. Adrian parked around the back of the hotel to hide my monstrous disguise from other guests, and once I'd been hustled inside the room, he followed his usual protocol. That meant drawing the drapes and then sprinkling the interior with holy oil to render the room temporarily hallowed.

I waited until Adrian took his turn in the bathroom before I wrote on the little pad of paper every hotel room seemed to have. Then I handed it to Costa, hoping my Hound disguise didn't somehow screw up the words he saw on the page.

Need to talk to Adrian alone. Give us a couple of hours?

Relief washed over me when Costa nodded, then crumpled up the page, tossing it into the trash.

"Gonna go clear my head, bro," Costa called out, grabbing some money from the duffel bag. "I'll be at the bar next door."

He left before Adrian could argue. Or maybe he wouldn't have. When Adrian emerged from the bathroom, his expression was serious and water clung to his hairline, as though he'd splashed some on his face while he was in there.

I sat on one of the double beds, suddenly finding it hard to look him in the eye. Knowing what I had to do didn't make doing it any easier.

"I know you're not really sick," Adrian stated, his gaze searching mine as he came nearer. "Just upset. Is it from finding out my real age, or because I used to rule the Bennington realm?"

"Both," I admitted. A surge of anger made me able to look at him fully. "After the new section was swallowed, was it your idea to restore the bed-and-breakfast on this side so minions could use it like a Venus flytrap?"

That must have been how Jasmine had been taken. None of the other Bennington hotel employees had recognized her picture. How simple it would've been for Mrs. Paulson to make all records of Jasmine's stay at the B and B disappear. Add in more minions on the police force to take care of any snooping family, and it was the perfect setup for funneling humans into the demon realm.

"No, that was Demetrius's idea," Adrian replied, sitting on the bed opposite mine. "But he's not alone. Demons have rackets like that all over the world. Hotels, guided tours, boat rentals, chauffeur services…any business that gets people alone and vulnerable, there's a chance a minion's planted in it."

"And nobody cares." My snort was bitter. "People like Jasmine disappear every day, and the world shrugs because she's not their sister." Pain sharpened my voice as I added, "Or daughter. Minions killed my parents, too, didn't they?"

Adrian sighed before running his hand through his hair. "Probably. They'd be considered too old to be decent slaves, and if they were making waves over her disappearance, their having an 'accident' would be the simplest solution."

I stared at him, silently daring him to look away. "Then I showed up making more waves, but I'm young, so they tried to make me a slave instead."

"Yes," he said, his gaze boring into mine while varying emotions flitted across his features. Disgust, anger and the most telling of all. Guilt.

"You did that to people, too." My accusation filled the space between us, creating an invisible barrier that seemed to grow with every second.

"Yes, I did." Something too bitter to be a smile twisted his mouth. "I told you, for a while, the demons had convinced me that humans were no better than they were. Just more hypocritical, because on this side, human slavers, murderers and oppressors were called dictators, kings and presidents, if they did it to enough people. Only the humans who did it to just a few were called criminals."

"Our race has issues," I acknowledged, still holding his stare. "Doesn't excuse what you or the rest of them did."

"No, Ivy, it doesn't," he replied, his voice very soft. "And I see the faces of everyone I harmed whenever I close my eyes. That's why I started working for Zach. Every person I save feels like washing a drop of blood from my hands, but deep down, I know I'll never even the score. Some things can't be atoned for, and all the lives I've saved will never restore the ones I've taken or ruined."

I wanted to believe the regret resonating in his tone. Wanted to trust the pain etched on his features, or the look in his eyes

that seemed to urge me to revile him for all the things he re-
viled himself for. But Jasmine's life—and mine—hung in the
balance, so I couldn't trust him. He'd told me that enough
times, and this time, I'd believe him.

I looked away and forced out a shaky laugh. "I don't know
about you, but I could really use a beer. Aren't there still some
that didn't get used for target practice in the trunk?"

He didn't say anything. I sneaked a glance at him. Adrian
still sat exactly as he had been, his elbows braced on his legs
while he leaned forward. The only thing new was his frown.

"After everything I just said, your response is to start drinking?"

More than a hint of disbelief tinged his tone. I scrambled
for a convincing reply and found myself answering with the
truth. Part of it, anyway.

"You might want to keep stewing over all the horrible
things in your past, but I want to move forward. Right now,
that involves getting a drink."

A slight snort escaped him. "Guess there are worse ways to
move on with our lives."

He went to the door, but as he opened it, I couldn't stop
from asking a question that had nagged at me. This was the
last chance I'd get, even if his answer was just another lie.

"Forget our roles, fates, whatever for a minute. When it's
all said and done, who do you think is going to win this war?
Archons or demons?"

He half turned. Though his face was only in profile, I could
see that his expression matched the absolute certainty in his
tone when he spoke.

"Archons."

I let out a short laugh. "Is it me, or do they seem outnumbered? I've seen several demons, but only one of them."

"You're right, they're outnumbered." Something else lurked

in his voice now. A pained sort of wistfulness. "When it's light versus dark, that doesn't matter. One shadow in a brightly lit room goes unnoticed, but shine a ray of light into even the darkest corner…and everything changes."

Then he left, splitting my emotions right down the middle. If he believed Archons would win, how could he betray me to the losing side? Was he that brainwashed by what he'd been told was his fate, or was he just saying that to play me?

Jasmine's face flashed in my mind, reminding me that I didn't have time for second-guessing. I ran over to Adrian's duffel bag, quickly rifling through it. Once I had what I needed, I dragged a chair over to the hotel room door and stood on it. Despite my preparations, two sides of myself remained locked in battle.

Believe him! my hopeful half screamed. *Just because he thinks his awful past has doomed him doesn't mean it has!*

It's too late! my cynical half roared. *You can't trust him, he's already admitted that he's too far gone!*

Somewhere in the parking lot, a trunk slammed closed, then footsteps approached the door. I sucked in a breath, my vision blurring as I raised my hands. I didn't want to do this. I didn't.

But I had to.

The door opened—and I slammed the same large rock we kept to smash mirrors down onto Adrian's head before he even cleared the threshold. His fist shot out with his lightning-fast reflexes, but in the instant before it landed, his eyes met mine. His sapphire ones widened, then his hand buried into the wall instead of my face.

"Ivy?" he asked, as though confused.

Tears streamed from my eyes as I whacked him in the head again. This time, Adrian fell to the floor, and the thump his body made seemed to reverberate all through me. I dropped the rock, sickened at how it was now stained with blood.

"I'm sorry," I choked out.

He didn't reply. In fact, Adrian was so still, I wasn't even sure if he was breathing. I knelt, my whole body rigid from fear as I checked his pulse.

It throbbed beneath my fingers, sending an instant wave of relief through me. He was alive! Even if he'd always meant to betray me, I never would have forgiven myself if I'd killed him. I didn't think I'd be able to forgive myself for doing this, and I wasn't done yet.

I grabbed the slingshot from his bag, tying his hands and feet together with it. Then I put duct tape over his mouth, deciding to add a few more layers to his wrists and ankles, too. When he woke up, he'd be pissed, and that was only if he were innocent. If he *had* intended to deliver me to Demetrius after I found the weapon... Well, maybe I should use all the tape.

When Adrian's wrists, arms, ankles and mouth were covered by the thick gray tape, I paused. There was one more thing I had to do, and I dreaded it even more than I'd dreaded knocking him out.

With shaking hands, I went back to his duffel bag and pulled out his knife.

chapter thirty-two

I tried to ignore the screech of brakes from the car next to me, but I couldn't ignore it suddenly swerving into my lane. I veered left, avoiding that crash, yet swiping the front of the Challenger against another vehicle in the process.

Forget everything else I'd done. Adrian was going to kill me for damaging his precious ride.

The driver I'd sideswiped blasted his horn and slowed down, but when he drew even with me, his expression changed from anger to pure terror. I hunched down and drew the bedspread over my head until I could barely see. Too late. Another screech of brakes and he was driving off the road, coming to a stop in the grassy shoulder along the highway.

It was dark out, and I used the hotel bedspread like a veil, but one look at my face destroyed the notion that I was just your average commuter. Seeing a hulking demon lizard behind the wheel was too much for my fellow drivers. At least it was well past rush hour, so while I'd caused a few individual spinouts, I hadn't been responsible for a real accident yet.

If I wanted to keep it that way, I had to get off the road. Sooner or later, some cop would finish a hysterical motorist's sobriety test and decide to check out their story of a monster driving a vintage Challenger. Add in the fact that some of the Bennington cops were minions and I'd *really* be screwed.

Still, I had to get as close to Bennington as I could. Ditching the car to run around in the open raised my chances of being seen. Not driving also meant it would take longer to get where I needed to be. I'd left Adrian back at the motel over two hours ago, so at any minute, Costa would return to the room and find him.

Adrian. I forced back the guilt that made me feel like I'd swallowed a bellyful of acid. He'd *told* me he'd betray me if we continued to spend time together! Demetrius and Zach had thought so, too, and with Adrian's admittedly bloody history, many people would agree he deserved what I'd done.

So why was I the one who felt like a betrayer?

To keep myself from brooding over that, I turned off at the next exit. According to the map on Adrian's phone—yes, I'd swiped that, too—the Green Mountain National Forest bordered the part of Bennington where the B and B was located. I vaguely remembered the woods from my visit to the B and B, so if I kept to the trees, I'd be able to stay hidden until I reached it. The realm gateway was in there, Adrian had said. Too bad he hadn't specified *where* in the B and B, but I had a plan for that, too.

I ditched the Challenger in the woods behind a gas station, but only after I wrapped some supplies in my blanket. Then I hoisted it over my shoulder like a sack, held Adrian's phone out in front of me so I could see the map, and started running.

Once, I would have found the dark expanse of woods creepy, but not now. Maybe it was because no animal in its right mind would attack me with my Hound disguise. Same went for people, and though the air was distinctly chilly, the

cold didn't affect me like it once would have. Must be my
growing abilities. After all, it couldn't be coincidence that I
barely needed the light from Adrian's cell phone to see.

You can do everything I can do…. It's in your blood. Adrian's
words stole through my mind, encouraging me and slamming
me with guilt at the same time. Dammit, I needed to stop
thinking about him! I'd made the only choice I could by not
trusting him, same thing he'd urged me to do over and over
again. Jasmine was the person I should feel guilty about. If
Adrian had been lying and she was dead, then I'd failed my
only remaining family. Worse, I'd lost my best friend.

Memories began to assail me. *Jasmine screaming with excitement
because she'd been accepted to the same college as me. Her countless
pranks, like adding BENGAY to my suntan lotion or replacing my
shampoo with bubble bath. How she'd hugged me after my disastrous
prom night, and how she'd never told any of my friends—or hers—
why I really went to the doctors so frequently. Jasmine as a little girl,
sitting with me in a psychologist's waiting room, her blue eyes somber
as she whispered, "If you say you see stuff, Ivy, I believe you…."*

The cell phone vibrated, startling me so much I almost
dropped it. *Incoming call,* read the screen. *Unknown.*

I slowed, torn between curiosity and caution. If I answered
and heard Demetrius's voice on the other line, it would con
firm all my suspicions. But what if it was Zach? I could really use the Archon's help, and for all I knew, Zach contacted
Adrian by phone; not to mention *unknown* would be a damn
good description of where *his* calls were routed from.

I hit Accept but didn't say anything, hoping whoever was
on the other line would speak first.

My gamble paid off.

"Ivy." Adrian's voice was hoarse from anger or urgency.
"Don't go in there alone. Don't—"

I hit the End button so hard, it cracked the screen. Then

I threw the phone down, as if that would further sever the connection between us. Still, the forest seemed to fill with Adrian's presence, until I could swear that the breeze ruffling through the trees was whispering his name.

"Leave me alone!" I yelled, sinking to the ground next to his phone. "You were going to betray me, so I had to do it."

Saying it didn't make me feel any better. Believing it hurt almost as much as hoping I was wrong. If I was, I'd ruined any chance between us by doing the one thing Adrian had managed *not* to do, despite heaven and hell telling him he had no choice. He wouldn't forgive me for that. No one would, myself included.

With a hard swipe at the tears filling my eyes, I grabbed the phone, got up and started to run again. Right or wrong, I'd made my choice. Whether Adrian intended to stop me or betray me, he knew where I was headed, so I didn't have much time.

Last time I'd seen the Paulson bed-and-breakfast, autumn leaves had been swirling around the lovely white house. Now, all the trees were bare and a dark, decrepit shell hung over the B and B, like the negative of a double-exposed photo. It didn't vanish after a couple blinks, either. It stayed, mute testament to how much my abilities had grown.

That's also why I could now see words carved into the side of the house, like "LEAVE!" "HELP!" and "DEMONS." Of course, no one else could see the warnings from people trapped in the other realm. Tourists who pulled up would only see a sign that said "Welcome, Friends!" on the portico over the front door.

I lurked at the far end of the yard, concealed by the trees that butted up against the foothills of the green mountains. Lights were on inside, giving off a warm amber glow, and two cars were in the gravel section where I'd parked the first time I came here. The B and B had guests.

And I was going to crash the party.

I started taking off my clothes, not stopping until I was down to only boots and the itchy leather bikini that doubled as Hound straps. I put the clothes in the blanket with my other supplies and hefted it over my shoulder again. Then I ran toward the house. When I reached the front door, I tried the knob. Just like before, it was unlocked. Silently, I entered the house, trying to focus on the *here* instead of the dark, double image that showed a place far different than this one.

No one was in the parlor where I'd first encountered Mrs. Paulson, but laughter came from farther down the hallway. I followed it, ending at the dining room. Two youngish-looking couples sat at the table, and for a frozen second as their heads swung toward me, no one moved.

Then screams coincided with the sound of chairs and other items crashing as they knocked things over in their panic to leave. I bared my teeth, hissing and waving my arms, hoping to scare them right into their cars. They needed to get out of here for more reasons than what Mrs. Paulson had probably been planning for them.

Not that the guests were grateful for my saving them. I had to dodge several plates one of the guys threw at me before he ran down the hallway. Finally, the woman I'd been waiting for appeared, looking flustered as she entered the dining room.

"What is going on—". Mrs. Paulson began, only to stop dead at the sight of me.

"*Dyate,*" she whispered.

chapter thirty-three

My grin must've looked savage, because I felt every inch the fearsome creature she thought I was as I came toward her. The innkeeper looked like the same salt-and-ginger-haired old lady I'd first met. She even still had on an apron, as if I'd interrupted her while she was baking dessert, but out of the two of us, she was the real monster.

This bitch had delivered my sister to demons. She'd also sent Detective Kroger after me, and for all I knew, might've been the person who'd messed with the brakes on my parents' car. I wanted her dead so badly, it burned. But first...

I dropped my sack when I was a few feet away. She still didn't move, following protocol on how to avoid being mauled by a Hound, but her gaze flicked to the sack in surprise. Guess she hadn't noticed it before, what with not expecting a hulking demon lizard to show up in her dining room. Then I pulled out the note I'd written earlier, shoving it in front of her.

Take me to the gateway.

Her face puckered into a frown as she stared at it. I knew she could read what I'd written; my note to Costa had proven that. My hope was that she'd think I was a stray who'd gotten separated from its handler, but that had a note telling whichever minion that found me to send me back home. As for the sack, well, dogs carried stuff sometimes. Maybe I should've held the sack in my teeth to look more Hound-like.

When her frown cleared and she looked at me with palpable hatred, I knew my plan had backfired.

"Davidian," she hissed, yanking something out of her apron.

I lunged to the left when I caught sight of a barrel. Her first shot missed me by inches and her second one went over my head as I ducked. Then I charged, steamrolling into her, fueled by hatred and strength from a legacy I still didn't understand. She went down, the back of her head smacking against the tile floor. But she still didn't let go of the gun.

I yanked its barrel to the side just in time, sending the shot she fired into the wall instead of my stomach. Despite her aged appearance, she had a grip like a bear. Teeth like one, too. She tore into my shoulder, making me yelp with pained surprise. I couldn't get the gun free, yet I didn't dare let go of it to pull her mouth off me.

As if Adrian were whispering instructions into my ear, I suddenly knew what he would do. So I did it.

I threw myself forward, my momentum causing Mrs. Paulson's head to smack against the tile again. Her scream reverberated against my aching shoulder, yet she didn't let go of the gun or stop biting me. I flung forward several more times, ignoring how it drove her teeth deeper into my flesh. Finally, her grip on the gun loosened and I was able to yank it away. My shoulder throbbed—I'd need a tetanus shot now, dammit!—but my grip didn't waver when I pointed the gun in her face.

"Where's the gateway?" I snapped, forgetting for a second that she couldn't understand me.

Mrs. Paulson spat at me, landing a disgusting glop on my cheek. I wiped it off with my other hand before grabbing the note that had fluttered to the floor near us.

"Where?" I said, shaking it at her.

She responded with a torrent of Demonish, some of which I recognized as more curse words. My jaw clenched. Adrian was on his way, and I didn't know whose side he was on, so I had to be gone before he arrived. That meant I couldn't waste any more time asking Mrs. Paulson nicely.

I lowered the gun and shot her in the arm. At this range, it blew a large chunk off, coating me in an instant spatter of red. She howled, her agonized writhing almost dislodging me, but I held on and shoved the note in front of her again.

"Where?" I yelled, putting the barrel to her leg next.

She didn't need to understand my words to translate the threat. "In my office!" she gasped. "Please, no more!"

She deserved more. So, so much more, but I didn't have the time or the stomach to give it to her. I hauled her up, planting the barrel of the gun into her side. She sagged, leaning against me so heavily, she almost toppled us over.

"Show me," I said, jerking my head at the hallway.

Once again, she got the gist and began staggering down the hallway. From the quiet around us, we were now alone in the inn. Guess if a massive demon lizard hadn't been enough to scare the guests off, hearing several gunshots had done the trick.

"Here," she said, leaning against the doorway to an office.

I couldn't see through to the dark realm here, but then again, I hadn't with any of the other gateways, either. Still, I wasn't going to take her word for it. I jabbed her harder in the side with the gun and shook the note for emphasis.

"Where?" I said, shoving her into the room.

Blood had turned her graying hair crimson, and more dripped from what was left of her upper arm, but she still managed to catch herself instead of falling. Again I was reminded that minions might look human, but they weren't, so while Mrs. Paulson was acting weak and defeated, the bitch still had lots of fight left in her.

"There," she said, pointing at the corner. Then she braced herself against her desk, as if she didn't have the strength to hold herself up on her own.

Sure she didn't. I kept the gun aimed at her as I went inside. The corner had a bookshelf on one side and an oil painting on the other. Certainly nothing that screamed "Demon door!" but when had any of them been helpfully marked? I stretched out my hand toward the center of the corner—and gasped when the blood coating it suddenly pulsed with an almost painful energy.

Adrian was right. It *did* feel like an electric shock, but only for the parts of me that Mrs. Paulson had bled on. That's why I'd done the most awful, unforgivable thing to him before I left him tied up and alone in that room.

I'd bled him.

Adrian told me I needed minion, demon or Judian blood to cross through a gateway. I hadn't been sure if Mrs. Paulson would be here tonight, so I'd taken precautions to ensure that I could get through the gateway anyway, and by precautions, I mean about two beer bottles' worth of Adrian's blood.

Maybe now, I wouldn't need it. The last thing I wanted to do was paint my skin with the proof of my awful deed. I could barely look at the bottles without feeling guilty enough to cry, so hopefully Mrs. Paulson had bled on me enough to—

An ominous click had me throwing myself to the side, and not a moment too soon. White hot pain grazed my arm, but my otherworldly speed had saved my life. While I'd let thoughts of Adrian distract me, Mrs. Paulson had gotten another gun from somewhere.

I fired back, not even getting a chance to really aim because I was too busy running out of the room. Just as quickly, I ran back in, cursing myself the whole time. *Don't leave a minion alone with a demon realm gateway, dumb ass!*

Mrs. Paulson was on the floor, one hand stretched toward the gateway as if she were trying to claw her way inside. She wouldn't be going anywhere, though. A single smoking hole dotted her forehead and the back of her head was gone. Then the rest of her disappeared as her body disintegrated into ashes.

I didn't have time to marvel at my shot, celebrate this small revenge for Jasmine, or be worried about how little it bothered me to kill someone. Again. Instead, I went back to the dining room to grab my sack and rub more of Mrs. Paulson's blood on me. Then, bracing myself, I went back to her office and ran straight for the corner.

Every other time I'd entered a realm, I'd tumbled out of the gateway into a barren landscape of frozen darkness. This time, I landed in a decrepit version of the same bed-and-breakfast, with lights glowing from the nearby hallway.

Mrs. Paulson's office looked a lot different on this side. It didn't have a stick of furniture and the only decorations on the walls were holes. Aside from some ratty-looking blankets, it was also empty. When I crept out into the hallway, however, I found out that the rest of the B and B wasn't.

"Hound!" a brown-haired guy who looked about my age yelled. Then he froze, giving me a chance to take in his ragged clothes, unkempt hair and wiry build. If I'd seen him in the real world, I'd have expected him to be holding up a sign asking for money. For a human in a demon realm, he looked great. His clothes were dirty and torn, but they were *real* clothes. Not disgusting human hides, and though he was lean, he didn't look half-starved.

Was the Bennington realm slightly less appalling than the other ones? The thought gave me hope that my sister was still alive. I wished I could ask the guy about Jasmine, but all he'd hear were hisses, and I'd left my notepad back on the other side.

Adrian had told me that Jasmine wouldn't be in the B and B, yet I checked it anyway. All the people stood like statues in whatever posture they'd been in when they heard the "Hound" warning, making them look like exhibits in a wax museum. They were in their teens or twenties and looked as disheveled as the first guy I'd seen. Still, no one looked abused, and the kitchen had real food in it. From the makeshift beds in almost every room, these people seemed to live here, yet I hadn't come across a minion yet.

I also didn't see Jasmine, but she'd been here. One of the girls had on a sweater that I recognized as hers. Again, I ached to ask, but I didn't have time to find a way to communicate, not to mention that minions could show up here any minute.

So could Adrian. I let that thought spur me as I left the B and B, dropping my sack by a nearby tree stump so I could grab it on my way back. Then I ran toward the lights in the distance. The temperatures made my teeth chatter, but being here filled me with a desperate sort of hope.

Soon, I'd know for myself if Jasmine was really still alive. If she was, I'd keep up my search for the weapon, even if I'd be doing it without Adrian. Zach would help me, if only because he didn't want the demons to get it. After I found the slingshot, I'd use it to free Jasmine. Then we'd hide out from the demons and I'd help her get over her captivity while helping myself get over my feelings for Adrian.

Bleakness threaded through me. Guess I should focus on one impossible task at a time.

Growling sounds made me skid to a stop midway up the hill. Lots of trees remained in this realm, standing like tall, petrified monuments to the world they'd been snatched from. That made it hard to see, even with my abilities working at full capacity. Had to be Hounds patrolling the woods.

Those odd snarls came nearer, echoing in ways that almost sounded like they were coming from above. I looked around, expecting a demon lizard to pounce out from behind a tree, but none did. Since I wasn't supposed to act afraid, I continued back up the hill, though going at a walk instead of a run.

Crashing noises above were my only warning. Then I had to run to avoid being flattened by a pile of frozen tree branches. Even at top speed, I still got struck, but I forgot about the pain when I saw what had caused them to come down around me.

Gray, leathery wings snapped back from their protective circle, revealing a creature that had to be nine feet tall. It crouched in almost apelike style, with its straight, massive arms resting between its bent legs. Shoulder and chest muscles bulged as it raised its head, showing red, glowing eyes and a face that was wider than a Hound's, but no less animalistic.

If Hounds looked like what would happen if a werewolf mated with a Komodo dragon, then this thing looked like the love child of a Komodo-werewolf-pterodactyl threesome. Worse, the way it stared at me said that moving or standing still made no difference. It could see me either way.

Gargoyle ran through my mind with a morbid sort of fascination. The Bennington realm had a gargoyle.

chapter thirty-four

I did the only thing I could think of when confronted by a much-larger creature who thought I was a dog-lizard: I rolled on my back and showed it my belly, hoping the "Don't kill me, I'm friendly!" gesture was as universal among animals here as it was in my realm.

The gargoyle cocked its head, staring at me as if I was the strangest thing it had ever seen. It didn't start tearing into me with those knifelike claws or teeth, though, so I considered my move a win. Cautiously, I rolled over, twitching so much from nervousness that my Archon-glamoured tail probably looked like it was wagging. I wasn't just in over my head with this situation—I was a thousand feet underwater.

The gargoyle chuffed at me. That's the closest way I could describe it, but at least it didn't start speaking Demonish. Hey, gargoyles could talk in cartoons; how the hell did I know if they could talk in real life, too?

"Hiya," I said back, hoping what it heard was a similar-sounding chuff.

It chuffed again, beating its wings for emphasis. Clearly I was supposed to do something. Damned if I knew what.

"Uh, follow you?" I guessed, taking a hesitant step back up the hill.

It rose with an explosion of air from those powerful wings, which I took as a yes. Then I had to scramble to avoid another shower of frozen branches as it blasted through the tops of the trees. Triumph and terror mingled inside me. I'd met a real-life gargoyle and survived. Now *there* was a Facebook update for a later time, not that anyone would believe me. Besides, what if gargoyles weren't the only unexpected creatures in this realm?

For the space of a few heartbeats, I wasn't sure what to do. Run toward the demon town over the hill? Or go back to the gateway inside the B and B? Adrian hadn't been kidding when he said the demons in this realm would beef up their security. No wonder there hadn't been any minions at the B and B. They didn't need them to keep the humans in line. Not when death flew from above.

And prowled along the ground, I realized as familiar hissing noises heralded the approach of three Hounds.

"You're late," I told them dryly, letting the beasts smear me with disgusting, slimy licks as they said their versions of hello. Between meeting a gargoyle and getting a Hound tongue-bath, I'd have nightmares forever from this realm alone.

Decision made, I followed the Hounds back up the hill. Since I was already scarred for life, I wasn't leaving until I'd seen for myself that Jasmine was still alive.

When we reached the top of the hill and I caught my first look at the city, I paused. *Beautiful,* I thought grudgingly.

A lot more time had passed since this section of the realm had been swallowed. Most of the forest had been cut down, leaving smooth, flat ground. Frozen rivers snaked through the valley in zigzags, ice reflecting the lights from the castle. The effect made the castle look like it sat on silver necklaces, and the significance of its blue stone walls wasn't lost on me.

Silver and sapphire, the same color as Adrian's eyes. I was staring at his former home, and it was barbarically magnificent.

I felt like I was leaving pieces of my heart behind as I followed the Hounds down the hill to the huge castle. Of course Adrian must have been playing me. No one raised by demons would have the fortitude to give all this up. People *not* raised by demons would struggle with saying no to all the power, money and supernatural bling that was Adrian's for the taking.

Like his castle. It could double as an icy version of Hogwarts with its massive size. Add in stone gates with elaborate frozen carvings glittering along their tops like cake frosting, and it was breathtaking. The minions who guarded it had shadow markings in their skin, showing they belonged to Demetrius, but their silvery breastplates all had an elaborately scripted *A* stenciled into the metal. So did the frescos in the outer courtyards, as if I needed more proof that I was in Adrian's former realm.

And all of this would be his again, if only he turned me over to the demons like everyone expected him to.

One of the Hounds nudged me, almost knocking me over. Okay, so I'd stopped running to stare at Adrian's once and future kingdom. It had all the extravagance of the other realms, but with one notable difference. Where were the slaves? I hadn't passed any ramshackle villages on the way, and most of the people milling around the courtyards were minions. Had—?

Something at the top of one of the towers caught my eye. This tower was lit up more than the others—that I'd noticed from the top of the hill—and it also had more open spaces, allowing for easier viewing inside.

That's why I could see the girl in the cage. Amber light surrounded her, coating her hair and body in varying shades of gold. The cage hung by a thick chain from the tower's roof, and the girl was sitting in it, her back resting against a corner. She wasn't wearing much more than I was, making me wonder how she hadn't frozen to death, until the humming noises coming from the tower clicked with the golden lights bathing her.

She was surrounded by portable heating devices. When she glanced down at the Hounds, who'd started to bay in annoyance because I'd stopped moving again, I glimpsed her face. Even though she was more than forty feet above me, my heart started to pound while my soul felt like it sucked in a breath.

Jasmine. My sister was alive and in that cage!

An avalanche of emotions rolled over me, making my eyes blur with a surge of tears. All these weeks, I'd been risking my life to save her, but an ugly, hidden part of me had thought she was already dead. Everyone else I cared for had been snatched away from me, so why should she be any different? That's why, for the space of several stunned seconds, I couldn't stop staring at Jasmine. That hopeless, jaded part of me was convinced that if I blinked or looked away, she'd disappear.

She didn't, despite my finally being brave enough to close my eyes. When I opened them and saw that she was still there, a noise tore from my throat that was part sob, part laugh. She was alive! Really, truly alive, and unhurt, from what I could see of her. If I hadn't been surrounded by minions who'd kill me the second they realized who I was, I might have giggled from the maelstrom of relief that flooded me, joining all the other feelings that seemed to compete with each other for maximum intensity.

Then something unexpected happened. My hallowed-hunting abilities kicked into gear. Maybe my sudden overload of emotions had activated them. I hadn't tried using them because the weapon couldn't be here. It was in a weak ruler's realm, and Demetrius ruled this one in Adrian's absence.

Yet the instant flare that thrummed through me wasn't relief at discovering that Jasmine was alive, though I was beyond relieved at that. It wasn't even anger over how she was displayed like a taunting trophy, and that made me damned angry. It was something completely different.

The only other time I'd felt anything similar was when I'd found hallowed ground for Adrian and me to flee to. If that had been a blip on my internal radar, this was a *boom!* that shook me from the inside out. Even feeling Mrs. Paulson's blood react to the demon gateway paled by comparison, and that meant one thing: something hallowed was here. Something *so* hallowed my entire body felt like it had multiple alarms blaring inside me, all pointing toward a single location as if it were a tracking transmitter and I was the antennae.

Shock turned into wild, inconceivable hope. Not only was Jasmine alive, she was in the same realm as the weapon that could save her.

chapter thirty-five

I followed the Hounds inside the castle, but instead of turning down the low hallway that must've led to their version
of a spa mud bath, I veered off into a corner. A baying hiss
was probably one of them cursing me for not keeping up again,
yet the lure of getting warm kept them from coming after me.

Good. One Hound roaming though the castle would already garner suspicion. A pack of them? I might as well write
my name on my chest so everybody would know who I was.

Then again, maybe it didn't matter. I could *feel* the weapon
yanking on my abilities, urging me to free it from its hidden
location. Once I did, I wouldn't need to be afraid anymore.
Instead, the demons and minions would fear.

The thought emboldened me. I left the corner, ignoring
the startled looks I got as I ran through the inner courtyards.
At least these food vendors sold cow, pig and poultry instead
of human meat, which meant I didn't have the urge to vomit
as I wove through them. Then I was past the vendor area and
running for the first stone staircase I saw. The weapon was

several floors above me, according to what I could feel, and its power pulsed through my emotions like a beacon.

I passed some humans on the way, so this realm did have more. In fact, they seemed to live in the castle, judging from the instant slamming of doors as they caught sight of me and hid. The ones I came across on the staircase froze in mid-step, only their eyes moving as I dashed past them. Just as I'd thought, Hounds must have certain designated areas, and the main castle interior wasn't one of them.

A voice shouted in Demonish behind me. Had someone sent the Hound handlers after me? I ignored the shout, running faster, a fearful exhilaration rising up to almost strangle me. I couldn't let someone stop me when I was so close to my goal. I just couldn't.

I left the staircase at the fourth-floor landing, the slingshot pulling me toward it like I was a fish being reeled in on a line. Following that inner pull, I dashed down the hallway to an ornate, wood-paneled room that looked like a library, of all things. Either word of a Hound on the loose had preceded me or this room wasn't used a lot, because no one was in it.

That didn't mean it was empty. My body pulsed from the weapon's nearness, drawing me toward the center of the room. A huge, four-sided fireplace rose up through the floor, the stone chimney disappearing into the soaring ceiling. Shields adorned the side facing me, with wicked-looking battle-axes on the opposing sides. The hearth was almost as tall as I was, and warmth radiated from the crackling flames, but that wasn't why I stood next to it, reaching as high as I could to touch the stones above the mantel.

There. The slingshot was right up *there,* and I was too short to reach it!

I spun around, grabbing the nearest chair and hauling it over to the fireplace. Then I paused, eyeing the polished stone chimney. I couldn't punch through it without breaking every bone in my hand, and then I wouldn't be able to use the sling-shot.

Seized with inspiration, I stood on the chair and yanked one of the battle-axes off. It felt heavy and solid like a real weapon. Time to see if it worked like one.

Stone shards pelted me with my first swing, their sharp edges stinging. Okay, so the ax worked! I swung it again, harder, and a bigger chunk of stone split off. The chair tilted from my momentum, reminding me to watch my balance. I used my legs to counter my force as I swung the ax again and again, until I was whacking at the chimney like a lumberjack trying to chop down a tree.

My heart pounded when enough stone crumbled away to reveal a smooth wall beneath, like a hidden panel. Something brown and twisted clumped at the bottom of it, and I threw the ax away. No way would I risk severing the slingshot by chopping my way to it. Instead, I used my hands to pry the rest of the stones away before reaching down into the panel.

Power sizzled up my arm, the sensation so sudden and strong, it was painful. Instinctively, I snatched my hand back, then grinned, bracing myself as I reached down again. This time, I pulled up a long, braided rope that was identical to Adrian's slingshot—except this one was stained brown from age.

"*Hondalte!*" someone shouted behind me.

I turned, seeing two armor-wearing minions and a third minion with so much mud covering him, he had to be a Hound handler. Muddy Minion had a harness in one hand and what looked like raw pot roast meat in the other. My en-ticement to come quietly, I supposed.

I jumped off the chair, which made all of them flinch. Guess they hadn't expected to see a Hound standing on the furniture. They also didn't expect one to use a slingshot, and as I slid my finger through the loop on the weapon, I smiled.

This was it. Jasmine's freedom and our ticket out of here, all courtesy of the raggedy-looking weapon that vibrated with so much power, my arm throbbed just from touching it. I picked up one of the rounder pieces of stone that had chipped off the chimney, and placed it in the thicker section of the sling. Adrian might have intended to betray me, but he'd taught me how to use this, and I didn't hesitate as I began to spin the rope, walking toward the minions while savage anticipation flooded me.

The minions began to back away, either in incredulity at seeing a Hound wield a slingshot, or in realization of what was really going on. I spun the rope faster, determined not to let them or any of the other awful creatures in this realm get away. Then I aimed, sending the stone hurtling toward them with a snapping sound that was music to my ears.

Take that, bastards!

The stone hit the blond minion in the chest, denting his armor right in the middle of its elaborately embroidered "A." Then it dropped to the floor, which is what I expected the blond minion to do. In fact, I expected *all* of them to drop dead on the spot, but the blond minion only stared at me. Then he stared at the stone and his friends, his expression changing from fear to bewilderment.

"That's it?" he asked in English.

My exultation turned to ashes, which is what the minions should have done. Yet they stood there, a dent in Blond Minion's armor the only sign that I'd hit him with the famed, long-sought-after weapon.

I grabbed another chunk of stone, desperation making my fingers tremble as I slid it into the slight pouch. *This has to work, it has to!* my mind roared. No way was this the wrong weapon. Not only had it been hidden in a wall within a demon realm, its power made my arm ache. So why wasn't it killing everyone like it was *supposed* to?

I whipped the stone toward them without really aiming this time. It hit Muddy Minion, and he let out a yelp that gave me a wild flash of hope before I realized I'd only pissed him off.

Then the three minions lunged toward me, all their former wariness gone, and I did the only thing I could do.

I ran.

chapter thirty-six

Trying to hide while looking like a half-ton demon lizard would be impossible. That's why I ran straight to the tunnel in the lower courtyard where I'd seen the other Hounds disappear to. As expected, it led to the mud room and I submerged myself into the warm, stinky water along with the rest of them. I even took off my leather bikini since I'd noticed that none of these Hounds wore straps, but I kept the slingshot. I intended to choke Zach with it as soon as I saw him—if I managed to live through this.

All for nothing! I kept inwardly howling. I'd risked my life repeatedly based on the promise that if I found the slingshot, I'd be able to save my sister. Now I had the stupid, ancient weapon, and it couldn't even help me save myself.

After about ten minutes, the Hounds decided they were warm enough to patrol again. I got out with them, intending to run straight for the B and B as soon as I cleared the castle grounds. When we rounded a corner in the stone hallway, however, a barricade of minions blocked our path, lined so deep that I couldn't count them all.

The other Hounds turned, deciding this must mean they got more time in the mud bath. I followed them, hoping like crazy that there was another way out except the one that was blocked. Just in case, as soon as we were back in the small room, I slipped the slingshot under a pile of animal bones in the corner. Much as I wanted to throttle Zach with the useless weapon, I didn't want to get caught because I was the only Hound that appeared to be carrying its own leash.

It took just a few seconds to realize there was no exit down here. Out of options, I got into the water with the other Hounds, feeling as naked and helpless as I was. *Why'd you run to the only place that didn't have another way out?* I silently lashed myself. So much for my plan to blend in.

My situation went from bad to worse when Demetrius strode into the underground room. The demon's shadows filled the small space, brushing across my head and shoulders like tiny, icy fingers. I sank farther beneath the water, suddenly glad to be covered by the smelly, muddy liquid.

Three more people filed in after him. With sinking spirits, I recognized Blond Minion, Muddy Minion and their friend, whom I now dubbed as Scowling Minion for obvious reasons.

Demetrius said something to them in Demonish. Muddy Minion came up to the edge of the water and barked out one word. The Hounds sprang forward like he'd yelled "Lunch!" I did, too, standing at attention as they seemed to be doing.

Demetrius walked along the length of us. Whatever word the Hound handler had used, it kept all of them in perfect formation like dutiful lizard soldiers. So much for my hope that they'd charge anyone moving and I could slip out in the ensuing melee. No, I had to stand in line with them, all the while feeling like I had a neon sign over my head that flashed

"Davidian." Terror slithered through me, making me almost oblivious to the fact that I was stark naked in front of Demetrius and a few other men. If Demetrius could tell I wasn't a Hound, I was dead.

Or worse.

Demetrius spoke sharply to Muddy Minion, who looked at the other Hounds and me with such obvious confusion that I almost whooped in relief. He couldn't tell us apart! Okay, I wasn't going to strangle Zach if I got out of this. I'd only punch him in the face. His Hound disguise was so good, not even their handler could tell me apart from the others—

"Ivy."

Willpower alone kept my head from snapping up at the sound of my name. Demetrius wasn't getting me to out myself that easily. My fortitude must've surprised him because he went to the nearest Hound, petting it in apparent bemusement.

"I know you're here," Demetrius went on, flashing his cruel smile as he fondled the beast. "No Hound would use an ax to smash through a chimney, so it's obvious you came to this realm looking for the weapon. Very clever of the Archons to disguise you as one of our pets. We're so used to having Hounds run about, we don't even notice when we have an extra one."

I said nothing, of course. Didn't even breathe loudly. My continued pretense was just staving off the inevitable, but what was I supposed to do? Serve myself up with a smile?

"Clever also of you to soak yourself in here," Demetrius continued, leaning in to smell the next Hound in line. "That mud bath reeks so much, I can't pick up anything that might give you away, like the lingering trace of perfume."

Haven't worn any lately, I thought to distract myself from the fear that made me want to start shaking. Being on the run with Adrian hadn't allowed for many shopping trips to the mall.

"But I will discover which one you are," Demetrius all but purred as he reached me. I forced myself not to recoil when his hand slid over me, brushing my breast on its way to my back. His touch was somehow burning cold, like holding an icicle for too long. Still, I tried to school my features into the bland, compliant mask the other Hounds wore. My situation might be hopeless, but if Demetrius wanted to kill me, he had to figure out on his own which one I was.

His hand slipped down my arm and he leaned in, taking a deep breath. *Please, let me stink as badly as the rest of them!* I silently prayed. What if he could smell the shampoo I'd used when I washed my hair this morning? Or the deodorant I'd put on because it hadn't occurred to me that I'd be demon-sniff-tested tonight?

It was all I could do not to sag in relief when Demetrius moved on to the Hound after me. *How I love you, filthy reeking mud bath!* I inwardly crowed. *If I get out of this, I'll take a mud bath every night in your honor—*

Two more minions came into the room, freezing my thoughts in midvow. Not because the minions were the largest men I'd ever seen, but because they didn't come alone.

They thrust Jasmine out from between them, causing her to stumble for a few feet before Demetrius caught her. My sister looked at the demon with all the horror I felt, and when he ran a hand over her dirt-matted blond hair, a tremor of pure rage shook me. *Don't touch her!* I silently seethed. *I'll kill you, I'll kill you!*

But I couldn't. The weapon was across the room under a pile of animal bones, and even if I *could* reach it, the damn thing didn't work. Despair threaded into my rage, forming a toxic mixture that ran like poison through my veins. Everything I'd risked, all the pain I'd endured, everything Jasmine had been through…it had all been for nothing.

"With you here, Ivy, I don't need her anymore," Demetrius said, his tone filled with the surety of victory. "So you have a choice—reveal yourself, or watch your sister die."

"Ivy?" my sister asked, looking around. "Where?"

I drew in a breath that was probably going to be my last. I didn't want to give the demon the satisfaction of making me reveal myself, but no matter what he'd do to me, I couldn't watch my sister die.

"Don't bother."

Adrian's voice filled the room, chilling and thrilling me as my traitorous emotions responded in wildly conflicting ways. Then my heart nearly stopped at his next words, which were delivered in a flatly emotionless tone.

"I can see which one she is."

Adrian pushed past the huge minions like they were nothing more than toy soldiers. Then his gaze landed on me, and the coldness I saw devastated me. For a split second, I actually *wanted* to die. My worst fears were confirmed in those merciless sapphire depths, and the curl to his mouth seemed to mock me for ever believing the lies he'd told me.

And I *had* believed them. Even when I'd knocked him out and tied him up, part of me had hoped I was making a terrible mistake. Yeah, I had, but not by doing that. By not listening to him the first time he'd told me not to trust him.

Demetrius's dark gaze flared as Adrian walked toward him. "My son," he said almost reverently. "I never doubted that this moment would come."

I suppressed a bitter snort. A demon with unwavering faith, how ironic. And his faith would soon be rewarded, how unfair.

Adrian smiled as he embraced his foster father, practically shoving Jasmine out of the way to get to him. I don't know why I didn't run to my sister in the last few seconds I had left. Maybe shock froze me in place, keeping me from doing anything except staring at the man who'd proven to be every bit as traitorous as his infamous ancestor. *Everyone* had warned me about Adrian, yet just like my gullible or well-intentioned family members, I hadn't listened.

Now, just like my ancestors, I'd also die after being betrayed by a Judian.

"I kept everything in this realm the way you left it," Demetrius murmured, pulling away. "Even your ridiculously burdensome means of feeding and housing your slaves."

Adrian chuckled like Demetrius had told a joke. "Makes them work harder to avoid being sent to one of your realms... Father."

The word was the final nail into my heart, but Demetrius smiled with such joy, it transformed his face, making him appear as he must have once looked however many aeons ago.

Angelic.

"Let us finish this," he said, kissing Adrian's forehead. Then he turned toward the other Hounds and me, his arm still around Adrian's shoulders as though he couldn't bear to let him go. "Which one is she?"

Adrian met my gaze—and strode over to the Hound next to me, shoving it toward Demetrius with such force that he actually managed to make the huge creature stumble.

"Here she is," he said clearly.

chapter thirty-seven

I looked at the Hound, then at Adrian, emotion after emotion crushing me as though I were being hit by multiple tidal waves. He hadn't come here to betray me. Once again, against all odds and destinies, he was trying to save me.

I wanted to throw my arms around him and sob out an apology for ever doubting him, let alone all the other terrible things I'd done. Then I wanted to kiss him until neither of us could breathe. But I couldn't do either of those things. If I so much as moved, I'd undo the ruse he was trying to pull off.

"That thing isn't Ivy."

My sister's confused whisper cut through my inner battle, but the surge had already activated my abilities, and they zeroed in on Adrian. Granted, my hallowed-sensor should've picked up on what was in his pocket before, but in my defense, I'd been a little preoccupied thinking I was about to die.

"Her appearance is disguised," Adrian responded, flashing a nasty smile at the Hound. "Not that it does any good with me."

The Hound looked mildly irritated at being shoved around, but it didn't attack. Talk about well-trained. Demetrius pulled a knife out of the sheath on his belt, and I braced in pity for the creature. Here's hoping the demon would make it quick—

Faster than I could blink, he had Jasmine in his grip, the knife against my sister's throat. The Hound barely spared them a glance, but I lunged forward with an anguished cry.

"No!"

Adrian caught me before I reached the demon, and for a split second, his eyes met mine. So many feelings spilled from his gaze that I could barely believe he was the same person who'd looked at me so coldly moments before. Then four incensed words brought our attention back to Demetrius.

"You lied to me."

Adrian took off his long coat, putting it around me. The whole time, his gaze never left Demetrius's, even when I felt him furtively remove something from the coat's pocket.

"You wanted me to be a betrayer." Adrian's voice was thick with sarcasm. "Be careful what you wish for, *father.*"

"If you won't rule with me, then you can die with your whore," Demetrius hissed, digging the knife deeper into Jasmine's throat. "But not before she tells me where the weapon is. I know you found it, Davidian. Where did you put it?"

Adrian's gaze swung to me. "It was *here?*"

I nodded, too horrified by the line of blood trailing down Jasmine's throat to answer audibly. Another ounce of pressure, and her jugular would be severed.

Adrian let out a short laugh. "Right under your nose this whole time. Must've been hidden here before you stole this realm from Ciscero."

"Give it to me, Davidian, or watch her die," Demetrius ordered, ignoring that.

I tightened the coat around me, then went over to the pile

of bones and pulled the slingshot out from under it. Damned thing didn't work anyway, but maybe it would provide enough distraction for Adrian to use whatever he'd brought with him.

"Ivy, don't," Adrian said, grasping my arm.

I glanced at his hand and then back at him, trying to tell him with my eyes to get ready.

"If he has this, he doesn't need us anymore," I said, knowing the demon would try to kill us anyway, but hoping Demetrius believed *I* was that naïve.

The two minions who'd brought Jasmine began to circle around us. Blondie, Muddy Minion and Scowling Minion moved to block the tunnel entrance, as if the dozens more behind them weren't enough to prevent our escape. Demetrius didn't seem to notice the extra activity. He stared at the braided rope dangling from my hand with something akin to rapture.

"So let us all go," I continued, "and it's yours."

Adrian translated my words to the demon. He dropped my arm, too, his hooded sapphire gaze flicking between me and Demetrius.

I hoped that meant he understood and was on board. Demetrius was. He lowered the knife, revealing a small, still-bleeding cut on Jasmine's neck. Then he shoved my sister toward me. She caught herself before she reached me, staring at me with horrified confusion. Right, I still looked like a Hound. How could I keep forgetting that?

"A deal's a deal," I said, tossing the slingshot toward the demon.

He reached out to catch it—and Adrian hurled the small object he'd concealed in his coat. Dazzling white exploded in the underground room, throwing Demetrius backward while briefly blinding me. The demon's agonized scream seared my ears as Adrian yanked me into his arms, and I felt rather than saw him haul my sister against him next.

When my vision cleared, the five minions were dissolving into ashes from the Archon grenade and the Hounds were dead, but Demetrius was still alive. And mad as hell.

"You failed," the demon spat, hauling himself over to block the exit to the tunnel. "You may have killed these men, but you will not escape!"

Adrian's response was to whistle, loud and long. Demetrius cocked his head, confusion replacing the pain on his pale features. Then his eyes widened as screams erupted from farther down the tunnel. He sprang aside right as a huge gray form hurtled into the room. Dark gray wings unfolded, revealing the monstrous, massive gargoyle I'd encountered earlier.

"Thanks for keeping everything just the way I left it," Adrian told Demetrius before throwing Jasmine at the gargoyle. "Especially for keeping my most loyal pet, Brutus."

Jasmine screamed as the gargoyle caught her against its chest with one leathery, muscled arm. Then it was my turn to yelp as Adrian shoved me at the creature. The gargoyle pressed me next to Jasmine, its arm an unbreakable band across our stomachs. Adrian ran across the room, snatched up the slingshot and then threw himself at the gargoyle right as it began to beat its massive wings. The gargoyle caught Adrian and shot forward, the powerful expulsion of air propelling us down the tunnel.

The gargoyle was so strong that it could hold us without difficulty, but the weight of our three bodies proved too heavy for it to fly. We smashed into some of the minions lining the tunnel, resulting in a brief, fierce fight before another rush of the gargoyle's wings cleared us over them in a sort of hop. Then we plowed back down again.

Demetrius's enraged scream filled the tunnel behind us. "Kill them, kill them!"

Countless hands seemed to pull at us, weighing the gargoyle down even more. Adrian punched and kicked while the creature rallied valiantly, another burst of power clearing us over the seething mass in this section of the tunnel. Before we could reach the end, though, we dropped back down again. Only fifty yards away, a wall of minions rushed toward us, urged on by Demetrius's furious commands in English and Demonish.

Adrian looked at me, then barked out a few words that made the gargoyle halt and, unbelievably, let him go.

"What are you doing?" I gasped.

He took my head, his silvery-sapphire gaze almost burning into mine.

"He can't fly with all of us, and I'm the heaviest. Brutus'll take you to the B and B, then you need to cross through the gateway." A dark, quick smile. "You already know how."

I was appalled. "Adrian, you can't—"

He pulled my head down, his mouth searing mine in a kiss that matched the blazing intensity in his eyes. Desperation, desire and despair seemed to pour from him into me, but when he broke the kiss and pulled away, he was smiling.

"I love you, Ivy. I love you, and I didn't betray you. For the first time in my life, I feel like I can do anything."

Then he stuffed the slingshot in my coat pocket, smacked the gargoyle on the side and yelled, *"Tarate!"* Those mighty wings began to beat at once.

"No!" I screamed, struggling to get free.

The gargoyle rose up, no longer encumbered by too much weight. The last thing I saw before we cleared the tunnel and the realm's eternally dark skyline enveloped us was Adrian turning toward the horde of minions that was almost upon him.

chapter thirty-eight

Jasmine screamed in terror the whole way to the B and B. I screamed, too. In anguish. Adrian was strong, but he couldn't beat dozens of minions when they were armed and he wasn't. He was going to die, and he knew it, but he'd willingly doomed himself to save me.

I love you, Ivy.

I thought my heart had been wounded before. Now, I could feel it ripping wide-open, scalding my insides with the kind of pain that would never heal. There had to be a way to save him.

As soon as the gargoyle released us at the entrance to the B and B, I started yelling the same word Adrian had used to make it leave him.

"*Tarate, tarate!* Go back and get Adrian!"

The creature only stared at me. Jasmine backed away a few feet, rubbing her arms against the chill I barely noticed in my desperation.

"If you're really Ivy, do something to prove it."

Do something? Like what, start miming out the letters to

my name? Couldn't she see that I was trying to get the winged monstrosity to save Adrian, yet the stupid thing just kept *looking* at me!

In complete frustration, I flipped Jasmine off. She blinked in disbelief, then threw herself at me.

"Ivy!"

She started crying in the loud, hiccupping way she used to do when she was a child. I held her with one arm, flapping the other at the gargoyle in a last-ditch attempt to get it to understand that it had to *fly*. Now.

The creature chuffed at me in obvious annoyance. Then its wing whipped out so fast, for a second, wild hope filled me. I shoved Jasmine back, screaming "That's it!" while flapping both my arms. Then I noticed something rolling on the ground toward me. What was—?

Jasmine shrieked and I recoiled. It was a head, and as it dissolved into a small pile of ashes, I noticed the form to the right of the gargoyle just before it, too, dissipated into ashes.

The gargoyle angled its wings flat like two massive, leathery blades. Then it took one step toward me, and a burst of motion behind me made me spin around.

The minion who'd been sneaking up on us turned around and started hightailing it into the woods. The gargoyle chuffed loudly, as if saying, "Yeah, you'd better run!" before folding its wings into two compact piles on its back.

I wanted to thank it and rail at it at the same time. Yes, it had just saved my life, but it should be saving *Adrian's*. Not standing here like a dinosaur version of a knight in shining armor. Since I couldn't seem to communicate that, I ran to the tree stump where I'd left my supplies. Where there were two minions, there'd soon be more, so I had to get Jasmine out of here while I still could. Besides, maybe Costa and a lot of weapons were waiting on the other side of this realm. If I couldn't make the gargoyle rescue Adrian, maybe I could find a way to do it myself.

Once I had my sack, I took Jasmine's hand and led her into the B and B. Unbelievably, the gargoyle followed us, though it stayed bent down because it was taller than the ceiling. The human residents of the B and B stood stock-still in terror at the sight of a Hound and the winged creature in the house, and I had no way of telling them that neither one of us were dangerous.

Well, the gargoyle probably wasn't dangerous.

I drew Jasmine into Mrs. Paulson's office, pain knifing my heart again when I pulled out one of the two beer bottles filled with Adrian's blood. *I'm coming back for you,* I silently promised, hating myself for what I'd done. Then, because I had no choice, I smeared my hands with Adrian's blood and started running them over Jasmine.

She let out a noise that was half whimper, half fearful sob. "W-what are you doing, Ivy?"

I wasn't about to waste Adrian's blood by using it to write out an explanation, so I held my finger to my lips in the universal gesture for silence. Once I estimated that she was covered enough, I used the rest of his blood on myself. *Betrayer!* those red smears seemed to scream at me.

My eyes blurred with tears. Yes, I was a betrayer and Adrian wasn't. Now, to make sure he lived so I could apologize to him for the rest of my life.

I put the second bottle in the opposite corner of the office, then grabbed Jasmine around the waist and hurtled us both toward the gateway. That push-pull-stretch-puke sensation as we crossed through the realms seemed worse, but we tumbled out into the non-demon version of Mrs. Paulson's office.

Unfortunately, we weren't alone.

"What the *hell?*" the young, sandy-haired cop sputtered.

Right, the guests would've called the police after I'd scared them out of here with my rampaging monster act. I let go of Jasmine, but put myself in front of her. If the cop went for his gun, I had a better chance at stopping him since I was faster than Jaz.

Then something knocked me over from behind. I didn't have time to register what had caused me to suddenly face-plant before the cop's head was on the floor in front of me. The rest of him was still up where I couldn't see.

I rolled over, stunned to see the gargoyle looming like a dark shadow over me and Jasmine. His one wing was still extended in that chopping formation, and a thump nearby had to be the guard's body falling next to his severed head.

"Why'd you do that?" I snapped, only to feel a small "poof" by my face. When I looked again, the head had turned into ashes.

The cop was a minion. Of course. Detective Kroger wasn't the only one at the Bennington police department, and who else would investigate stories of a monster at the same inn that doubled as a demonic Brimstone and Breakfast?

"Uh, good boy," I told the gargoyle awkwardly.

"What is *that* doing here?" a familiar voice asked, his tone heavy with disapproval.

Zach! I bolted up, so excited to see the Archon in the doorway that I knocked Jasmine over in my haste to get to him.

"Get me out of this disguise, I need to talk to the gargoyle!" I said in a rush. It hadn't understood me as a Hound, but maybe Adrian had taught it to speak English.

Zach touched the top of my head. I knew the instant my disguise disappeared because Jasmine choked, "Oh, Ivy!" and threw her arms around me again.

I wanted to hug her back. A big part of me even needed

to after everything we'd been through, but I was too terrified for Adrian to do anything except gently shove her aside.

"Brutus, you have to go back and save Adrian," I told the
gargoyle, grabbing the edge of its wing in my urgency. "Please,
go back now!"

The gargoyle cocked its head, the wing beneath my hand
quivering. From his expression, he seemed to *want* to do what
I asked, yet he made no move toward the gateway.

"Go, now!" I repeated, trying to shove him in the right direction, but the gargoyle was way too heavy for me.

"He doesn't understand you," Zach said, sounding bemused
this time. "This must be Adrian's pet. Why did he follow you
here?"

"Adrian said something to him and he hasn't left my side
since, but that doesn't matter." I let go of the gargoyle's wing
to grasp the Archon's trademark sweater. "Adrian's fighting
for his life, so I need all the weapons you have, now!"

"I don't have any weapons," Zach said, as if the idea was
preposterous.

"Then glamour some up," I all but snarled. "Didn't you
hear me? Adrian's going to *die!*"

"I can't. Glamour is illusion—it's not creating something
out of nothing." Zach's dark gaze narrowed as he looked at
my pocket. "But you already have a weapon, don't you?"

I don't know why, but I backed away, my hand flying to
cover my pocket. "It doesn't work," I said breathily.

Zach snorted with something like contempt. "Without faith,
it wouldn't." Then his expression became deadly serious. "Give
me the slingshot, Ivy."

I edged away farther, glancing at the invisible gateway.
"Why? You can't cross into a dark realm, so you're not going
to use it to save Adrian."

"Demetrius won't allow him to be killed," Zach replied,

sounding almost careless now. "He may take out his anger on him, but Adrian should survive that."

"And that's okay with you?" I snapped, fury boiling over. "Wait, of course it is. This wouldn't be the first time you left him at the mercy of demons, would it?"

Zach's features hardened, and he held out his hand in silent, imperious command. *Give me the weapon,* his stare warned.

He really would just take the slingshot, give it to his boss and call it a day, regardless if it meant Adrian's torture or death. *We can only depend on each other. To Archons and demons, we're just pawns that they move around for their own purposes,* Adrian had said. From the unyielding expression on Zach's face, he'd been right.

And I'd betrayed him just as awfully as Zach had all those years ago. I'd believed the worst of Adrian's words when his actions should've shown me that he would never hand me over to Demetrius. In the end, it was our actions that defined us. Not words.

I glanced at Jasmine, who was looking out the window as if she couldn't believe she was back in the real world. She was and so was I, all because of Adrian's sacrifice. Now, it was my turn. *I love you, Jaz,* I thought, choking back a sob. *But you're not the only one I love.*

Then I looked at Zach. "You might be willing to abandon Adrian again. I'm not."

His shout was cut off as I ran into the gateway, leaving him, my sister and the rest of my world behind.

chapter thirty-nine

I landed in the icy, decrepit version of the B and B on top of a dark-haired boy, who shoved me aside with a yelp.

"What the—?" he began, only to stop talking so fast, I whirled, expecting to see a minion or a demon behind me.

Nothing. I spun back around to see the boy staring at my chest with widened eyes. I looked down—and then yanked the coat together. It had flown open during my tumble, and I no longer had my Hound disguise, so not only had I landed on a kid who looked about ten, I'd done so while mostly naked.

And being a prepubescent boy, he'd fixated on that even while trapped inside a demon realm. My hand went to my coat pocket, anxiously checking for the slingshot. Still there.

"Sorry," I said, then stopped when I saw what the boy had in his hand. He must've found the beer bottle of blood that I'd left here.

"Rub some of that on your arms and legs," I said quickly. "Then run at the corner I just came through. You'll come out in the real world, promise."

"Are you a minion?" the boy asked suspiciously.

I let out a snort. "No. In fact, I'm here to kill them and all the demons."

"You're crazy," the boy scoffed.

I didn't believe that I could do it either, but that was the problem. *It doesn't work*, I'd told Zach. *Without faith, it wouldn't*, he'd replied. And Costa had said, *thousands of years ago, a shepherd boy killed a giant with nothing more than a slingshot and blind faith*. All right, I had the weapon. Now, I had to find the blind faith. Fast.

"Rub that stuff on you, and you can get out of here," I repeated. "Tell the others."

"You're gonna die, crazy naked lady," he muttered.

The scary truth was, he was probably right. After Zach's cold dismissal of Adrian's situation, I had less faith now than I'd had the last time I'd tried to use the weapon. Let's face it: it was too hard to believe in a benevolent, cosmic "boss" when his employees were made of so much suck!

Fear urged me to turn around and run back through the gateway. A far stronger emotion had me pulling out the slingshot and running out of the B and B as fast as I could. Yes, I was probably crazy, and yes, I'd probably die, but if there was even a chance that I could save Adrian, I had to try. Besides, if the Archons' boss didn't want the equivalent of a nuclear bomb in His enemies' hands, then He *had* to show up—

The braided rope pulsed with a sudden flare of power. I was so surprised, I almost stumbled during my mad dash up the hill. What had caused that? I hadn't been thinking anything pious. I'd been thinking that only an idiot would fail to realize the weapon would either work for me, or I'd be delivering it right into the demons' hands—

The slingshot pulsed again, stronger this time, until my

right arm almost felt numb. The reason why hit me then, and I began to laugh with wild, ragged whoops.

I didn't need to have pious faith. I didn't even need to have complimentary faith. No, this weapon's batteries ran on the same juices that had kept Adrian going when no one else had believed in him. *You can trust my hatred of demons,* he'd always told me. That had been his faith. Mine, apparently, was believing that the Archons' boss didn't want the slingshot to end up in demon hands. I didn't trust the Great Being with much, but it seemed that I trusted Him not to be stupid.

Power sizzled up my arm and light infused the rope, making it glow against the darkness. At the same time, shouts sounded about a hundred yards ahead of me, with more close behind those. With the Hounds dead and the gargoyle gone, minions must be on patrol, and I didn't have a disguise anymore.

I stopped running to grab a stone for the slingshot. Since nothing was around except frozen ground, all I managed to get was a ragged piece of ice. I put it in the glowing, pulsating rope, starting to spin it as soon as I reached the top of the hill where the trees abruptly ended.

The valley spread out below, faint, iridescent lights from the castle showing three minions dashing up the hill toward me. Worse, it looked like a larger group of them weren't far behind. Demetrius must've been hoping I'd come back.

Well, here I was, armed with nothing except cynical faith and a weapon that hadn't worked in thousands of years. I spun the rope faster, my emotions feelings like they were whirling in circles alongside the ancient weapon. I was scared beyond belief, yet I also felt the strangest sort of exultation. I was about to die or about to kick some serious ass, but either way, I'd be doing it for Adrian. Prophecies, destinies…they weren't why I was here. He was, and in life or in death, I wasn't going to fail him again.

Raising the weapon, I ran down the hill to meet my enemies.

The three closest minions leaped forward with such ferocity, they were briefly airborne. At the same time, an incredible surge of power caused pain to rocket through my whole body. Then light shot out from the weapon. As soon it touched the minions, they stopped moving so abruptly, it looked like they'd hit a wall in midair. Another agonizing surge caused those thin streams of light to hit the group of minions behind them. They froze, too, some with weapons still pointed in my direction.

I staggered, trying not to fall over from the searing sensations that made my insides feel like they were boiling. The beams of light coming from the slingshot kept the minions frozen into place, but the overwhelming pain made me want to fling the weapon aside. My body must have been the power conduit, and if this was what two supernatural blasts felt like, would I survive more?

Sirens came from farther down the hill. Someone must've seen the strange lights and sounded the alarm. I clenched my jaw, trying to keep from screaming as I spun the rope into a tighter, faster circle. This hurt so much, my bones actually ached. Who knew they could do that?

Then I walked past the first group of minions. If I only had one shot, I needed it for saving Adrian. The lights coming from the slingshot stayed on them, though, until the weapon had glowing strings both behind it and ahead. By the time I reached the bottom of the hill, the castle was in full defense mode.

Gunfire sounded, making me duck while holding the weapon aloft enough to keep the rope spinning. Another blast of power emanated from the slingshot, the subsequent pain almost driving me to my knees. As soon as that light touched them, the bullets stopped with the same suddenness as on that day in the desert when Zach had intervened. Hope clawed through my agony. The slingshot held the same power as an Archon. It really could do everything it was supposed to, as long as I could stand to wield it.

I forced myself to keep walking toward the castle. This time, I didn't duck as a barrage of gunfire came my way. I braced, a cry ripping out of me at the sizzling pain of dozens of bullets being supernaturally frozen in midair. Then more light shot from the weapon, landing on the guards like laser sights on a rifle. The new surge of power had me shaking in torment. I wasn't sure I could walk, let along keep the rope spinning. The slingshot felt like a thousand pounds of molten agony being funneled from my arm into the rest of my body.

A new wave of minions began to flood the lower section of the castle. The weapon reacted, beaming light onto every one of them and freezing them in place. I screamed, tears almost blinding me as I used both hands to keep the rope spinning. *Adrian, Adrian,* I repeated feverishly, forcing my feet to keep moving even though shudders racked me so fiercely, I staggered. He was trapped in the tunnel, but if I could get close enough, the weapon would incapacitate his attackers. No minion or demon could stop me, as long as I kept walking. The weapon took them out as soon as its light touched them.

Problem was, the weapon might also take me out.

Somehow, I made it past the gates and into the outer courtyards of the castle. By that time, I couldn't stop my screams at the merciless blasts of pain. Each new minion the light landed on sent agony shooting through me, until everything else faded beneath the constant, brutal onslaught. After a few minutes, I couldn't be sure if I was still holding the weapon anymore. A few minutes after that, I couldn't remember where I was or why I'd come here. Only the pain was real, and it was excruciating. I couldn't take it, and the pressure building inside me warned me that I wouldn't have to for much longer. Something was about to happen. Something big.

I fell to my knees from the next surge of power, which felt like a thousand knives ripping into me at once. *This is it,* I thought dazedly. *I'm dying.* Instead of being afraid, the thought filled me with profound relief. Anything to escape the pain.

Release the stone.

The whisper somehow made it past the torturous insanity strafing my mind. That's right, the stone. Until it was free, this wasn't over. With my last reserves of strength, I stood up and snapped the slingshot, releasing the ice rock into the nothingness that was coming for me.

My whole body convulsed as the light marking every minion suddenly exploded with sunlike brightness, until I couldn't see anything except burning, dazzling white. Just as swiftly, my agony disappeared, leaving me almost paralyzed with weakness. Unable to move or see, I fell onto the ground, feeling countless brushes of something light across me.

Slowly, that blinding whiteness faded, though at first, I thought the swirls around me were snowflakes. Then, as my vision returned even more, they changed color, turning from white to gray to charcoal. *Ashes,* I realized, shock giving me enough strength to sit up. Ashes were blowing everywhere, yet I didn't see a single minion or demon. I *did* see several humans venturing into the courtyard, their expressions mirroring the same sort of hopeful disbelief I felt, now that I could think again.

The slingshot seemed to have done the impossible, killing all the demons and minions without harming any of the humans. I'd kiss the weapon, if I knew where it was. My hand only had smudges from ashes in it at the moment.

Then a horrible thought crept into my mind, demolishing my happiness with one brutal question.

What if the slingshot had killed Adrian, too?

Fear got me to my feet, though I swayed so much, I expected to fall when I took my first step. Adrian was human, but his lineage had so much dark power, he could cross into demon realms. Did that same power cause the weapon to mark him for death as it had the minions and demons? Had he survived the attack Demetrius ordered against him, only to have me kill him?

God, please, no! I half ran, half staggered toward the Hound tunnel where I'd last seen him. The low, enclosed space kept the wind out, so the thick layer of ashes lining the floor weren't swirling around. They were ominously, deathly still.

"Adrian!" I cried out, sloshing through the grayish-black mess. "Adrian, please, answer me!"

I heard nothing but my own voice echoing hollowly back at me. I'd almost made it to the end of the tunnel when my legs gave out. Then I sank into the ashes, despair filling me as the pile I knelt in came nearly to my waist. From all the minion remains, the fighting must've been thickest here, so this was probably where Adrian had died. I plunged my hands into the embers, tears making everything blur as the particles either fell from my fingers or curled into wisps and floated away.

Gone, just like Adrian was now gone. More tears fell, making pale trails through the stains on my hands. I wanted to scream the way I had before, but though this pain was just as intense, it tore at my soul instead of my body, so there was no outlet for it. I hadn't been able to tell Adrian how sorry I was for what I'd done. Or tell him that I'd come back for him, or tell him the most important thing of all.

"I love you, too," I whispered to the ashes.

I'd never said that to a man before. Now, with Adrian gone,

I'd never say it again. I didn't need the gift of prophecy to know that I wouldn't feel this way about anyone else. Ever.

"Are you okay?" a hesitant voice asked.

My head jerked up, and through the tears, I saw the outline of a woman at the entrance to the tunnel.

"I saw you go down here," she went on. "You won't find anyone in here, though. This was where they kept the Hounds."

"I know." My voice was thick from anguish.

She took a few steps toward me. "Are you...her?"

"Her who?" I asked wearily.

"The one who killed them," she replied in an awed whisper.

Her words were a fresh blow to my heart. Yes, I'd killed them. All of them.

I didn't say that. As I heaved myself to my feet, I said the only thing I could think of to make her go away. I needed a few minutes to pull myself together. Or a few lifetimes.

"Go to the B and B. The dark-haired boy knows how to get through the gateway, if he hasn't left already."

She turned around and left. Moments later, I heard her excitedly telling someone that she knew a way out. I dragged a hand through my hair, feeling physically and emotionally beaten beyond my ability to cope. I didn't want to move from this spot, but the single bottle of blood at the B and B wouldn't be enough. More minion blood would be needed to bring everyone through the gateway. Fast, too, before other demons showed up to commandeer this realm. The slingshot only worked once, so even if I knew where it was, it was useless to prevent other demons from re-enslaving the people here.

That meant I'd have to leave this realm to find a minion, capture it and bleed the hell out of it. Tonight. The realization had me shuffling toward the exit to the tunnel. My body ached like I'd been pummeled from the inside out, but I forced myself to keep moving. If I didn't, I'd stay here and cry my eyes out, which wouldn't help the people trapped in this realm. Besides, my tears were already starting to mess with my vision. For a second, I'd thought the ash pile next to me had shifted.

I had gone about ten feet when a distinct rustling sound made me freeze. That wasn't a figment of my imagination. Something was in the tunnel with me.

Very slowly, I turned around. It looked like a dark pillar had appeared at the entrance to the Hound spa. Then the pillar doubled in height as the person beneath the embers stood up, revealing the form of a tall, broad-shouldered man. When he wiped his face, a layer of blood showed beneath the soot, and the hair he brushed back was stained black from the ashes swirling around him, but I didn't care. Right now, they were the most beautiful things I'd ever seen.

"Adrian," I whispered, my tears starting to flow faster.

His head snapped up—and then he moved with his incredible speed, gripping me in those powerful arms. Tilting my head back and covering my mouth in a bruising kiss that made joy rip through me with all the intensity of the pain I'd felt before. When he finally broke away several minutes later, I could hardly breathe, but I still managed to speak.

"I love you," I choked out. "I love you, I love you, I love you—"

His kiss cut me off again, and this time, I wasn't crying when I kissed him back. I was smiling.

epilogue

We didn't need to leave to catch a minion for its blood. Adrian pulled through the remaining people in the realm, taking them in groups of twos and threes. It still took the rest of the night, but I wasn't afraid of demons stopping us. Not when Zach stayed at the B and B, which rapidly filled to overflowing from all the survivors of the Bennington realm. I might still be mad at him, but no demon would take on one Archon, let alone three of them.

One moment, Jasmine and I were passing out blankets to the people who'd spilled out onto the lawn; the next, I was staring at two people whom I knew were not human despite their normal appearance. The brunette girl had freckles and the guy had blond dreadlocks, of all things, but for an instant, both of them radiated light like Zach had the first time we met.

"Uh…hi," I said, so surprised I stumbled over my words.

Screams erupted from the people outside. I whirled, groaning when I saw the gargoyle coming toward us. Adrian had *told* Brutus to stay hidden in the trees. Dreadlocks gave it a single glare. "Tell your creature to stay back."

"Admanta!" I yelled, using the word Adrian had taught me. The gargoyle chuffed warningly at the Archons but turned around and disappeared into the trees again.

"Sorry," I muttered, glad that Freckles was calming the people down.

"He's not hers," Jasmine offered, staring at the stranger curiously. "He, uh, belongs to Adrian."

"Not anymore," Dreadlocks said, with another grunt of disapproval. "Adrian bound him to your sister as her protector before he sent the two of you out of the realm."

"What?" Jasmine gasped.

I stared at the Archon, too stunned to speak. Thoughts, accusations and questions bombarded my mind, and after a moment, he began to answer them.

"No, Zacchaeus did not lie to you. Archons cannot lie, as he told you. We also cannot enter the dark realms, as he told you, but we can see into them. You never asked him that."

"Sonofa—" I began furiously, only to have his warning look stop me. "You mean Zach knew my sister was alive this whole time and never *bothered* to tell me?"

Jasmine wiped her eyes. This was too much, too soon for her. The Archon merely shrugged. "Those weren't his orders."

Orders. A slew of curses ran through my mind. The Archon gave me another glare, but I snapped, "Oh, please! I didn't *say* any of them, so give me a break!"

"Mortals," he muttered. "So obsessed with technicalities."

"Jaz," I said, controlling my anger with great difficulty. "Can you see if Adrian's back, please?"

I didn't want him to stop transporting humans, but I wanted to get my sister out of here for a few minutes. She was running on shock and adrenaline, so at any moment, she could snap.

She disappeared into the house without arguing, another
indicator that she wasn't herself. Moments later, Adrian came
out onto the lawn, eyeing the two Archons with guarded optimism.

"I hope you came to help. We'll need several buses to get
all these people out of here."

"We will not," Freckles replied. With those words, she and
everyone else vanished, leaving me, Adrian and Dreadlocks
alone on the lawn. From the sudden silence in the house, that
had been cleared out, too.

"What. Just. Happened?" I managed. Even Adrian appeared
startled.

The blond Archon wasn't. If anything, I'd say he looked
bored. "These people needed to be taken to safety. Sarai has
done that."

"But they're just *gone*," I stressed, as if I was the only one
who'd noticed that.

A shrug. "Archons aren't limited by your laws of physics."

After everything I'd seen, why did that surprise me? "Is Jasmine still here?" I asked in sudden anxiousness.

"Yes. We will provide care for the others, but she is yours
to look out for."

Good. I didn't want it any other way.

Adrian drew me next to him, his arm a welcome weight
across my shoulders. Aside from those few, blissful minutes
in the tunnel, we hadn't had a moment together since I found
him alive. He'd been ferrying people through the gateway
and I'd tried to do what I could for the traumatized survivors. I hadn't even had time to wash my hands. Calling dibs
on the bathroom when so many of these people hadn't had a
hot shower in years would've been selfish in the extreme, so
I was still covered in ashes. So was Adrian. We looked like
coal miners after a cave-in.

Zach came out onto the lawn. He exchanged a glance with the blond Archon that had Adrian tensing into stonelike stillness.

"Don't," he said low.

"It is too late," Zach replied, his voice equally soft. "The second trial has already begun."

"What trial?" I asked, stiffening, as well.

Zach's dark brown gaze rested on me. "Adrian no longer needs to transport the survivors. They are crossing through to this realm on their own."

I was incredulous. "How?"

"The gateways are opening," Zach said simply.

Adrian's arm dropped from my shoulders as he ran both hands through his hair. They were still covered in blood beneath the soot from all his injuries. Without Zach healing him the first time he'd crossed over to this side, I didn't think Adrian would even be conscious now. Zach's statement backburnered my concern for Adrian, however.

"The gateways are opening," I repeated. "From your tone and Adrian's reaction, that's bad, but why? If trapped people can now get out of the realms without the aid of a demon, Judian or minion, isn't that a good thing?"

"The gateways are opening because the walls between our worlds have started to crumble," Zach said. "The gateways are affected first, since they connect the realms."

Now I understood, and horror filled me. "But if the walls crumble until nothing separates the demon realms from ours, it'll be hell on earth in no time at all."

"Exactly," the blond Archon stated in a mild tone.

His nonchalance made me want to slap him. "Well, someone's got to *do* something!"

A pained sound came out of Adrian right as Zach said, "That someone is you, Ivy."

"Me?" I sputtered. "What can I do? I lost the slingshot, not that it matters since I already used it—"

"It's not lost," the blond Archon interrupted. "It's been forever embedded in your flesh."

I gaped at him, then shoved my coat sleeve up. I couldn't see anything beneath the grime, so I ran to the hose people had been drinking from and splashed water onto my arm.

As the soot cleared away, I began to tremble. The outline of a brown, braided rope ran from the loop on my finger all the way up to my elbow, the length of the slingshot curling around my arm several times. It looked like an extremely detailed tattoo, only this wasn't ink. It was like a supernatural brand.

Large hands gripped my shoulders and I turned in Adrian's arms. He was shaking, I realized with shock, and when his cheek brushed against mine, it was wet.

"Whatever happens next," he whispered. "Remember I love you. I didn't lie about that, Ivy."

Whoa. I pushed him away, a foreboding chill sweeping through me at his stricken expression, not to mention his words.

"What don't I know?" I asked, starting to tremble.

"Your destiny, Davidian, was not merely to find the slingshot," the blond Archon stated. "You must acquire the remaining two hallowed weapons before the demons get them, or the world you know will cease to exist."

"Wait, *what* other weapons?" I blurted before memory seared me with pitiless clarity.

To take down demons, you need one of three weapons, Adrian had said the day we met, *and the second and third ones will probably kill you.* Then when he'd taken me into the first realm, he'd said, *That's why I still hide things from you, Ivy. If you can't accept the way the board's set up, you're not nearly ready to learn the endgame yet....*

"You knew," I breathed, staring into his tormented jeweled gaze. "You knew *all along* that finding the slingshot was only the beginning, but you let me believe that if I did, this would all be over. You lied to me, Adrian!"

He flinched as if my words had struck him like a physical blow. Amidst my anger, disbelief and blistering hurt, I also felt a fresh wave of exhaustion. I'd thought if I got the slingshot and saved Jasmine, I'd be done with demons and their horrible realms. I didn't have it in me to take on one more fight against them, let alone two. Right now, I didn't even know if I had it in me to keep standing.

Zach came over to me, his brown eyes filled with a knowing sort of pity.

"Judas was guilty of three betrayals. The first was trust when he robbed the money set aside for the poor. The second was greed when he accepted thirty pieces of silver, and the third—"

"Was death," I finished, my heart breaking all over again. "You did betray me, Adrian, just like everyone said you would. You just haven't killed me yet."

"Ivy, I'm sorry," he said, catching my hands and holding on when I tried to yank away. "I didn't believe I could beat my fate before, but I do now. *You* made me believe, and—"

My laughter cut him off. It was dark, ugly and filled with all the anguish of love lost, found and lost again.

"How ironic. Now you believe, and I don't." He opened his mouth, and I let out a harsh scoff. It was that or I'd start to cry, and it was taking all the fading strength I had not to do that already. "Just leave. I can't listen to you right now. It hurts too much to even look at you."

He released my hands but gripped my shoulders, his sapphire gaze blazing into mine. "I'll leave, but not for long. I'll make you believe again, Ivy, if it's the last thing I do."

Then he was gone, using his blinding speed to disappear into the trees. I waited until I was sure he wasn't coming back before I finally allowed myself to sink to my knees, tears leaking past my clenched eyelids. Everyone had warned me, but not only had I trusted Adrian, I'd fallen in love with him. Worse, even after all this, I still loved him. Was that because I had the world's worst case of stupidity? Or was it another example of the curse of my fate?

"What's this second weapon and what's it supposed to do?" I asked, not really wanting to know but needing something to distract me from my urge to call out for Adrian.

Zach knelt until he was eye level with me. "The staff of Moses. It parted the Red Sea, sent ten plagues upon Egypt and caused water to pour from rocks in the desert. In short, it controls nature, so it can repair the walls between the realms."

My head dropped into my hands while a gasping laugh escaped me. "No wonder the thing's supposed to kill me if I use it."

"It might," Zach said steadily. "But the slingshot didn't, and it could have, too. You're strong, Ivy. Now you need to be stronger, so you can stave off the destruction of your world."

Another gasping laugh. "Oh, is that all?" We were all doomed. *Doomed.*

"If you succeed, you will save Adrian, too," the blond Archon said almost casually.

My head snapped up. "How? He's destined to betray me, remember?"

"And so he has," Zach said in a mild tone. "Yet now there is a chance that he won't do it again. Adrian's hatred of demons was the first thing that made him struggle against his fate, but hate was never going to be enough for him to overcome it. Only light can defeat darkness. Loving you is his light, Ivy. Without it, he was doomed to fail, but with it, his fate is truly in his own hands."

I stared at him, thunderstruck, as different details started falling into place.

If Zach hadn't abandoned him all those years ago, Adrian wouldn't have learned how to be the insanely strong fighter that he was. He also wouldn't have hated demons for their countless deceptions, giving him a reason to fight them in the first place. Then later, his hate ensured that he went with me when I was looking for the only weapon that could kill them. As I'd accused Adrian before, he wouldn't have gone with me otherwise, no matter how Zach tried to persuade him...

Hope began to spiral through my wildly swinging emotions. That's right, Zach had *wanted* Adrian to go with me, so maybe the Archon was using the supernatural tie between us to help Adrian, not to doom him. After all, if Adrian hadn't gone with me to search for the slingshot, we wouldn't have fallen in love. Yes, Adrian had horribly betrayed my trust, but I'd betrayed his, too, and he'd forgiven me. Could I really refuse to forgive him, if there might be a future for us after all?

I drew in a deep breath. I wasn't ready to throw myself back in his arms, but what if the Archons were right? What if love was the wild card that gave us a chance to beat the demons, save the walls between the realms from crumbling *and* save ourselves from our fates? It was a long shot, true, but I now had a three-thousand-year-old weapon tattooed into my arm, so anything was possible.

I rose, giving the two Archons a nervous yet determined look.

"All right, when do we start?"

★ ★ ★ ★ ★

acknowledgments

Before anyone else, I have to thank God for continuing to give me the ability and the opportunity to live out my dreams. Ten years ago, I first started trying to get published. Twelve novels, five novellas and two short stories later, part of me still can't believe that my dream has become my reality.

Sincerest thanks also go to my husband, Matthew, whose love and support is the stuff romance novels are made of. Further gratitude goes to my agent, Nancy Yost, who's been riding this roller coaster with me almost from the beginning. This book also wouldn't be possible without the wonderful people at Harlequin, who've championed *The Beautiful Ashes* as though they wrote it themselves. There are too many of you to list, so in the interest of space, I'm only highlighting my editor, Margo Lipschultz, Shara Alexander from Publicity and Reka Rubin from Subrights. "Thanks" doesn't even begin to cover everything you and the rest of the Harlequin HQN team have done.

Finally, a huge thank-you to readers, book sellers, librarians, reviewers and bloggers. Without your enthusiasm for reading and spreading the word about books, authors like me would have no one to share our stories with, and that would be very sad indeed.